CRAVE
BENEATH THE SECRETS

LUNA MASON

Here's to finding someone who loves you not despite your flaws, but because of them.
*There is someone out there who **will** give you the whole world, not just half of it.*
And maybe, it will be an unhinged biker who tells you to look at your reflection in his visor to see how pretty you are when you come undone for him.

*It's time to **get on your knees** and welcome Alexei...*
He's ready to take you on a wild ride.

AUTHOR NOTE

CRAVE is a dark, stand-alone mafia romance. It is the second book in the Beneath The Secrets Series.

It does contain content and situations that could be triggering to some readers. This book is explicit and has explicit sexual content, intended for readers 18+.

The FMC in this book battles with bulimia and body dysmorphia.

A full list of triggers and information can be found on my website: www.lunamasonauthor.com

PLAYLIST

- Nightmare, Halsey
- *Self-Destruction, I Prevail*
- *Who We Are, Hozier*
- *Rescue, Lauren Daigle*
- *DOA, I Prevail*
- *Silence, Marshmello, Khalid*
- *What If I Told You That I Love You, Ali Gatie.*
- *Circus Psycho, Diggy Graves*
- *Mistake, NF*
- *ALWAYS BEEN YOU, Chris Grey*
- *Joy Ride, Hueston*
- *The Best I Ever Had, Limi*
- *DIE FOR ME, Chase Atlantic*
- *DARK, WesGhost*
- *i know (faded) Ex Habit*
- *Sleep Token- Fall For Me.*
- *Fire Up The Night, New Medicine*
- *I'll Look After You, The Fray*
- *breathe, mxze*
- *Sleep Token, Sugar*
- *Gasoline, I Prevail*

PLAYLIST

- *Sleep, Citizen*
- *The Other Side, Ruelle*
- *Sleep Token, Alkaline*
- *Euclid, Sleep Token*
- *Ocean, Martin Garrix, Khalid*
- *DIAMONDS, MIKOLAS*
- *Body Loud, SWIM, Limi.*
- *I Wouldn't Mind, He Is We*
- *Lollipop, Framing Henley*

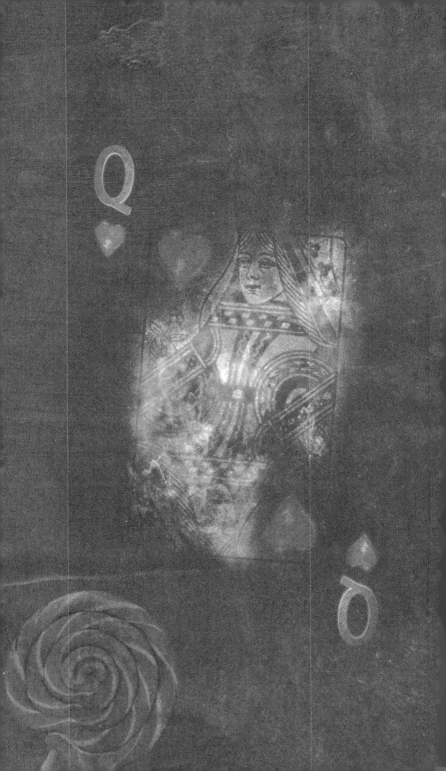

PROLOGUE
ALEXEI

Twenty Years Ago

I'll go home when my candy's gone.

If Papa catches me with it when he's drunk, he'll beat me again for stealing. My lip hasn't healed from last time, but I can finally take a full breath again from my sore ribs.

I don't hate him. Not that I know what that would feel like.

But I avoid him.

My feet trace the puddle under the swing in half-moon circles. The air is cold enough to see my breath, so I know I'll have to find a warm place to hide until my treats are gone.

I didn't take them. He shouldn't make up stories. Papa always tells me lying is wrong, but then punishes me, even when I tell the truth.

"You, kid! Why are you always here?" A brown haired boy, bigger than me, yells across the desolate playground.

I thought I was alone.

There's two of them, both taller and wider than me.

I bet they're teenagers.

I can't wait until I'm one. I'd stand up to Papa if I were.

The black haired one moves closer. "Didn't you hear my brother?" Bending at the waist, he peers at me with his dark eyes.

He doesn't look mean, at least.

"What happened to your face?" His tone softens, like he's talking to a child younger than me.

I'm almost a teenager, not a baby.

Defiantly, I stick up my chin and meet his gaze. "None of your business." The hard candy clicks against my teeth as I shift it to the other side of my mouth.

The smile makes him look nicer. Maybe they aren't going to take my treat?

"What's your name?" The brown haired one stands behind his brother who drops to a squat in front of me. "I'm Nikolai. You can call me Niki. This—" He drops a hand on his brother's shoulder. "—is Mikhail. We won't hurt you."

Niki has blue eyes. I've had to learn to watch people's faces. I'm not very good at guessing emotions, but their features usually tell me what they're thinking.

Papa's mouth will twist and his eyebrows drop into a line across his nose just before he starts swinging.

"Do I call you Miki?" I stare at the squatted boy. He looks almost like a grown up with the stubble on his jaw.

Nikolai grins. "Not if you want to live."

Mikhail winks at me as he shakes his head.

Confusing.

Does that mean sometimes?

"So, you kill people? Can you teach me?" I can use that the next time Papa gets mean.

Mikhail's brows knit, and it reminds me of Papa.

Sliding off the swing seat, I back away and put the pole between us. I don't want him mad at me.

Mikhail glances up at his brother, then softens his features. "Why do you want to know? Who hurt you? It looks like you can barely see out of your eye."

I forgot about that. I'm so used to one or both being swollen, I don't notice as much.

"Papa said I was stealing, but I wasn't." My arms cross over my threadbare coat, tucking the edges together.

Nikolai bends over and whispers something in his brother's ear.

Mikhail nods and looks back at me. "Is your father Akim?"

My chin bobs, but I don't answer. If I don't say it out loud, I won't get in trouble.

Mikhail sighs, and pushes his hands against his thighs to stand. "Tell you what kid, if you want help, you be here next time we come through, and you can show me where you live. Khorosho?"

"Okay." I watch their heads go close, and they talk too quietly for me to hear.

It's only as they start to leave I remember I didn't answer their question.

Papa always said it's rude to ignore him when he asks me something.

"Alexei!" I yell.

Nikolai turns back. "What's that?"

"My name! It's Alexei!"

I should be used to it. One of the teachers at school told us that scar tissue is tougher.

All of the scars Papa gives me should make me invincible.

But I can't see out of my eye again, and my tongue is fat in my mouth from when I bit it.

He hits too hard when I'm not watching.

I watch the alley for any movement. They should be here today.

It's almost time for me to leave. Hanging out on this swing waiting for them makes my toes tingle.

The fear of missing the boys makes my feet seem like a tiny problem. If they don't show up, I'll have to go home.

I don't want to anymore.

Long shadows stretch from the old brick building. When they reach the sandbox, I'll leave.

Just a few more minutes.

Footsteps echo from the alcove.

Maybe it's them?

My chin juts out, hoping they'll be able to see the fresh bruises when they pass.

"Hey, Alexei! We haven't seen you in days." Nikolia is the first to see me.

He smiles and moves closer. But his mouth drops into a frown. "Mikhail, look." He gestures at me.

Like I'm a thing.

Mikhail tugs a small girl with him. She looks younger than me with light tufts of hair poking out from her bright pink hat.

She pulls against him when she spies me.

"You should say 'Hi'." Mikhail encourages her. "I have to take care of something. Do you want to stay here and play while I do?"

Her pink lower lip rolls between her teeth as she looks at me with big blue eyes.

Nikolai squats down in front of me, and reaches his palm towards my head.

He pauses when I try to jerk away. "Be still," he grunts. "I'm not going to hurt you. Is your father at home?"

I don't move, but let him twist my face left and right. "Yes. The blue house at the end of the street." My arm raises to point, showing off the holes in my coat.

He squints and his mouth thins.

That usually means irritation.

"He did a number this time," Nikolai calls to Mikhail.

Mikhail sighs and pulls the girl closer.

"Alexei? This is Lara. She's very important to me. I have one job for you in exchange for helping you with your father. You need to keep an eye on her and keep her safe while we're gone. Can you do that?" He places his hand on her back and leads her closer. "When I get back, you come home with us, okay?"

I nod solemnly.

Putting my hand across my heart, I look into Nikolai's face with as much seriousness as I can muster. "I swear to you I'll do whatever you want for, um." I can feel my nose wrinkle. It hurts the right side of my face. "What's the word for forever? The fancy one?"

Mikhail gives me a lopsided smile. "Do you mean 'eternity'?"

Bobbing my chin makes my neck hurt. It's still hard to turn after Papa kicked me when I fell.

"Yea, I swear I'll do whatever you want me to do for eternity." One side of my mouth grins.

The other side tries to split and starts bleeding again.

"What happened to you?" The girl asks. Her voice is sweet and musical. With wide eyes sits in the swing next to me.

Do I tell her how I accidently broke a glass, and that made Papa so mad he beat me to the ground and kicked me?

"A giant grizzly bear broke into my house. He broke some stuff, but I chased him away." That sounds better.

Nikolai's brows raise.

My arms move as I shrug. "What? That's better than the real thing."

Lara giggles. "I know it isn't true. But you're funny. Can you tell me another?"

Nikolai pats my leg and stands. "We'll be back. Keep her company."

"I promise. For eternity."

CHAPTER 1
LARA

20 Years Later…

No one understands how hard this is.

I need to be perfect *all* the time, or I get judged.

My father was the worst. Always looking over my shoulder for him is exhausting. Sometimes, it all becomes too much.

He expected everything from my big brothers, Nikolai and Mikhail, but from me, it was to be immaculate. The mafia princess he needed me to be.

People can't see me out of control. The days when I barely have the strength to pull myself out of bed. It's always after I fuck up and decide to cheat.

Stupid. That's weak.

I should be stronger than that. There are just so many days when I can't stop.

Then it comes back to punish me.

At least Alexei seems to understand. Well, he accepts me.

He told me about this cabin years ago, when we first came to Vegas. Small, quiet, and remote.

It's a safe place that isn't surrounded by coffee shops and bakeries.

They're the worst.

Being able to smell fresh pastries while I'm walking down the street should be a crime. How do they expect anyone to resist?

Luring me in. Practically forcing me to eat.

No. Out here, all I can smell are the pines. It's easier to forget. I always make sure that I pack lightly, so I'm never tempted.

Alexei swears he never comes out here, but it's clean and fresh every time I show up.

He must have someone who checks on it regularly. Otherwise, how would it be so cozy?

I know it drives him crazy when I disappear. It's just so hard to deal with the overwhelming pressures.

Looking a certain way.

Acting like I know what is going on.

Never missing a step.

Who did they call when Jax and Sofia's world was crashing down?

Me.

Who did Niki trust to judge Mila's character?

Me again.

I tried to warn him I had a weird feeling about her, then she stabbed him.

Maybe I should have tried harder. It's my fault he got hurt.

If I hadn't eaten so much sugar, I would have been able to be clearer.

Like my father used to say. The sweets make me dull and fat.

Nikolai needed me. I let my own brother get hurt because I wasn't paying attention.

I just need a few days to detox. A good fast and I'll be sharp again. I'll lose this extra weight that I put on while worrying.

Then I'll be better. The treats won't get to me next time.

I'll resist.

CHAPTER 2
ALEXEI

I DON'T KNOW why she thinks she's hiding from me, but I'm always glad when she comes back to town.

The video feed from the cabin isn't as clear. Maybe I need to talk to Enzo about a better internet connection. But that would mean telling him I'm watching her.

He spies on everyone, what difference is there?

I don't want him knowing.

She's *my* responsibility.

"Can you go that way?" I yell at Mikhail in the cockpit.

Without turning around, he taps his headset, then raises his middle finger at me. It's not like I could see his face, he always wears that black balaclava now.

Shit. I always forget.

I key the button to activate the mic on mine. "Cut to the left. I want to go over that hill face."

Mikhail nods and his Cessna tilts as the wing dips into the turn.

This is always a good distraction when Lara hides.

A buzzer rings through the speakers. When I glance at him, Mikhail gives me a thumbs up.

Pulling the door open, the rush of hot Vegas wind pours into the tiny cabin of the plane.

I have to brace myself to keep from stumbling with the force of it.

It's time.

I hang my headset on the heavy hook, and go through the last minute pattern of patting my straps and buckles.

Yep. Everything in place.

Without a word, I leap out into the sky.

The air is so loud as I fall that it's almost quiet, drowning out every thought.

There's a shadow from Mikhail that flickers over me. He's circling like he always does to make sure I land safely.

He shouldn't bother. We've done this a million times.

Well. At least a hundred.

I feel free. Guided only with the resistance of my arms and legs against the wind itself, I buck and roll. Spin and dive.

Completely untethered by anything except gravity.

Faster.

Streamlining my body, I rocket towards the earth.

I'm a missile, streaking through the dusk.

Does she know I can almost see her? That the roof of the cabin she's in peeks through the dense trees like it's waving at me?

The cameras never show enough.

Mikhail always thinks I like to jump here because of the craggy waterfall that works its way through the desert.

I tell him it's my quiet place.

Really, it's watching Lara to make sure she's okay.

I'm supposed to. It isn't only my job, it's my purpose.

My entire being revolves around her.

Her spirals always make her want to disappear. So I gave her somewhere she can run to, where she is safe. I know she's there trying to reset, to clear her mind, to get a fresh outlook.

Sometimes, they're longer than others.

But knowing that Nikolai and I will be leaving for Russia soon, I just need to check on her.

She'll come around.

Like always.

CHAPTER 3
LARA

JUST BECAUSE I dragged myself from the woods, didn't mean I wanted to come back and get thrown into taking care of Elena.

Nikolai and Alexei leaving to track down Mila? Melissa? Whatever her name is, it's important I return to take care of my niece.

I had a bad feeling about that woman. I knew she was hiding something.

"When is Daddy coming home?" Elena looks up at me with her big brown eyes. She favors her mom more than my brother.

Things have been so much different since the night my father killed Katerina.

"I don't know, sweetie. Did you want to watch a cartoon while I call Uncle Mikhail and see if he's heard anything?" Guilt shudders through me.

Nikolai could be dead for all I know. I haven't heard from him in days.

Even Alexei isn't keeping me up to date. He usually overshares.

But I can't tell her I'm worried.

Her little pink lip sticks out in a pout. "Okay. Do you have any cereal? I don't like those rice cakes." She crosses her arms on the counter and raises her eyebrows.

"I'm afraid I'm out." I don't ever want that in my house.

I might eat it.

"But I do have some strawberries. How does that sound?" I don't wait, grabbing them out of the fridge.

If I give her a chance to argue, she will.

"Fine. Thank you." She doesn't sound enthused.

I get her a bowl set up on the coffee table. "I'm going to make some phone calls. Let me know if you need anything."

"I will, Aunt Lara." She doesn't look up. She's already focused on the animated characters on the screen behind me.

Oh, to be seven again and not have the stresses of adult life.

Mikhail may be the head of the entire Las Vegas mafia, but he always makes a point of being there for me.

"Lara. How are you and Elena?" he asks gruffly. He always sounds like that, rough and busy.

"It's been a bit. I need to know if Nikolai and Alexei are okay? Have you heard anything?" Chewing on my thumbnail doesn't fix anything.

I need to chew on something though.

"Alexei called. I'm getting a flight ready to go pick them up. They're all fine and will be home tomorrow." He sounds distracted.

Hmm. "All?" What does he mean by that?

"They're bringing Mila and her brother back," he says flatly. That's his "I don't want an argument" voice.

Tough shit.

"What the fuck do you mean? She tried to kill him!" Damn. I have to stop yelling before Elena hears me.

"According to Nikolai, it was all a big misunderstanding. But our father was at the root of it all in his own insane way." He sighs.

"Oh." Whenever Ivan is involved, he ruins lives. Maybe I need to rethink hating Mila.

She was probably coerced by Father as only he can.

Sick bastard.

"After I get back, we'll discuss it further. I think there's some things you need to know."

"Wait? You're going? You swore you'd never—"

Mikhail cuts me off. "It's Nikolai and Alexei. Yes, I'm going. I'll be fine." His voice is gentle, almost crooning.

I'm getting loud again.

"Let me know as soon as you're back." My stomach growls. Is it really hungry, or is this new anxiety eating at my belly making the noise?

"Will do." There isn't a click when he hangs up.

He's going back.

Away from Vegas, and safety. Everyone I care for is in Russia. They almost didn't escape last time.

Why did they all have to go?

Silence. The low hum of Elena's cartoons bring me back to reality.

My belly growls again.

I better eat something. It will keep me busy while I wait.

CHAPTER 4
ALEXEI

"Mikhail, your plane needs internet." Waving my useless cell above my head doesn't make a signal magically appear.

He and Nikolai are like two giant boulders that have been deep in conversation for most of the flight home. I've heard it all, but don't care.

None of it really pertains to me. Or Lara.

Those are my only concerns. Well, and my pet flamingo, Sheila. But the neighbor is taking care of her while I'm gone.

I hope she's eaten her fish. It's good for her, keeps her strong and pink.

"Alexei, we're touching down soon. You can go back to searching porn," Nikolai grumbles as he steps past me, heading towards the rear of the jet.

"I'm not!" I protest. I'm checking my house camera to make sure Sheila is safe.

Mila stands up to greet him, and he gives her a kiss before they sit.

I noticed they did the same when they were rescued from Ivan.

As soon as the plane touches down, I watch the little waves on my phone screen until they show a connection.

ME

We're back

LARA

I'm glad. Everyone okay?

ME

I guess. Niki and Miki just talked. Don't tell Miki I called him that.

LARA

I never do.

My black BMW is still sitting where I parked it in Mikhail's casino garage. I'm itching to get away from everyone else and feel the wind on my face again.

When Lara gets done dropping off Elena, I'll need to see her.

She gets stressed when things change. Having Elena is one, and sending her home is another.

Yes. I'll check on her next.

Fuck, this feels good to ride. My toes slide to the tips of the pegs and I wedge the gas can between my knees so I can stand and stretch, throwing my arms out as I weave between the traffic with no hands.

Seeing their faces is the best part.

It's easy to tell their emotions when they're mouths are hanging open and their eyebrows are raised to their hair.

Except that one. Why is that girl smiling and curling her finger at me like that?

When I wave, it throws me off balance enough that the tires wobble beneath me and I swerve in front of a big truck.

He slams on his brakes, but I move out of his path.

The sound of steel crunching follows me.

Too bad I'm already gone.

I don't see anyone else making strange expressions.

Hitting the garage opener, I motor in and park my bike just as my phone pings.

Accident on the Vegas strip.

Hmm. Glad I missed that, I was just there.

Peeling my helmet off, I toss it on the table by the door and work my way through the house until I hit the back veranda.

Sheila stands there, gorgeous against the hot afternoon sun.

The pink shade has deepened, so at least I know she's eating.

"Hello, beautiful." I saunter closer, but she startles and moves away.

"Oh, being shy today? Fine, I'll stare from over here." Digging into my stash, I pull out a root beer flavored sucker and peel the wrapper.

Cherry is my second favorite. It reminds me of Lara's lips when she purses them at me.

Well, she usually does that right before she snaps at me for something. But I like them anyway.

"I'm going to fill up your pool. Are you going to be a good girl and stay here? No more escaping. I'll have to chase you down again." Unwinding the hose, the water scorches me when it comes out.

It's so hot here, all of the time. Do I like it more than Russia?

Yes. Less clothes, more motorcycle time.

There are many months of ice and slick roads in Russia. Not so much here.

And, my Sheila is here.

"There. I need to make sure Lara is okay now. Do you need more shrimpies?" The small feeding aquarium is set up in the shade, and is full of the tiny creatures.

I pull out a hefty scoop and dump it into her pool.

"Pretty bird, I have to leave. I'll be late, don't stay up." I give her a wave like the one I gave to the woman in the car before going inside.

It makes my stomach hurt to go too long without seeing Lara. Like when someone eats the last piece of pizza.

I wish I could have more.

Just because we were thrown together as kids, doesn't mean I'd have to enjoy my time with her like I do.

She's my person. Easy to be around. She doesn't judge me. I can be myself.

The others, they expect me to act like them. That's hard.

When I have a thought, I want to say it.

I shouldn't have to hold it back, but they expect me to. Or look at me strangely when I tell them something that is so obvious to me.

I'm not weird, they are. But I have to hide what's in me.

Not with Lara.

She opens the door before I can knock, then simply lets it hang as she continues into the kitchen.

"So fill me in on the trip. Mikhail didn't tell me much." She pours herself a glass of water, then hands me a soda from the stash she keeps for me in the fridge.

I shrug, and toss myself onto the couch. "She stabbed him again. I think they're in love. It's what Nikolai said." I can feel my face twist. "Is that what people in love do?"

"No, Alexei. That isn't normal. Remember when Nikolai was married? They didn't stab each other. That's what it's supposed to be like." Lara pushes her long blond braid over her shoulder and sits next to me, tucking her toes under my thigh.

I like it when she does that. It usually means she's not mad at me.

She flicks her hand. "Okay, so they're fucked up together. What else happened?"

"They got taken by Ivan. He fucked them up. I bet it takes Nikolai weeks to heal from being turned into a pot cushion."

When I shift the candy to the other side of my mouth, it makes my cheek pucker.

She has an eyebrow raised and her lips are crooked. "Pin."

"Pin what? You want me to write it down for you?"

Her blue eyes close and she shakes her head. "No, it's 'pincushion'. Like for sewing. Never mind. What did Ivan want? He never does anything without a reason."

My feet prop up onto the coffee table, then I push the buttons on the remote to turn on the TV. "I dunno. He was asking about someone named Zoya. I don't know her so I stopped listening."

Cartoons. Horse racing. Shampoo commercial.

Nothing's on.

"Can we watch Yellowstone?" We started it before I left.

I want to see what happens next. Those cowboys are just as ruthless as we are.

Bigger hats, though.

Lara lets out a long sigh. "Sure." She fidgets with her phone while I bring up the show.

I can feel her big blue eyes on me.

"What?" I click the candy over to the other side of my mouth.

"So, there's this guy…" She trails off.

Ugh. I hate it when she does this. "Okay? Is he trouble? I can take care of him." I have before, I can do it again.

Her eyebrows drop.

I must have said something wrong.

"No, he isn't trouble, Alexei. I am supposed to meet him for dinner tomorrow." Her thumbs type into the screen. "So, if everything goes well…" Her voice fades.

I hate it when she does that.

"And? What? Use your words. I suck at reading your thoughts," I grumble, turning back to the television.

"If all goes well, we might come back here." Her lower lip curls between her teeth.

I shrug. "He can watch Yellowstone with us." The sucker crumbles when I bite it as I turn to her. Using the wet stick, I point to emphasize myself. "We are *not* rewatching episodes to get caught up though."

There's still too many left to backtrack.

Her toes disappear from under my thigh and she crosses her legs.

Is she mad? I think she is.

Pausing the show, I look at her. "What do you want me to do?"

She narrows her eyes and stares at me for a long time. "You might have to try spending an evening in your own house."

"Oh. Is that all? Why didn't you just say that?" My palm lands on her knee. "You don't have to be subtle. I don't understand that well."

Her breath hitches as she looks at the back of my hand. "Okay."

"See? Easy." Threading my fingers behind my head, I kick back into the heavy cushions to continue watching the show.

CHAPTER 5
LARA

SLAMMING the door shut behind me, I storm through the hallway and toss my bag across the floor.

That motherfucker.

I can't believe he said I was the slowest eater he's ever met? He has no idea how much I had to hype myself up just to go on the damn date, *in a restaurant.*

Bile rises in my throat. After he made that comment, despite rapidly losing my appetite, I ate most of the plate of grease. I feel disgusting.

I thought I had a better handle on myself until Nikolai took off running after Mila around Russia. It was hard not to panic constantly worrying that he and Alexei wouldn't come home. Memories flood back of that night five years ago.

Nikolai's anguished yelling. Mikhail was injured, but trying to hurry us away.

Alexei never left my side, even though I was terrified.

Our whole lives were crashing around us.

We've all had to rebuild in our own ways, away from our evil father. The man who made me starve to stay in shape so he could marry me off for an alliance one day.

Gripping onto the kitchen counter, I take a few deep breaths, before grabbing a glass of cold water.

Maybe, if I don't eat tomorrow I won't gain any weight.

Sliding out my phone, my finger hovers above Alexei's number. With all of his crazy, he brings me calm. When he crashes into my life daily, I get so lost in his unpredictability and his deranged humor, I can forget about the anxious gnawing which always seems to exist in my belly.

After that disastrous date, he is the one I need more than anything,

Just as I hit dial, he answers before it even rings.

"Pchelka. Are you okay?" His gravely voice mellows the frustration of earlier.

I smile at the screen. "Yes, sladkiy. I'm fine."

There's a raspy sound, I bet he's scratching at his stubble.

"Hmm. Why don't I believe you?" He pauses. "Open the front door."

I frown, looking at the time. It's nearly midnight. Following his orders, I open it and find him leaning against the porch rail, one leg over the other, hand in pocket and his cell up to his ear.

His broad grin reveals his silver tooth shining in the security lights.

I might be happy to see him, but I don't want him to know it. "What are you doing here?"

With a shrug, he stands up in front of me. "I was passing by, thought I'd check in on my favorite Volkov." He chews his bottom lip. "And to see if you'd filled up that candy jar."

I'm surprised that his silver tooth is the only one that's been replaced. As much sugar as he eats, I'd expect his whole mouth to be rotten by now.

Yet, he still has the perfect white smile.

"I did." I twist the diamond ring on my finger and turn away. I know I can't even look at the container tonight, or I'll be eating half of it by myself.

He brushes past me and pulls the lid off to scowl inside before making a selection.

"Is that the only reason you're here? I'm not sure I'm in the mood for company tonight." As much as I love Alexei, he's my best friend and can't give me what I need tonight.

I just want to feel sorry for myself. There's no way to explain that to him.

"I want to watch the next episode of Yellowstone." He pushes past me and flops onto the couch. "Where's your friend?" He looks over the backrest at me. The tattoos on his neck are a sharp contrast with the beige of the cushion.

Standing in front of the fridge, I really wish a cheesecake would appear.

One night of cheating won't count, will it?

"It didn't work out." My stomach is still rolling from the heavy food. Probably a good thing I don't have any dessert here, besides Alexei's stash.

"Did you watch one? It tried to skip ahead." He pushes buttons on the remote before tossing it onto the glass coffee table.

"Like I'd dare watch it without your annoying commentary," I grumble into my empty freezer.

"It needs it. It makes you laugh." He pounds on the seat next to him.

Which is just what I need, a night of Alexei induced laughter.

"It does." I admit. Finally settling on strawberries, I fill a small bowl and join him in front of the TV.

When he left with Nikolai, it almost made my skin itch. My world was quiet, and boring without him.

Curling my feet under me, I tug up a blanket and lean against his warm arm. His comforting scent surrounds me as I relax.

Sometimes I wish we were something more than close friends.

But I screw up every romantic relationship I've ever been in. I'd rather have this much of Alexei than to mess it all up and have none.

He's the only thing that keeps me sane most days.

Seeing how happy Nikolai was when he came home makes me ache for that, though. Someone to love every part of me.

I don't know if Alexei is even capable of that. So I won't push it.

He doesn't judge. He doesn't try to change me. Of all of the people in the world, he accepts me for who I am.

And I'm terrified to lose that.

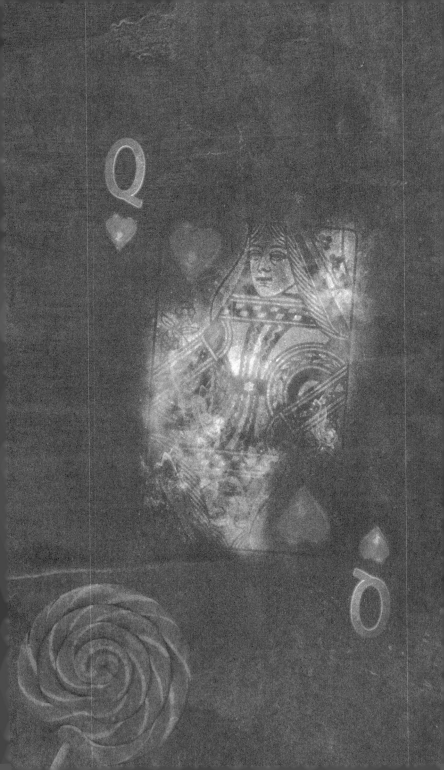

CHAPTER 6
ALEXEI

She had a date tonight. Following previous patterns, they always go wrong.

I don't know why. She is the most amazing girl to ever walk this earth.

No one compares to my Lara. It makes me want to murder the men that upset her.

Well, I have. On many occasions, I've killed men and women who have hurt her.

I know, when she calls me late at night, or gives me her slight smile, she isn't okay.

When she fiddles with her rings, tugs on her clothes, and bites on her thumb nail, it tells me something isn't right.

She did all of those things today.

"You know we won't be able to do this forever?"

I frown, processing her words.

"I don't understand. Why not?"

There is not a future where I am not here with her. It doesn't exist. I won't let it.

"One of these times, I'll find someone who likes me." She stares hard at me, like I'm supposed to say something in return.

But the answer is obvious. Shrugging, I look back at the TV. "I like you. It's enough."

She chews on her lower lip in silence. Her breath catches a few times, like she's getting ready to say something, but doesn't.

"There's more to a relationship than just watching silly shows. What happens when one of us wants, um…" Her voice trails off.

"What? I can make some popcorn if that's what you want?" I watch her eyebrows draw together.

No, that wasn't what she's going for.

"I mean, something more? Niki ran off to bring home a woman who stabbed him, and yet still loves her." Her pink lips turn and she chews on the inside of her cheek.

I have no idea what she's trying to say.

The look on my face must show my confusion because she makes an exasperated sigh.

"What if one of us gets a partner? Then this—" Her finger points back and forth between us. "—won't work anymore."

"Huh? I have partners. Niki, Jax. Mikhail, too." Leaning back, I tuck my arm behind my head.

When she talks in circles like this, it gets tiring.

"No. Nikolai has Mila now. Jax has Sofia. That's the kind of relationship I'm talking about." Her thumb works up to find its way between her teeth.

She's stressed over Niki, I bet. She was convinced he was leaving to die in Russia.

"What if I get a boyfriend?" She twists the blanket around her hand and finds the television suddenly fascinating.

"Oh. Well, nothing would change." I push the blanket off and grab my empty cup. "Here, give me your glass." I stand in front of her and gesture with my hand.

Why does she turn her head away? I'm right here.

"Alexei. If I find someone, we can't do this anymore." She

circles her arm around where I was sitting under the covers next to her.

Blinking, I try to figure out what she's implying.

I go into the kitchen to buy some time. When she's stressed out, she only drinks water.

Everything else is "bad" for her, or so she says.

After I set her drink next to her, I crawl over her legs to my side. "It's simple then. No boyfriends allowed."

She scoffs. "What, then no girlfriends for you?"

Swirling my cup, the ice cubes clink against the side before I swallow. "I have you."

Her eyes narrow so tightly, I can barely see the blue. "Not the same, Alexei."

When she crosses her arms and slumps against the back-rest, I know she's done.

She's so confusing.

CHAPTER 7
LARA

Song- Nightmare, Halsey

My LUNGS BURN with one more mile left to run. Except I don't know if I'll be able to, the protein shake I had this morning probably isn't enough to fuel me. But I can't afford more calories after a bad week of eating. My jeans are already starting to feel too tight again.

Wiping the sweat from my forehead, I hold onto the bar, blinking as my vision starts to cloud. I hit the red stop button that puts me back into a gentle stroll as I heave for breath.

Fuck.

It rolls to a stop, and I try to regain my breath while downing some water. My shaking legs just about get me off the machine, but I can't let go as the room starts to spin around me.

I know this feeling too well. I keep drinking the cold liquid, remaining still and focusing on deep breaths in and out. It'll pass.

It will be worth it to lose the weight.

When I'm confident I can actually walk, I make my way out of my home gym and head straight to the shower.

Peeling off my sweaty workout gear, I toss it in the laundry. The hot mist starts to fill the room, but I can still see myself in the huge mirror on the wall. As I push my hair out of my face, I study my reflection.

I can see my hip bones again, hell, even my ribs through my skin.

Still hideous.

Tears prick in my eyes as I focus on the faint white stretch marks on my thighs. The more I look, the more I find wrong with myself.

Never good enough. Never pretty enough. Not even to be sold off as a wife.

I want to scream and punch the mirror so it shatters into a million pieces. There's a piece of me that wants to do it to every single one so I never have to look at myself again.

All I can hear in my mind is the comments over the years.

"Are you sick? You've lost so much weight, Lara."

"No man is going to want you looking like that."

"You look like you need to eat."

"You need to tone up if you want to keep a man."

I slam my hands down on the vanity sink and let the tears flow and step under the steamy spray. This is my daily ritual.

Maybe I need to go back to Alexei's cabin to adjust my brain again. It is the only thing that works. No social media, no people and only he knows where I am. I tell him when I am ready to come back and no questions are asked.

An hour later, I have a full face of make-up and blow dried hair. I don't have plans other than visiting Mikhail at the casino to get some more admin work done for him. My brothers are smart and ruthless when it comes to the mafia business. However, the casinos and bars, they couldn't give a shit about. That's where I come in, keeping the records clean so they don't land up in jail.

We don't trust anyone outside enough to deal with it and it's good, it keeps my brain busy.

I put on my gold Chanel heels to match my bag, perfect with my white slip dress. Thankfully I tanned yesterday, so my skin is glowing.

Just as I toss my bag on the passenger seat, I hear the familiar rumble of Alexei's BMW. As I look at the rear-view mirror, his black bike comes into view and of course, he pulls a wheelie as he crosses through the gate.

Every drive safe text I send him is utterly pointless, yet I'll never stop trying. I need him too much to ever leave me. He pulls up next to my car and I put down my window as he pulls his helmet and mask off, shaking out his dark curls.

With his teeth he pulls off his gloves.

"Where are you off to?" he asks, climbing off his bike and opening my door.

"Work."

"You got time for some lunch?"

I look at my Rolex and tap my chin.

"Hmm, I really don't know. My boss is kinda harsh, I don't wanna lose my job."

He holds out his hand and I place mine there as he pulls me up to my feet.

"You could lose him ten million and blow up the building and you'd still have a job."

I scoff but he's not wrong.

"See, you can't deny it either. You know you have all three of us wrapped around your big finger." He grins and falls into step next to me.

"Little, Alexei."

"Nothing little about me." He shrugs, putting his helmet under his arm and dragging me towards my own front door. He keys in the security pin and makes himself at home, rummaging through my refrigerator.

I sit up on the barstool and shoot a quick text to Mikhail that I'm running late.

He responds right away.

MIKI

Bring Alexei with you. Need to speak to both of you.

"Hey, A? You pissed off my brother?"

He pauses, turning to me with a tomato in his hand. "Which one?"

I flip my phone around to show him the screen. "Mikhail. He wants to speak to you."

He scratches his head. "I've behaved. I think."

I bite back a laugh at the fact he's genuinely trying to figure out what he's been doing.

"Oh." His face falls along with his shoulders.

One of my eyebrows raise. "What did you do?"

He chews on his lip and looks to the side. "There was a little mix up on the word 'blow' yesterday."

I rub my temple. This is no doubt going to cause me a headache. "In what way?"

"Well, when Nikolai told me to get the blow, I assumed he meant, you know, like boom." He mimics an explosion with his hands and pops the tomato which runs down his hands.

"Ew." He tosses it in the sink and washes his hands.

"So you blew the place up instead of getting the cocaine?" I shake my head. Nikolai should know better, especially with words like that.

He holds up his wet palms. "Yeah, my bad."

"Do I want to know how much drugs were in there?"

He pouts, grabbing a bottle of water from the fridge. "Enough for him to have me working like a donkey for the next year."

"I'll speak to him." I can sweet talk my brother about half

the time. I don't think even Mikhail can really be upset at Alexei, not after everything he does for this family.

He hands me one of the frigid drinks and motions to the vehicles. "I guess if the king is calling, we must go?" His grin shows his silver tooth as he holds the door for me.

"Are you riding with me?" Most of the time, I prefer it. I worry about how cocky he is on his motorcycle.

He shrugs and moves to the passenger side. "You'll be able to carry my body to the car? I want to be buried with my bike."

His palm flattens against the window when I back down the driveway. "Goodbye, Betty. We had a fun life."

My eyes roll. "You're being ridiculous. Mikhail would have told me if he was really that upset."

Alexei runs his fingers through his dark hair. "He's too hard to read with that mask on. I can never tell. At least in the plane, it's a thumbs up, or thumb down. I don't see his face."

My stomach tightens. "You're still doing those jumps?" I hate that he loves to skydive. Almost as much as I dislike that Mikhail is a pilot.

They're both too dangerous.

I can feel Alexei squinting at me, but I keep my face neutral.

"Maybe?" He draws the word out, still staring at me.

It makes my stomach grumble, thinking of him falling through the air.

What if his parachute doesn't open?

"I wish you wouldn't." Chewing on my thumbnail won't ease the rolling in my belly.

He turns away when the shadows of the building darken the car. "How else would I get out of the plane?" he grumbles towards the window.

I don't even have a reply to that.

When we pull into the parking garage, I find my designated spot near the main entrance.

The fact that Mikhail owns the casino does have its perks.

My heels click over the hard marble floor when we step through the glass automatic doors.

The wash of the air conditioning is refreshing after the stifling heat of the Vegas afternoon.

"I need an iced coffee first." I'll pay for the sugar later. It will help to soothe the nerves in my belly.

An extra half hour on the treadmill. I might skip dinner.

Alexei picks up two chocolate chip cookies and raises his eyebrows at me.

"I don't want one." I'm already going to be paying for this drink.

He looks confused. "They're both for me. See how little they are?" Holding them up separately, each is nearly the size of his hand.

How is that fair? He can eat whatever he wants without worry?

Yet I have to agonize about every single calorie.

Waving my hand in annoyance, I turn on my heel and head for the elevators. The girl in the kiosk knows to put it all on my account.

Working for my brother for so many years has earned me the right to walk into his office without knocking.

"Lara." Mikhail looks up from his desk over the black balaclava that covers the lower half of his face. His dark eyes narrow when he glances at Alexei sauntering in. "I'm glad to see you brought the fool." He points at Alexei with his thick index finger then jabs it towards the couch against the wall. "Sit. You're not useful to me today, but you're here for her."

The knot in my stomach tightens.

Any time Mikhail or Nikolai push Alexei to me, it's because something horrible is about to happen.

Alexei takes a huge bite of one of his cookies, spilling crumbs down his chest and onto the floor as he walks.

I bet he did that on purpose. I make sure to scowl at him when I sit next to him.

The disgruntled sigh that Mikhail makes when he stands indicates he saw what he did, too.

"I swear, Alexei." He shakes his head and steps around the edge of his big desk.

Mikhail is huge on his own, but when he gets closer he towers over us.

"I need to talk to you about what happened to Nikolai." His arms bulge as he crosses them over his chest. "It's about something I've kept from you." Mikhail's dark eyes slip to the side, averting his gaze.

What the hell did he do?

The iced coffee isn't cutting it, my stomach starts to roll with anxiety.

"Let me back up. You know that asshole Kirill? The one who got tied up with Knox and helped to try and kill Jax?" Mikhail growls the name.

"Yes, have you found him?" I know that guy has been elusive. Even Alexei has voiced frustration in trying to track him down.

"Well, he's the one who had a hand in sending Mila after Niki. He works for Ivan." He spits our father's name.

I just call him evil in my own head.

Alexei fidgets next to me. "Ivan makes my own father look nice."

When I glance at him, he smiles with chocolate on his lips. "That's saying something."

"It is." I don't know the details, but I've picked up through the years just how awful Alexei's parents were.

And that Mikhail took care of the problem.

"Ivan caused all of that chaos looking for Zoya." Mikhail runs his hand over his eyes, then rubs his temple.

Wait, I think Alexei mentioned that name. "Who is that?"

Mikhail takes a deep breath and lets it out slowly, fluttering the mask over his lower face. "Father's bride. She escaped *that night* and sought out our mother for help."

My straw makes a slurping sound as I suck up the last of my drink.

It needs alcohol.

Mikhail had already shuffled us to a safehouse away from Ivan before that night. It's like he knew our father was planning on creating havoc with us.

"Where did she come from? We weren't gone that long before the fire." I'll never forget the pain that Nikolai suffered when his wife died.

That was the last time I saw Mikhail's face.

"Our father like's them young, apparently. She was barely eighteen, and he didn't waste any time." His voice falls into hushed tones. "She was pregnant."

My hand flies over my mouth. "That poor girl. She was in the fire?" I squeak.

He nods. "She's who Ivan was after."

"What?" That makes me sit up and scream.

So many died that night.

The chaos has affected us for years.

Nikolai lost his wife.

And Elena, her mom.

I lost mine.

Jax lost his father and sister.

All because of her?

"I don't understand. Why does he still think she's alive?" I know Mikhail was the only survivor, besides Ivan who started the blaze.

Mikhail looks at me, then Alexei for a long moment.

"Because she is. And she was pregnant."

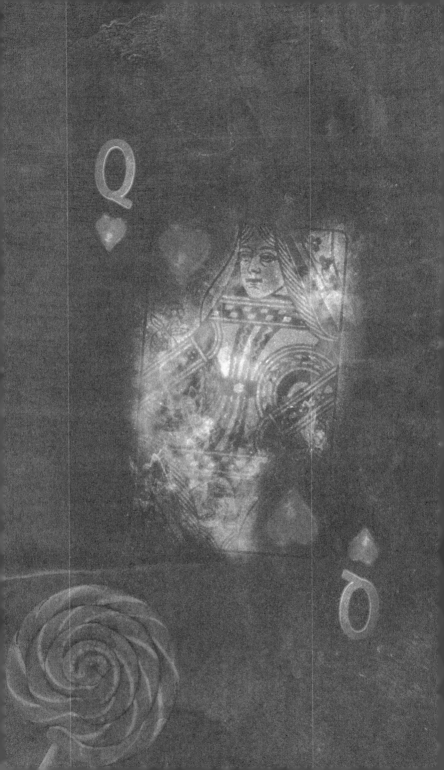

CHAPTER 8
ALEXEI

I WATCH her as Mikhail hits her with the surprise.

How is she going to react? What do I need to do to help her?

"What are you saying, Mikhail?" Her voice gets a squeaky high note in it.

She must be very stressed.

I hold out half of a cookie to her, and she takes it without looking at me.

Three big bites, then she swallows.

"She escaped and had a baby girl. We have a half-sister named Galena." Mikhail keeps his words even, his dark eyes studying her as intently as I am.

With a gasp, Lara cups her hand over her mouth and falls backwards against the cushions. When she looks at me, her cheeks are streaked with tears.

Oh boy.

I pull out my phone and text the housekeeper for the cabin. She needs to make sure it's fully restocked.

Every time Lara gets upset, she needs a time out. It's my job to make sure she has someplace safe to hide.

I just miss her when she's gone.

"What is she? Four? Maybe Five? Where is she? Are they here? Can I see her?" Lara's questions hit rapid fire, so quickly they turn into a blur.

Mikhail holds up his palms. "She's almost five. They're still in Russia in hiding. I've made sure they've stayed safe."

"You *knew* this whole time?" Lara almost shrieks.

Umm. Another message to send to the cabin saying extra wine.

I wish I knew another way to make her feel better, without crossing a line I can never return from.

"She needed to get away from Ivan. She is a victim of him, too." Mikhail squats in front of Lara so he's level with her. "It was easier to keep her hidden if as few people as possible knew about her."

Lara's blond hair whips as she turns to me. "Did you know?"

"Nope." I pop the "P" emphatically.

"Who else knows?" Her lower lip quivers as it juts out.

"Enzo," Mikhail grunts. "It's how I met him. I needed someone to keep an eye on things and move stuff anonymously."

Lara groans and crosses her arms. "No wonder he's going to Russia. I thought it was just to hire girls for his clubs."

"It's a convenient excuse. But I think he pays the girls very well since he makes his money in information." Mikhail pushes himself up and moves to his desk. "He's an incredible asset. I'm glad he's on our side."

Enzo saved Nikolai's ass when we were in Russia.

He's a mystery to me.

I don't think he likes me though. There's always a twitch of annoyance around his eyes when he looks at me.

"I can't believe you kept all of this from me." Lara buries her face in her hands and her shoulders begin to shake as she cries.

Glaring at Mikhail, I instinctively lean forward and start rubbing my palm up and down her back.

She falls against me, shuddering with sobs.

His brows drop, and I can see the muscles in his jaw work.

"What? You did this." My middle finger raises towards him.

He could fold me in half and not break a sweat. I don't care.

Lara is hurting. Every piece of me wants to make it better.

"Should we go?" My neck moves against her head.

I can feel her nod against my chest. Did I text already about the cabin?

Oh, yes. It'll be ready for her. She's going to need it.

Mikhail clears his throat before we leave.

"Alexei?" he asks.

Letting out an exasperated sigh, I pause Lara at the door. "What?" I don't hide the annoyance in my voice.

"You need to swing downstairs and talk to Nikolai after getting her home. They just got back from, um, vacation." His dark eyes bounce between Lara and I.

It's irritating that I can't see his face and read him better.

But I get the impression he's trying to tell me something else.

"Yes, Miki," I say curtly, then turn her down the hall.

Lara holds out her keys silently in the elevator. She's looking at a blank part of the wall and blinking really fast.

Two bottles of wine.

Leading her to the car, she pauses at the passenger door, letting me open it for her.

"I have a sister," she whispers before she focuses on me. "Can we stop at a drive through?" she asks as she clips her seat belt on.

"Yep, I know the perfect one." I wink at her then start the engine.

I fucking knew it.

As soon as I pulled in her driveway, she jumped out to begin packing.

"I feel sick." She runs out of her bedroom to her ensuite while I lean against her door frame.

I'm glad the sound of vomiting doesn't bother me. She always has a weak stomach when she gets stressed out.

Or eats a lot, like the great big greasy burger she had on the way home.

All I can do is wait.

She dabs her mouth as she leaves the bathroom and gives me a weak smile. "I should be ready soon. Maybe just a short trip?"

"Do you want me to drive you out there?" I'll know if she makes it safely either way.

But maybe I can talk her out of it if I'm driving?

"No, you have to go talk to Nikolai, remember?" Her hand burns as she puts in on my arm.

I wish I knew how to make her better. So she could not care about stuff out of her control like I do.

"Find out where he went? I can't believe he decided to go on a vacation so soon after barely surviving Russia. And being stabbed by Mila so many times." Her eyes roll before she turns to her suitcase on the bed.

"Okay." I saw Nikolai hug Mila fiercely in Russia to make her feel better.

I grab Lara by the wrist and pull her close. Wrapping my arms around her, I squeeze her against me. The heat of her body presses tightly to mine, and her hands lock briefly behind my waist.

It feels good to hold her.

"Have a safe trip to the cabin," I say as I step away.

Why did she look at me funny afterwards?

That was her confused expression, with her eyebrows peaked in the middle of her forehead and her eyes all squinty.

I don't understand what she could have mistaken it for.

Pulling my bike out onto the street, I'm confident that she was so shocked at the comfort she got it made her question herself.

That has to be it.

Nikolai is at Mikhail's casino. It's strange that I had to drop Lara off before talking to him.

It's her brother, after all.

His hulking frame is folded into one of the tables near the coffee stand, flipping through his phone.

"Mikhail said you wanted to talk with me?" The metal legs of the chair screeches as I pull it out and sit.

His blue eyes glance up and past me. "Lara with you?"

It irritates me that I had to leave her. "No. I had to abandon her in her time of *need*, Niki. Why am I here?"

He runs his fingers through his hair, and I catch a glint of a ring.

No way.

"I need your help breaking the news to her." He looks down at his cup of coffee. "I did a thing." The gold band on his hand clinks against the cup.

"Have you told Lara?"

He twists it with his thumb. "Not yet, I will."

"You know how much it hurt her with you going back to Russia? I keep her safe, now you go and upset her again."

"We didn't mean to."

I stand up quickly, knocking the flimsy chair over. "I'll look after her, don't worry."

Stomping away from him, I barely have the patience to wait for the glass doors to open, so I barrel through the manual one on the side.

Only on the streets of Vegas can a green haired clown

hang out in the same spot every day without getting in trouble.

The same one seems like it lives in front of Mikhail's casino.

Sometimes Lara giggles at his antics.

That's what I need. She has to laugh.

I push through the small crowd that is always gathered around him and grab his arm.

"Buddy. Do you do birthday parties?"

CHAPTER 9

LARA

WHICH ONES DO I BRING? My open toed sandals, or my flip flops?

Both. Why not?

It's not like anyone is going to see me. Or wants to.

I still can't believe Mikhail hid something so important from me for so long. I thought I meant more to him?

He's my brother!

It makes me want to scream and shake him. If only he wasn't so huge. I doubt I could budge him.

My bag has rollers that thrum across the tiles as I head into the living room.

And almost run directly into Alexei.

His silver tooth shows in a wide grin and he holds out a large bouquet of roses.

"What is this for?" Doubt tinges my words.

The last time he showed up with flowers, it was because he "borrowed" my Audi then "accidently" drove it into a pond at a golf course.

At least he paid for all of the repairs.

I can feel my eyes narrow watching him fidget with one of the stems.

"Well, I know today was a long day. You learned a lot of new things about your family. How does that make you feel?" He squints, raising one cheek to look at me sideways.

"How I feel? Since when do you ask that?" My arms cross over my chest.

Alexei isn't an emotions guy. He runs off of sugar and intrusive thoughts.

I'm not sure if he knows what caring really is.

He shrugs, pushing the bouquet into my hands. "Yep. Was it the worst day ever, or could have been worse?"

His lips purse and he leans forward, scrutinizing my face.

How do I explain to him I feel broken? Hollow? Betrayed?

That I want to run away to the cabin so I can cry for days where no one will bother me?

It's the only place that even Alexei gives me space.

I wish he knew how to fill in those gaps when I need emotional support, not just companionship. He's already my best friend.

But that's all he'll ever be.

His eyebrows bunch and he leans back. "I'll wait until you get back. Will you be here for my birthday? I'm having a party."

"That's next week. Of course I'll be back. But why a get together? You usually don't make a big deal about it." It's my turn to peer at him.

What is he hiding?

"You're having a hard day and thought that a celebration with some cake and ice cream might help." He shrugs, then pulls out a package of chocolate covered strawberries. "I got you these for today."

The berry part is okay, they're low in calories. But I try not to cringe about the chocolate.

Or the idea of having to stare at all of the sweets I know he'll have.

He lives on sugar.

"Thank you." I put them into the fridge and go back to my bag. "I do wish you'd just tell me, then I'll have some time to think about it." Or cry about it.

Either way, I can process.

Alexei squeezes one eye shut and watches me heading towards the door. "I dunno. What if it was that I'm going jumping again with Mikhail?" He bounces on his toes as he follows me. "Or, maybe we're going to pull a job on the Reapers?"

That makes me cringe. They've been a rival faction in Vegas for years.

It's been a bloody and brutal battle against them.

I've come close to losing him and Nikolai so many times.

"Why?" I pause on the porch, waiting for his answer.

"Well, because they work with Kirill. And we need to find him so we know what Ivan knows." He pulls a piece of hard candy out of his pocket and twirls it open between his fingers.

The porch light highlights his tattoos that run up his neck and over each ear, then sparkle off of his silver tooth when he grins.

"Ugh." I shiver. "I don't want to know that part. Please just be safe." It's hard some days knowing we all are involved in constant threat of danger. That at any moment a brutal attack could swoop down over us.

I want to pretend it doesn't happen.

"Maybe I've been punishing your boyfriends for not being nice to you?" His lean frame slides down the guardrail from the porch and he lands with a flourish.

"That would be nice, but I know that they don't want to talk to me. Besides, you don't even know most of them." I roll my eyes and put my suitcase into my trunk.

"What if I told you, I got a pet flamingo?" He hops down the steps ahead of me to open my car door.

"That would be ridiculous. And highly irresponsible. You always try to give dessert to the girls when we babysit." I wave my hand. "That's a wild one. But if you don't want to tell me, don't tell me. No need to make stuff up, I'm not a child anymore."

I'm just a woman with enough anxiety to shake start a cement truck.

And I need a break.

"Elena and Maeve love me. A little treat doesn't hurt them." He clicks his candy along his teeth. It sounds like when Jax drags his tongue piercing.

"It's not the once or twice, Alexei." I try to calm myself.

He's right. What they get is okay.

I'm the one that is broken. My father always had cruel words about my body, and it ruined my perception of food.

That's on me, not him.

"I have to go. If you won't tell me, I at least want to get to the cabin before dark." I slide into the seat of my Audi, wincing against the hot leather.

It turns into an oven in no time in Las Vegas.

His inked fingers curl over the top of my window. "I'll tell. I really do have a flamingo. That's why I went swimming in your car."

My jaw drops open.

I have no words.

He grins, and pushes the door shut. "Have a safe trip!" Waving, he steps away into the shade of the garage.

A freaking bird?

CHAPTER 10
ALEXEI

"I DUNNO, Jax. I don't know why you're all worried. They can't hurt that bad." I flip through a flash catalog on the counter of the tattoo shop.

"I still can't believe you don't have any piercings. How can you have that much art on your body, but no metal?" Jax clicks his tongue bar against his teeth.

I've found myself rattling my candy in my mouth the same way. It always gets a response from Nikolai when I do.

Sometimes it's a smack to the back of the head, but it's a reaction.

"Why are you getting one? You already have that one." I gesture at my lips. Every now and then the English words slip away from me.

"I have more than just that one." Jax winks one of his dark eyes at me, then sits in the chair next to the artist.

"Oh, I guess your ears count?" I never paid attention, but see the studs in his lobes beneath his curly hair.

"More than them, too." Jax grins at the ceiling as he leans back, closing his eyes as the man wipes his eyebrow with a square cloth.

Glancing at the pictures on the wall of various jewelry, one with nipple rings stands out.

Great big breasts with heavy bars through the tips. They're hard not to look at now.

"Um, you got some of them?" I point up, afraid to avert my eyes in case the photo disappears.

A magazine flutters across the room and hits my upper arm. "Stop ogling," Jax laughs before settling into the chair again.

"Well, do you?" Fine, I won't stare any more.

"No," he grunts, not even opening his eyes.

"Then where?" Why haven't I asked him this before?

Jax holds up one ringed hand and makes a finger pistol before pointing it at his own crotch.

Wait.

"Why in the fuck would you do that?" I pinch my own cock in sympathy pain.

"Drives the women wild," he chuckles just as the tech shoves a needle through his eyebrow.

He didn't flinch.

"Didn't that hurt?"

"Not really. I wanted to get Sofia and the kid's birth-stones." He sits up and turns the silver new bar towards me. "What do you think?"

"I think I want one."

"Like this?" Jax points to his temple.

I shake my head and move to the case where all of the accessories are. "No, like that." There's a bar through the underside of a plastic dildo standing in the corner.

Jax breathes out, blinking. "Are you sure? That's a pretty hefty thing to start with. Why?"

Lara will need extra cheering up once she finds out about Nikolai.

Maybe this will help.

Her and I aren't "that way", but if I have it, I bet it will still make her smile.

"You said it didn't hurt." I glance at the artist who's watching me with a smirk. "I want that one."

Jax claps me on the back. "I'll wait out here. I don't want to see your junk, man."

How bad can it be?

"Follow me." The short tattooed man with a rod through his nostrils beckons me into the same seat that Jax had been in.

"Never done this before, huh?" He sits and snaps on a new pair of blue surgical gloves. "Unzip your pants."

I might regret this.

Pulling my dick out in public isn't an issue.

Having someone else touch it, is.

"I have to sterilize it, this might be cold." He swabs around the tip with the iciest piece of cloth I've ever felt.

And I've fallen into a snowbank. Naked. In Russia. In January.

It was not like this.

"Okay, you might feel a poke." He glances up at me with his forehead furrowed. "Ready?"

I grit my teeth and turn away. "Do it."

Then he stabs me.

Through my *penis*.

"Holy *der'movyye shary!*" I scream. "Jax! It hurts!" I hope he heard me.

His laughter confirms he did.

"All set. Looks good on you, big boy." The guy rolls away, peeling off his gloves.

My cock twitches under the fluorescent lights and the metal rod catches the glare.

It throbs, and not in a need to jack off.

But like, I should put some ice on it.

"Here, you put this on it until it heals up in a couple of days." He hands me a little tub with some sort of gel.

"Wait. Days? How long will it hurt?" I'm already regretting this. "I have a party to plan. It's the most important thing to me. I can't be slowed down with a sore dick."

The small man shrugs. "Then maybe you shouldn't have gotten a cock piercing today." He stands then walks to the counter. "Come on over, I'll ring you up."

I don't want to move.

When I push my aching bits back into my pants, it feels like fire in my crotch.

Keeping my legs spread to reduce the friction, I waddle into the office area in the front of the shop where Jax is waiting.

"How ya doing?" He grins at me, clicking his tongue bar.

I want to rip it out of his mouth.

"Stay away," I grumble, digging my wallet out.

He laughs again. "I still don't know why you did that. You get that for Lara?"

Jax throws up his hands and feigns away when I half-heartedly swing on him.

I know he's the King of Chaos in the boxing ring. I'm no match for him, but I could always get lucky.

"Don't be stupid. I got it because you said it didn't hurt." Waving off the receipt, I start hobbling towards the door.

Every step moves my pants against the tender tip of my dick.

"I meant the brow one." Jax points at his eye, shaking his head. "The fact that you thought getting your pecker poked wouldn't be painful makes you the crazy one, not me."

I'm only crazy when I'm not around her.

She mellows me.

But the last thing I want is for her to come back and see me walking like an old man.

Maybe I'll tell her about Niki, that way she stays a few more days and I can get rid of the last loser who hurt her feelings without trying to limp up on them.

I need to go home and put an icepack on my crotch.

Besides, Sheila misses me.

CHAPTER 11
LARA

THIS IS the first time in three days after coming to the cabin that I can wake up, sit on the porch sipping coffee, and honestly feel relaxed.

Well, up until the moment I glance down at my ringing phone and see Mikhail's name on the screen.

"Yes?" I hope he doesn't ruin the thread of peace I've found today.

"Lara. I was just calling to see if Alexei told you, and to see how you're doing with it." His gruff tone almost hides the note of concern in his voice.

Blood pulses in my temples, giving me a headache. "He told me a lot of things, none of which I believed."

A flamingo? Really?

Mikhail snorts. "Why wouldn't you believe that Niki got married?"

I nearly drop my cell, but catch it in my lap.

"He what?" I shriek. "No, he would have told me!"

I feel like I've been hit in the chest with a sledgehammer.

If Mikhail did that, I'd get it.

But, Niki?

He wouldn't, would he?

"He married the bitch that stabbed him?" I can't keep the shrill out of my words.

Mila doesn't seem awful, and Nikolai did seem much happier once they returned from Russia.

Yet, the *audacity* to not even tell me?

I'm his sister!

Mikhail chuckles over the line. "Settle down. I didn't get invited either. Not that I'd want to go to a wedding."

Now it's my turn to be skeptical. "How much longer until yours?"

"I doubt there's a woman out there that could deal with me." He lets out a long sigh.

"You aren't that bad, if Niki can find two, you will be able to find at least one wife in your life. You have a better sense of humor when you decide to show it. Although, you might wanna let them see that pretty face of yours."

"Not happening," he growls. "What about you? Still dating?"

I know what he's doing, trying to shift things away from himself. "First dates, quite a few, second, none." There's been a few that I thought went well, but they ghosted me afterwards.

He takes a long pause. "Hmm, that might not be your doing."

"What do you mean?"

"Nothing," he says quickly. "They just clearly aren't good enough for you."

"Well, thank you. I guess."

What the hell is that?

A small buzzing sound is slowly getting louder.

"I have to go." I don't wait for his protest, but hang up on my brother, the big, bad mafia boss.

He'll always be just 'Miki' to me.

Where is that noise coming from?

Stepping inside the open sliding glass door into the kitchen, it seems to get quieter.

Outside on the deck, I work my way around the thick log walls before I see it.

A drone is hovering just over the main entryway beneath the awning.

It has a wicker basket hanging under it.

I'm not sure if I should get any closer.

"It's okay. Take it off the hook." Alexei's voice comes through the small speaker.

"What is this?" I find myself asking the flying machine.

"You told me to not come up and visit, or bug you, under any circumferences. No, that's not right." There's muffled arguing, but it sounds like it's all with himself.

"Circumstances." I correct him, and move closer until the downdraft of the tiny propellers whip my loose strands of hair.

When I pluck the container from the hook, the drone jerks up, nearly hitting the roof.

"Shit," he grunts.

Ducking, I back away from the wild antics as he stabilizes it.

"Alexei, where did you get a drone?" I yell from a safe distance.

"This is Enzo's. I might need to get one, this is fun." His cackle makes it static.

I can't imagine him with a drone unsupervised.

Lifting up the edge of the basket, the first thing I see is a red rubber ball over wrapped packages.

It's so squishy, I'm surprised when a slit opens when I squeeze it.

Seriously? It's a clown nose.

Feeling goofy, I slide it on and peer inside to see what else he sent.

How does he always know when I need a pick me up the most?

I wave at the leaving drone, then carry it into the kitchen.

The next parcel has a package of chocolate covered strawberries. Today, after what Mikhail told me, I'm grateful for the sweet treat.

I'll just walk extra tonight to make up for the extra calories.

There's a small box that has a note on top. Never one to read first, I discover a pair of sunglasses with a tiny flamingo printed on them.

I told you I had a flamingo, now you do too.

It's written in Alexei's scrawl.

He makes me smile.

I wish things could be different sometimes between us. He always knows what I need, and when.

He comforts me before I even know I'm hurt.

There's still a line though, one I'll never cross. Losing him would be devastating.

I don't think I'd survive it.

Nope. It's better to keep things as they are, than risk ruining it in search of something more.

Besides, there has to be someone else out there who can give me the physical things I'm missing?

Why can't I just be content with what he gives me?

Because I *do* want more. There's been times where I've been too tipsy, and almost did something I knew I'd regret.

I'm glad I haven't.

The last package is wide and flat.

I can't miss the words scrawled across the front.

"Picture of the strongest person I know." Is in thick black marker.

A gold gilded hand mirror.

Holding it up, I can see the tears forming in my own blue eyes.

His gifts are always random, but perfect.

One last message is across the bottom of the basket.

"I bet you want to know what the clown nose is for. Come home to help me with my circus and keep me from going crazy?".

Huh? What is he talking about?

My reflection catches the smile tugging up my lips.

It's going to be hard the next time I see Nikolai.

Somehow, it seems a little easier knowing Alexei will be there with me.

CHAPTER 12
ALEXEI

"Come on, come on. This way." I grab Lara's hand and guide her out onto the veranda in the backyard.

"Hold it right there. Don't move." I square her shoulders so she can face just perfectly.

"Alexei, you know this is ridiculous, right?" She takes a deep breath and lets it out slowly. It's tinged with the sweet wine we just drank inside.

I know she's trying to look upset, but the lift of her mouth says she's enjoying herself.

"Okay, you can look." Holding my arms out, I direct her blinking attention to my beautiful Sheila.

Lara's eyes widen. "No shit?" She takes a half step forward, then pauses. "Does she bite?"

"Just when I caught her. She didn't want to come home with me, but after I made her, she likes it here." Cupping my hand around Sheila's long neck, I urge her closer to Lara.

"Alexei." Lara's brows drop. "You need to let her go. She's a wild animal."

Her features soften when she reaches out and slowly strokes Sheila's pink feathered head. "She's gorgeous though."

"That time I borrowed your car? The stupid throttle locked and zipped me across that golf course. I didn't mean to, but I clipped her with the tire and broke her leg." I bend over and point to the healed limb. "She's better now, but still is slow at walking. So I'm taking care of her."

Lara's palm flattens over my wrist. "That's so sweet! What are you going to do with her during the party? Is that big pool out front that you're having set up for her?"

My head shakes. "No. That's for anyone who wants to swim, and I think the guys have a dunk tank they were talking about setting up."

Shit.

"I have to go, will you watch her for me?" I start moving out of the patio, but my dick still pinches when I walk.

"Alexei? What is going on with you? Why are you walking funny?" Her voice has a tinge of concern.

"Nothing. It's Jax's fault." I don't want to tell her what happened.

"What did he do?" Her brows furrow as she glances down, making her cheeks flush pink.

"He lied to me." I'll leave it at that. "I'll be back."

She looks confused, but I don't want to explain any further.

It only takes me a moment to find the bushy green hair of the hired clown.

"Hey, Bubbles." I feel strange calling a grown man that. "Is everyone here? My friends will be showing up any time."

The big man with the wild chartreuse wig turns and smiles so wide that the white makeup he has plastering his face cracks around his mouth. "Yes, boss. I have someone running the desserts and bar, and someone else setting up a pin-the-tail-on-the-donkey game."

I never really noticed he has an accent like mine before.

"Ty iz Rossii?" I ask him.

"Yes, I'm from Russia, but came here as a child." His

grin freezes at the edges. "Is there anything else? I need to get set up for the balloon animals and the magic show." The oversized red shoes on his feet twitch as he starts to back away.

"Just one more thing. The most important part." I grab hold of his arm to stop him, pulling him around to look me level in the eyes.

"Um, okay?" He squints at me before looking to the side. The oversized shirt grows taut as he tries to pull slowly against my grip.

I reach out and seize his other sleeve, squaring him up. "I'm serious, clown. This is vital." I let my voice drop, hoping he understands.

His painted chin begins to quiver. "I swear I'll do it. Please, man." Leaning away, I notice his palm beginning to ease into his pocket.

I bet he's going to show me his balloons.

"Listen. I *need* you to be funny. Make Lara laugh." My teeth grit inches from his red, bulbous nose.

The breeze of his rapid inhale whisks past my face. "Oh." He blinks rapidly. "Of course." He tugs away, smoothing out his purple shirt.

When he turns away, I hear him muttering to himself in Russian, but I don't pay attention.

I got my point across.

Today is going to be hard on Lara when she sees Nikolai and Mila for the first time.

I'd do anything to make her happy.

The first cars begin to pull in the driveway. I catch a glimpse of Mikhail followed closely by Nikolai and Mila.

Uh oh. I better go check on Lara before she sees them.

More tires churn over the gravel marking Jax and Sofia.

At least everyone is here. That should make Lara smile.

Limping my way back towards the veranda, I pinch the tip of my dick one last time and try to dull back the pain.

It doesn't hurt nearly as bad, and doesn't hurt at all when I'm naked.

That wouldn't be a good look here. Maybe I should have worn my silk boxers. I never thought about my zipper rubbing without any underwear on.

"Alexei, I think your bird looks excited. I heard vehicles, is everyone here?" Lara gets up from the lounge chair on the deck.

"Um, I think so. Let me just get her in her cage—"

Lara opens the door to the patio, and Sheila rushes forward with a squawk.

"No!" I chase after her, grabbing my crotch to keep the chafing minimal as I try to run. "Sheila! Wait!"

She flaps her wings and hops into the large kiddy pool I had set up for the girls.

Everyone watches me, but I don't care.

"Sheila, come here!"

I can hear Lara laughing at me. "Alexei, if she wants to swim, let her."

Her footsteps fade towards where my friends are gathered near the bar.

But I have to rescue Sheila.

Circling from one side to the other just pushes her to swim away from me.

"Why did her brother get to go, and not me?" Lara's voice carries to me as she jabs a finger towards Mila.

Crap, she sounds upset.

It looks like Mikhail is trying to calm her.

"I didn't get invited either. Don't take it personally."

Lara glares at him. "You rarely go to anything you're invited to. I'm surprised you're here, to be honest."

Mikhail shrugs.

Nikolai sighs. "Lara, it's done. We're just as married as if there were a million people there."

I can hear Lara getting upset.

Maybe I can do something to stop them all from talking. Hobbling over to the balloons, I grab one and pull out my knife.

This should work for getting Sheila out of the water. She hates loud noises.

When I pop it, everyone startles.

But Sheila doesn't get out of the pool.

Guess I need another.

"Alexei? What the hell, man?" Jax turns and yells at me.

I walk over, spreading my legs apart with each step. "I'm trying to scare Sheila out."

Jax starts laughing. "It isn't working." He points at the lazy circles the flamingo is doing. "Still sore? I told you not to do that shit."

Nodding, I cup my crotch. "I think by next week it shouldn't sting anymore."

Nikolai grunts. "What the hell did you do?"

Good, Lara is watching me and not him.

With a wide grin, I start to drop my zipper. "I'll show you."

"No!" They all join voices in trying to stop me.

I roll my eyes. "I saw Jax get his, but I wanted to get one, too. I just don't have any kids, so the stones didn't make sense."

"So you pierced your dick? I still think you're a dumbass." Jax snickers over his beer before tossing the empty bottle into the garbage can.

Lara pokes Nikolai in the chest. "I'm not done. Why wasn't I invited? Am I not a close enough family member?" A droplet runs down her cheek. "Am I not good enough?" Her lower lip trembles.

Fuck. This isn't working. She's supposed to be *happy*.

Nikolai kisses the top of her head. "Don't be silly. I love you. We didn't want a big fuss. You know me."

A horn blows, signaling a line of servers to appear with an oversized cake and tubs of ice cream.

"Time for the birthday boy to blow out his candles!" The green haired clown calls out while carrying the cake to the table.

Now is my chance to get her away. "Come on, Lara. Let's get a snack. It always makes me feel better."

She pauses, wiping her eyes. "No," she says, shaking her head. "I can't. I just, well, I need some air." Turning, she pulls away from my grasp and heads towards the woods

Shit. "I'm going to get her a slice."

I care about Lara more than Sheila. If my flamingo wants to swim, fine.

But I need to make sure Lara is okay.

"What's up with you and Lara?" Jax follows me over to the plates.

"We're friends." I shrug, picking up two slices.

I don't look at him, I keep my eyes fixated on Lara as she walks away. I hate the way her cheeks are reddening. Her jaw is tense and she's tapping her fingers on her palm.

She's upset.

Jax watches me, then gestures at her moving towards the trees. "You don't look at her like you're just friends."

"Fine. We're best friends. Just don't tell Niki, he will get all jealous, okay?" For a split second, I drag my focus to Jax and find him smirking behind his bottle of beer.

"What?" I ask in frustration.

He chuckles and shakes his head. "You'll figure it out one day, Alexei."

I don't know what the hell he's talking about. Right now, Lara being upset is my main concern.

When I glance up to find her again, she's disappeared into the thick grove.

"I'll be back," I tell Jax.

Lara needs me.

CHAPTER 13

LARA

I THOUGHT I had a hold of myself. But seeing Nikolai and Mila, with those shiny new gold bands on their fingers, just made me feel shitty all over again.

Every time I turn around, no matter how hard I try, it seems like I'm being pushed away or left out.

Am I not good enough? Am I too fat and they're embarrassed by me?

My hand reflexively reaches down and pinches the soft skin of my belly through my shirt.

Probably. It has to be something like that?

What is wrong with me?

Tears stream down my face and leave a salty burn on my lips.

All I want is to be wanted. Not ostracized by my own family.

This hurts so fucking bad.

When I hear the footsteps behind me, it irritates me knowing I don't have any peace and quiet. "Alexei, I don't have the patience right now," I say without turning around.

I love him, but trying to explain to him why I'm needing to get away could be exhausting.

Knowing all he wants is to make me happy, I know it isn't fair to him.

But right now, I want more than a joke or a treat.

I just want someone to make me forget the pain. To distract me so I can disconnect from this doubt and self-loathing.

To tell me it isn't my fault.

The crunching of the leaves on the dry ground gets louder.

Leaning against a tree, my arms cross in frustration. "Alexei, unless you're here to bend me over and make me forget my name, I'd really like some time alone," I say, maybe just half sarcastically.

If only. It's hard to ignore how crazy hot Alexei is sometimes.

The little bit of wine I had this morning on an empty stomach would give me a sense of courage I normally don't have.

A strange click comes from behind me.

"Alexei, please?"

Something cold and metal presses against the back of my neck.

"I don't know why you keep calling his name, he isn't going to save you. But you keep begging. I like it." The deep voice has a tinge of an accent that I know too well.

I freeze, my stomach rolling in panic. "What do you want?"

"You're going to come with me." He presses the hard object into the bottom of my skull.

It has to be a gun barrel.

My hands fly up reflexively in surrender. I'm completely unarmed. I don't even think I have my phone with me.

Stupidly, my anger got the best of me.

"Fine, I'll go. Are you sure you don't want a good time here?" I try to wiggle my hips suggestively as I walk over the rough terrain.

If I can delay him for a few minutes, I know Alexei will come and find me.

He always does.

There's a forceful shove between my shoulder blades and I tumble forward into the dirt.

"Move, you Volkov bitch," he spits.

Rough wood digs into my palms.

He's pissing me off. "My brother is going to kill you for that." I turn in time to see a flash of green hair and a purple shirt. "You have got to be shitting me. I'm being taken by a fucking clown?"

This has to be a whole new level of low in my life.

"Get up." His oversized shoe lands against my ribs.

I guess I'm lucky, the blunt end softens the blow.

"Fine, asshole." I get up in a hurry, losing one of my heels in the process.

Dammit. That was one of my favorites.

Whatever. Limping on a four inch lift is a pain, so I pull my other pump off after only a few steps.

"Keep going." He prods. "To your left. The white van."

As I get closer, the rear doors open and a shorter, thin man pops out.

His trimmed beard doesn't cover the smirk beneath his dark glasses.

"Ah, the princess. Welcome, Lara. We're going to have such a nice time." He opens a black cloth bag just as my wrists are locked behind my back by the green haired asshole.

Why does he look familiar? I can't quite place it, but I feel like I should know.

"I can see you're confused. Let me clear things up. My name is Kirill."

As he drops the bag over my head, my blood runs cold.

I remember now.

He works for my father.

CHAPTER 14
ALEXI

Song- DOA, I Prevail

I DON'T KNOW what the heck Jax is talking about. Of course I look at Lara as a friend.

I'd look at her as more, if I thought it wouldn't mess things up.

But I've seen my father and his girl friends. He beat them like he did me.

Lara has dated a lot of guys.

Most treated her poorly, so I removed them. No one deserves to live who treats her badly.

She must have gone farther than I thought.

Carrying the cake in one hand, I push into the thicker trees, hoping to catch a glimpse of her blond hair between the trunks.

I can't seem to find her.

Zig zagging through the forest, I pick up speed.

I want to surprise her, but how can I if she's winning at hiding?

Fine.

"Lara? Are you out here? Come back to the party, pchel-ka." I know it gets to her when I call her a Russian name.

Maybe she's cranky enough it will make her yell at me, and I'll catch her.

"Lara?" Worry starts to gnaw at me.

Pausing, all I can hear is my heartbeat, and the distant sound of the music playing back at my circus.

The whole thing is for her.

Where is she?

"Lara? I'm sorry, please come out?" There's a set of low bushes. I bet she went in there.

Putting the plate on the ground, I crouch and push through the thicket to find nothing but a balled up garter snake.

"Have you seen Lara?" I call after him as he leaves.

I might as well be talking to Sheila.

Or Percy. But I doubt my motorcycle can tell me where she is either.

Would she leave completely? Did she cut back to the road and then walk around to her car?

Surely I'd have seen her leave.

No, I better check.

I'm halfway there when I remember the cake.

Fuck.

Running through the woods, I find it already covered in ants.

It's ruined. She's gone. The day is a failure.

Shit.

Turning back, I head towards where everyone is. Sitting on the picnic table, it's hard to be happy when she's not here.

"I can't believe I messed up. She's my responsibility," I groan. I'm such a fuck-up.

Mila looks up. "What do you mean? Aren't you guys a thing?"

My brows knot. "No. I keep her safe. It's always been that way. It's my purpose. And, I failed." My arms fall flat and I drop my forehead onto them.

She reaches out and pats my shoulder. "She'll turn up. She probably just went for a walk."

Lara should be back. She knows I'd worry.

There has to be something I'm missing.

Looking around, I don't see anything out of the ordinary.

Pin the tail on the donkey. A baggy panted clown is doing the balloon animals. The green haired one is doing the magic show.

Except he isn't.

Where is *he?*

It hits me. "The green one."

Nikolai has a puzzled expression.

I have to find Mikhail. He'll know what to do.

Grabbing his arm, I pull him away from his conversation with Jax near the balloons. "The magician. He had the green hair. Where is he?"

The clown dressed with the oversized pants shakes his head. "We don't have anyone like that. We thought he was a special hire for the gig." He holds his palms up towards Mikhail, his painted face exaggerating the scared look.

Mikhail yanks my shoulder and drags me with him towards the trees. "Where did you look?" he growls through his mask.

Nikolai and Jax jog up behind us.

"We'll go this way." Nikolai points in the direction I was going to cut through towards the road.

Mikhail pulls me through the trees. "Show me how far you went."

"I know I fucked up. I shouldn't have let her go." I can't keep the whine of worry out of my voice.

"Alexei." He pauses, stopping me. "I know you'd never do anything to hurt her. I trust her with you, and that isn't given lightly. I don't know what happened, but I know it wasn't your fault."

I didn't expect that.

It almost makes this whole thing slightly easier.

Nikolai will still be pissed at me.

"Here's the cake." The plate is covered with a mass of ants and beetles. "And then I crawled in there." I point into the bushes. "But she wasn't there."

"Okay. You go that way." Mikhail gestures to my right.

Frantically, I start running in the direction he pointed.

It isn't until my phone rings that I stop.

"Nikolai?" I'm out of breath.

"We found her—"

"Where is she?" Before I wait for a reply, I sprint back the way I came.

"She's gone, Alexei." His voice sounds so…final.

"No. She's not dead." Faster I bolt through the trees, my arms pushing limbs out of the way as they lash against my face.

"Alexei!" he yells. "We found her shoe."

It doesn't matter. I run until my lungs burn and my legs feel like they're going to give out.

If I'm fast enough, I'll catch her.

A thick arm snakes out and whips across my chest.

I almost strike out at whoever stopped me. They're keeping me from her.

She's mine.

My Lara.

"Alexei! Come on!" Jax wraps his thick biceps around me, squeezing me against the urge to keep going. "We need to make a plan," he grunts into my ear as I squirm.

"No! I'll find her!" My voice cracks.

I don't know a world without her.

She's always there. It's me who goes. Off on jobs. Off on adventures.

Lara is where I leave her. She's my anchor.

My base.

Tears stream down my face as the struggle starts to leave my body.

I can't stop looking for her. "She has to be here."

"We'll find her. I promise." Jax lets me go and watches me. "You good?" His dark eyebrows knot.

I nod. It's all I can do.

"Okay, let's head back." His hand sits on my shoulder as we walk.

I feel like I've lost every purpose I've ever known.

My chest is empty.

I didn't know she filled it like this. It aches.

We get back to the tables where Sofia and Mila look up at us.

Jax holds up the high heel he found.

It's her favorite. She never would have taken that off, especially not in the dirt.

Nikolai runs his hand over his jaw. "She's been taken."

CHAPTER 15
LARA

"Time to wake up, Lara." A deep, unfamiliar voice cuts through the fog of slumber.

When did I fall asleep? There's a filmy layer in my mouth that has a faint acrid aftertaste of chemicals.

Did they drug me?

Blinking, the room is somewhat dim, but bare.

The thin mattress does nothing to stop the creaking of the metal frame when I sit up.

Kirill sits in front of me, with a big man languishing on a chair behind him.

A tinge of white still cakes the skin around his eyes.

It's the fucking clown.

"What the hell am I doing here?" I demand. My rise is stopped by a handcuff around my wrist that's fastened to the end of the bed.

"Your brother was proven to be useless. So you're next on the list." Kirill crosses one leg over the other at the knee. "And there isn't anyone here to save you." He leans back and pulls a pack of cigarettes from his lapel.

"You know those things will kill you." I give up on trying to tug at my restraint, so I flop back against the lumpy pillow.

"Your kind thoughts on my wellbeing are noted." He flicks a brass lighter and holds it up.

"Oh. I'm sorry for the confusion. You misunderstood 'get fucked and die'." I throw my free arm over my eyes.

Kirill chuckles and takes a long drag, blowing smoke over me.

"You have your father's fire, I see." His foot hits the floor.

Grabbing my hand, he jerks me off of the bed onto the cold concrete and presses his knee into the middle of my shoulder blades.

The hard edge of the cuffs digs into my skin, stretching me painfully as I struggle to breathe.

"We need to set some rules, my dear." Kirill's lips rest almost against my ear. "I ask the questions, you answer." He shifts and holds the burning ember near my eye. "You don't have to see to talk."

A frigid chill runs through me, despite the heat from his body over me. "Okay. I get it." I can't keep the stammer out of my voice.

It must be enough to convince him, because the weight on me disappears, leaving me splayed out next to the small bed.

"Get up," he barks, already back in his reclining pose.

Shit. My tethered elbow feels like it popped out of joint and aches when I move it.

With a groan, I roll myself back onto the creaky cot.

My breasts feel squished and my ribs are sore, but mainly it's just my arm that hurts.

Am I supposed to feel lucky that's all the damage he's done yet?

"I just have a single question for you. Once you've answered it, you'll be let go." His thin lips wrap around the filter as he takes a long inhale.

"Fine. What is it?" I have a feeling I already know what it's going to be.

Kirill leans forward with his elbow on his knee. Smoke falls from his nostrils like a raging bull. "Where. Is. Zoya?"

My heart stops.

She's the mother to my *sister*.

There's no way I'll give her up.

"Who?" I bat my lashes with the best look of innocence I can muster.

Kirill's features fall neutral and he stares at me long enough it begins to make me uncomfortable. "Perhaps you just need some time to think about what is truly important." Standing abruptly, he slings his chair against the far wall and stomps from the room.

The silent guy in the corner doesn't move.

"What? Are you the muscle that's supposed to break my legs? How'd you even convince Alexei to hire you?" I'd throw something at him if I could.

Not my pillow. I might need that.

He stands with a grunt. "Just tell the boss what he wants, and I won't have to hurt you."

The door closes, leaving me alone in the bare room.

A bed, and two chairs.

How am I going to get out of here?

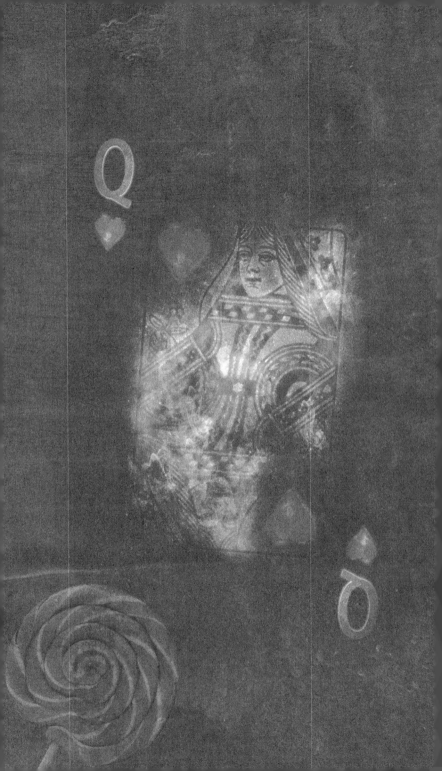

CHAPTER 16
ALEXEI

"THAT'S HIM!" My finger jabs the screen hard enough it flickers.

"Alexei, stop fucking up my laptop," Enzo growls at me, pushing my arm away.

Standing behind him, I can't keep still. Bouncing from one foot to the other, I drop my chin to hover above his shoulder so I can watch.

His typing pauses, and his head turns slowly. "You're breathing in my ear." His dark eyes narrow.

Mikhail grunts from his desk behind me. "Alexei. Do we need to take a trip?"

"No," I whine. "I need to stay and help." I can't go anywhere while Lara is missing.

My heart doesn't work the same since she's been gone.

Mikhail's heavy hand lands on my back. "Come on. I'll take you up and you can see if you can find her."

I know that it won't work.

But I *need* to do something.

At least jumping out of a plane will make me focus on something else.

It's been two days since Lara was taken.

I haven't slept. I haven't eaten.

Candy isn't as sweet.

The thought of a cowboy makes me almost cry because we can't finish Yellowstone together.

"I gotta watch and make sure Enzo doesn't miss anything." It's becoming a reflex holding the tip of my dick through my pants, even though it doesn't hurt anymore.

"Alexei. You're acting like a toddler who has to pee. Get your ass in the hall." Mikhail gives me a shove towards the door.

"Thank you, Mikhail. Alexei, I promise I'll let you know if I find out anything," Enzo calls out as we leave.

"But—"

Mikhail cuts me off. "We're doing everything we can. Once Enzo finds the van, he'll let us know. Or that green haired fucker decides to show his face again."

"Maybe he took her because of how funny Lara is," I grumble as I follow him.

Mikhail stops and stares hard at me over his mask. "Are you joking?"

I shake my head. "She makes me laugh all of the time. Is that how clowns are made? They just take people? I don't know anyone who grew up *wanting* to be one."

This void in my chest is gnawing at me.

It's like my skin doesn't fit right anymore and bugs keep crawling through the gaps.

Mikhail drops his head and doesn't answer, but pulls me with him.

He drives us to the airport and through the side gate to his plane.

"I don't feel like jumping today." My favorite reason was so I could hope to catch a glimpse of Lara standing on the deck of the cabin.

"You're gonna be my co-pilot." He hands me a headset and points to the seat next to him.

"Why are we doing this? We should be looking for Lara." Only half of what I say makes it into the mic as I slide it in front of my mouth.

He calls in to the tower and idles us onto the runway before glancing at me. "Sometimes, you work best when you don't know you're working."

Pushing the throttle, the g force pushes me back into the chair.

I usually like this part. The anticipation of a dive always makes my heart beat faster.

Today, it just feels like I'm running away.

As the trees grow smaller, I can hear the static before he talks.

"I want you to tell me about why you wanted a clown." Mikhail banks us away from the cabin.

"To make Lara happy." Easy.

"Why did you want to make her happy?" He prods.

"I knew she'd be upset about Niki and Mila. She was already mad about Zoya and your sister." I can't get the image of the tears in Lara's eyes out of my head.

Fuck, I need her back.

"Look over there." Mikhail's thick hand extends in front of me.

"Hey, I can see my house!" There's the backyard where Sheila lives.

It's the last place I saw Lara laugh.

"What did you tell the clown?" Mikhail's voice has almost a hypnotic cadence through the speakers.

"I told him to be funny." It was important to me. Ever since I was little, it's been my purpose.

The clown has been here since he was a small boy.

"He was from Russia, too." I'm still trying to keep my home in view when the wings tip the other direction. "Hey, where are we going?"

"You never mentioned that before." The set of his jaw beneath his balaclava means he's determined. Or pissed.

I'm confused. "That matters?"

"Very much. I bet that means he's somehow affiliated with my father," he growls before calling back into the tower to announce his landing.

"We're going back down?" I feel like I'm in a whirlwind.

If Lara was here, it'd be better.

"Yes. Mission accomplished, Alexei. You did good." He taxis back to the hangar at record speed, digging out his phone as we coast to a stop.

"Enzo. The clown was Russian. Start sweeping Kirill's known areas." He ends the call and drops his cell in his pocket.

I'm barely unbuckled before he's climbing into his car.

"That has to be the shortest flight we've ever taken." I barely close the door before he's rocketing us backwards and back to the casino.

Stalking into his office, he points at the couch, but doesn't look back at me. "Sit, Alexei."

"I want to help." I stand defiantly, jutting my chin.

"Oh, you will. I just need a minute to nail down the direction." Enzo glances up at me with a grin. "Knowing that the clown was Russian opened the floodgates."

Fuck. I wish I had said something about it sooner.

I didn't even think about it.

Not having Lara here is messing with my head. My thoughts are jumbled.

All I can focus on is her.

CHAPTER 17
LARA

"How much longer do I have to stay here?" I ask the big man when he comes in with my tray.

He looks down at the table, still piled with the food from this morning.

"Until you remember where Zoya is," he grunts before slamming the door shut.

My stomach grumbles as the fresh scent of bread wafts over me.

I can do this. I'm used to going long periods without eating to try and lose a few pounds.

Just imagine how thin I'll be.

Everyone will love me then.

I bet even Alexei.

I miss him terribly. Is he worried about me? He's always the one who leaves to run off on some adventure, or go work some job.

Does it bother him now that I'm the one gone?

Is he able to feel hollow like I do when he goes? Like a piece of me is missing.

I must be crazy. Thinking more about Alexei than even my own brothers?

Nikolai has his new wife, and Elena, my sweet, adorable niece.

Mikhail has secrets.

And the biggest one landed me here.

Captured and alone.

But Alexei, he's always been there for me.

And I might not survive to see him again.

I swear, if I get out of here, I'm going to do something wild. Show him that there could be more between us.

The thought of being without him terrifies me.

What if he meets someone else? She'd be prettier than me.

I wouldn't stand a chance.

With a squeak, the door opens and Kirill steps in.

This is becoming a routine.

"I see you haven't been hungry." He extends a single finger and tips the latest tray on the table near me.

"Did you come here to torture me?" I ask, watching him warily.

He pushes at one of the uneaten sandwiches. "It seems you've already been doing that to yourself."

Dragging a chair from the wall, he pulls it close, but just out of reach. His leg crosses at the knee as he lights a cigarette.

The acrid smoke burns my lungs long before he talks again. "Have you thought any more of my question?"

"I don't know anything about Zoya." I cross my arms as far as the cuffs allow me.

He adjusts his suit sleeve and scowls at me. "I find that hard to believe given the circumstances of her disappearance." Leaning forward, he exhales another billow of hot vapor. "Considering your mother died that night, I'd think the memory would be burned into you."

Long buried grief tries to well within me, making my chin quiver as I fight the tears.

I can't count the days I spent curled in Alexei's arms crying over the loss.

She was the only one who thought I was beautiful, and perfect.

Losing her broke something within me.

But Zoya had my sister. Mom helped her get away.

I can see my mother doing that. She gave of herself constantly to try and protect us against Father.

The monster.

My jaw sets and I tilt it up defiantly. "My mother died knowing she was protecting an innocent."

The corner of his mouth twitches and his dark eyes narrow. "So. You knew she was pregnant." His ember brightens as he takes a long drag. "I think you know more than you're letting on. A bit more time might loosen those lips."

Fuck. I messed up.

CHAPTER 18

ALEXEI

> **ME**
> Any news?

> **ENZO**
> This is the hundredth time you asked me today.

> **ME**
> But something might have changed.

> **ENZO**
> Well, you're right.

> **ME**
> I'll be there in ten minutes.

I BLOW through two stoplights on the way to Enzo's club. I don't even care. I'm not stopping when there could be news about Lara.

Skidding my motorcycle to a stop in front of the discrete blacked out entrance of his club, Ashes, I run through the main doors.

"Hiya, honey. Where can I direct you?" A scantily clad brunette with a bustier tries to saddle up to me.

"I need to talk to Enzo." Grabbing a hold of the inside glass door, it doesn't open.

"Sweetie, this is a member's only club." Her bottom lip sticks out in a pronounced pout. "Do you have an appointment?"

I try the handle again, just in case it unlocked in the last thirty seconds. "No. But he knows me."

"I bet he does, a handsome man like you. Can I get your name?" Her fingers trail down my chest.

I don't have time for this. Anger ignites in my belly and boils into my chest.

"Open. The. Door." My breathing comes in deep heaves.

"Just give me your name, hun. I'll make sure he gets the—"

A chair with steel legs makes a great way to shatter a window.

Another swing, and the slivers splinter away enough I can reach through and open the latch from the inside.

The glass crunches under my boots before I stride inside the dim foyer.

"You can't go in there!" she screams after me.

Two big, burly guys come running from the office and leap at me.

One drops when I connect my helmet with his face.

Beast number two wraps me in a bear hug.

Fuck, I can barely breathe.

Lashing my head back, I connect with his broad nose. There's a crack and a rush of hot fluid that runs down my neck.

He drops me with a grunt.

Running, I dodge another guard until I find Enzo's name on a placard.

Just as I'm about to grab the handle, the door flies open.

Enzo's eyes are wide, but they narrow quickly into a glower when he sees me.

"Why am I not surprised that all that bullshit was you?" He points towards the front hall and the lumbering men working their way closer. "You're paying for the glass." Turning on his heel, he gestures for me to follow.

"I need to know what you found about Lara." Giving the closest guard a smirk, I shut the office in his face.

"Not enough to warrant destroying my fucking club, Alexei. Next time, just give Bambi your damn name." Enzo sits in his leather chair with a sigh and glances up at the wall of monitors next to him. "I knew it was you." He waves at the camera feed above him. "You're on the fucking roster to come in." His palm runs over his face.

"What did you find out?" I'll worry about all of that other shit later.

Enzo blinks at me. "I already told you through a message." He holds up his phone and flashes the screen at me. "I found a flight to Russia booked under a known alias for Kirill. They're still here."

I dig out my cell and read the text, word for word what he just said.

"Oh."

My mind races. I still have a chance to find her.

"Did you look at their warehouse?" I ask.

"Yes."

"The Reaper hangout?"

"Yes, Alexei."

"What about the hotel they run near the airport?" I press him.

Enzo sighs again. "You think I don't know about those places? I'm the one that showed them to *you* in Mikhail's office."

"I came all the way down here just to know she's so close, but out of reach?" Frustration has me slumping against the wall.

I need to think. When Nikolai and Mila were taken, how did I find them?

Wait.

"I didn't tell you to," he growls, turning to his keyboard. "If you want me to keep you updated, stop being such a jack-ass." The back of his fingers wave me away.

"Fine. But please, tell me if you find out anything new?" I'm desperate.

"Go apologize to Bambi, and I'll think about it." He doesn't look at me, but I know it's time for me to leave.

The three big guards glare at me as I walk past. One has tissues stuffed up his nostrils and blood drying on his white shirt.

They follow me closely as I dodge the housekeeper vacuuming up the glass.

Bambi's eyes widen when I get closer.

"I apologize. My name is Alexei, so you know for next time." Pushing out into the hot sun, I don't wait for a reply.

I have an idea.

That woman in Russia, she would know how to get Lara back. She knew what to do to get Nikolai and Mila free from Ivan.

The real question is how do I find her?

Pulling out my phone, I scroll through my contacts until I find a name I haven't called in a very long time.

"Max? It's me, Alexei. I have a favor."

There's a grunt from the other end as I fill him in.

"Wait. You want me to find *Tatiana Novik?*" he groans. "She's a fucking dragon."

"Yea. I know. I need her fire to save my friend." I miss Lara like I miss breathing. Her being gone makes me feel like I'm suffocating.

"No, no, no. You must have gotten more crazy. No one is worth going into debt with Tatiana." Max makes a swallowing sound.

Knowing him, it was probably a long pull from a bottle of cheap vodka.

"Lara's worth it." I'd do anything to get her back.

Max laughs wryly. "There is no pussy in this world worth dealing with that vulture of death."

That makes me pause. I've never fucked Lara. It was always something I thought was against the rules.

Would I want to? Yes.

But do I want to risk losing her over it? No.

I'd stay celibate forever for her.

"She's worth it." I'm firm with my answer.

Max chuckles. "It's your funeral, friend. We had some wild times, it's too bad they'll all be in the past."

"Please, Max?" I hate to beg.

But I would crawl on my belly through the slivers of Enzo's shattered door if it meant I got to see Lara again.

"Fine, fine. I'll get word out. Be ready. Rest in peace, fucker." The line goes dead when he hangs up.

I'll be okay. I've been practically face to face with Tatiana before, and walked away.

Thirty-six hours and twelve minutes later, and I'm standing on a secluded corner in an alley off eighth street under a broken street lamp at four am.

Who the hell wakes up this early?

Las Vegas is a strange town. The street sweepers are the only ones working, cleaning up discarded fliers and cups. It's like the entire city revolves around the Strip.

I'm glad I'm away from prying eyes.

Well, maybe having a witness would be in my best interest.

Fuck. Of all the luck in the world, two Reapers are actually here when I am? I'd recognize their leather vests and heavy beards anywhere.

One is thick and tall, the other lean and shorter than me.

Shit.

All I have is a knife.

I try to press myself against the brick wall. Maybe they won't recognize me?

As they get closer, I catch them staring at me.

Slowly, I pull the knife from where it's hidden at my lower back. I won't go down without a fight.

"No need for that, Alexei." A woman's voice comes from the smaller man.

What?

When they are only a few feet away, I can see the dark eyes of Tatiana behind the beard.

"You beckoned?" she asks, a smile tugging up the thick fake fur covering her face.

"You're crazy, you know? Pretending to be one of them?" I glance up at the bigger guy.

He winks at me, then cracks his knuckles.

She shrugs. "I have insiders in every faction. It lets me go where I please." She crosses her arms over the vest. "My patience is wearing thin. Talk."

"Lara was taken and Mikhail thinks it was by one of Ivan's men." The words tumble out of me.

They make a knot in the back of my throat.

It's been over a week since I've seen her.

"So?" She raises one eyebrow.

I wonder if it's her real one. How detailed is that makeup?

When I lean closer, she bats me away. "I'm going to ask Damon to break your neck if you do that again." One long manicured nail bounces off of my chest. "Time's up."

"Wait, no." I reach out and grab her arm.

The big guy backhands me hard enough I bounce off the bricks. "No touching." He spits in a thick accent.

"I need her back. I need her here, with me." I can't stop the whine from lilting through.

Her mouth twists the hairs around it. "This is Nikolai's sister? Ivan's daughter?"

I nod.

"You know what it means, asking for my help?" Her fingers tap her chin as she watches me.

"Yes. I'll do anything." I look at her with the most sincerity I can muster.

"Max told me you have no limits. That can be handy. You'll work for me until I deem the debt paid. *Khorosho*?" She holds out her palm.

"Okay." I agree to her terms. I extend my arm to shake hands.

"No, fool. The knife. You're swearing a blood oath." She snaps her fingers and points to my back.

My blood runs cold. I could be signing over my life.

Shit.

Flipping the handle towards her, she takes it and hovers it over my open hand.

With a single slice, she marks me as hers.

CHAPTER 19

LARA

I'M SO TIRED, I can't keep my eyes open.

Weak.

It takes effort to focus on moving. Everything feels heavy.

I'll just lie here and count my heartbeats. That sounds like something I can do without too much work.

How can I be this calm? Like the stress of the world doesn't bother me anymore.

I just want to sleep.

So I do.

Drifting in and out, I have no idea how much time passes. It just takes more work every time I struggle to look around, I finally just give up.

A loud bang almost startles me enough to open my eyes.

But not quite.

Kirill's deep voice almost pierces the fog. "Fuck. We can't let her die, that isn't the plan. We need information."

Muffled sounds resemble an exchange, but I can't understand the words.

I don't care.

"We aren't ready to fight Mikhail, not yet." His smooth fingers slap against my cheek.

My eyelids flutter weakly letting in a flash of light.

Then darkness.

"Shit. She hasn't eaten this whole time?" he growls across the room.

"No, boss." The clown moves closer.

Kirill hits me again, harder. "Wake up," he commands.

I can't.

When the footsteps fade, I'm sure I'll be left alone again.

Good. I'm enjoying the lack of dreams. I guess my body thinks that takes too much energy too.

It's interrupted by rough hands jerking me upwards.

"Open your mouth."

No.

I'm too weak to utter the word.

Hard fingers dig around my jaw, trying to pry it apart far enough for something hard pressing against my lips.

Every bit of strength in my body goes to keeping my teeth firmly shut.

Screw him. He isn't going to win this battle of wills.

I've been doing this my whole life.

"Fucking bitch," he grunts. "Fine, I'll make you take it."

A metallic grating sound hits my ears just as the blinding pain explodes from my mouth.

Now I look.

The handle of a knife protrudes from my cheek where he twists the blade, forcing my chin down.

Both of my wrists are cuffed when I try to move them.

Screaming around the blood pouring into my throat, it bubbles down my chest.

He doesn't pause, but takes a thick tube and shoves it past my teeth and over my tongue, gagging me as he pushes it further.

"Pour the shit in," Kirill says over his shoulder to the other man.

The clown pops the top of a protein shake and dumps it messily into the tube.

My stomach tries to seize at the intrusion, twisting against the foreign food.

Trickles of it run down the outside of the plastic and mix with the blood on my lips in a chalky tang.

The empty can rattles against the wall when he throws it, then the length of tubing is ripped out of me.

I want to puke.

"No you don't." Kirill stuffs a pillow behind my head, then grabs a roll of thick duct tape next to him. "If you hurl that shit up, you're gonna choke to death. Eat up, Volkov. You don't get off that easy." He sticks a long piece over my mouth that wraps over the wound in my cheek.

He wipes his crimson stained hands on my mattress and sheathes his blade. "I'm going to start cutting off fingers and toes and shoving them down your gullet if you decide to keep testing me."

Squeezing my eyes shut, I try to wish my belly to stop being as queasy as he slams the door shut behind him.

I thought I had an out.

Shit my face hurts.

How bad is it?

Now, I'll be even more hideous. No one is coming to get to me.

I'm not sure what I'm clinging to.

CHAPTER 20
ALEXEI

Song- Self-Destruction, I Prevail

I'M NOT sure what I'm looking for.

The text I got from an unknown number just said to wait on this corner. I seem to be doing that a lot lately.

JAX

Where are you?

ME

I can't tell you.

JAX

WTF Alexei, we're supposed to go to Vox and pick up the payment.

ME

I'm on a corner. You'll have to go without me.

JAX

Just on a random corner? Looking to give your new piercing a spin?

That makes me involuntarily pinch the tip of my dick where the bar rubs against my zipper. It doesn't hurt anymore.

In fact, it feels pretty good when I mess with it.

When a woman walks by and gives me a grossed out expression, I let go.

ME

No. I'm saving that.

JAX

We'll find her.

I blink at the phone. He thinks I'm saving it for Lara?

Maybe I am.

Would that be so bad?

Except I promised Mikhail and Nikolai to protect her.

Every man she's been with has hurt her. Killing them may have removed the problem, but only temporarily.

Do I just eliminate every other man out there?

Or is there a chance she'd be happy with me?

I don't want to be the cause of her pain, though.

Fuck, I hate this. I don't even know what I'm supposed to be looking for.

Tipping my head back, I try to see on the tops of the buildings.

What is that up there?

Just a couple of steps back, and I might get a better angle.

Someone runs into me from behind.

"Hey, *zhopa*, watch where you're going." A big guy grunts from behind me.

Hey, I know that voice.

Turning quickly on my heel, I peer into the unpainted face of the clown.

He doesn't have green hair, but I know it's him.

And he recognizes me. His eyes flare wide and he begins

to back up.

"I almost know who you are." Leaping, I wrap my arms around his neck and bite the end of his thick nose until a piece shears off into my mouth.

Spitting it out, the blood pours before he screams and covers his face. "Now I'm sure."

Tatiana is brilliant.

There's an empty building so handy. It's almost like she planned this.

I'll have to remember not to piss her off.

Shoving the man through the unlocked door, I slam it shut behind me and kick him in the side of the knee.

"Where the fuck is Lara?" I shriek.

He stumbles before falling to the dusty floor. His hand reaches for his waistband, but I jump on him too quickly, driving my fist into the missing piece of his nose.

Tugging his hidden gun from his belt, I hold it idly on him while he cries into his fingers and pull out my phone.

"Jax? I need your help." I text him the pin to my location as soon as he answers. "Hurry." I hang up before he can reply.

What was this place? It looks like an old restaurant.

The big man lays his palm flat and starts to push himself up, but I drive my heel into the back of it hard enough that the bones crunch under my boot.

"Fuck," he grunts, rolling away from me.

"I know you took her." I land a solid kick under his chin, throwing his head back against a counter. "Where is she?" My fingers dig into the front of his shirt and I throw him again.

He claws at a drawer trying to get away. "You'll never find her." He spits at me, spraying my face.

My hand covers his, and I jerk the handle hard enough that a geyser of utensils falls over us, but the corner knocks him in the temple.

When he slumps to the floor, I don't quite trust that he's

really unconscious.

I've faked it before.

A gust of hot air is followed by a slam, then Jax is standing at my side.

He's panting, and drops to grab his thighs as he tries to catch his breath.

"Fuck, Alexei. I thought you'd be dead by now." His tongue bar rattles against his teeth.

"No, but this guy will be." Ripping a cord from a lamp, I wrap it around one of his limp wrists and tie it to one of the vertical burners.

Some kind of rotisserie thing. But the two bars make a perfect place to latch the clown to.

"Help me with lifting him," I grunt, wrestling the dead weight.

My feet slip on the small metal dowels that fell out of the cabinet. "What are those?"

Jax bends over and picks up one of the thin utensils. "They look like shish kabob sticks."

I stare at him blankly. "Explain? Is that English?"

Jax smiles and shakes his head. "No. Well, it is, but I don't think it is? Shit. You put meat on these and roast them. Veggies too." He holds one over a dead burner and pretends to turn it over. "See?"

All I see are thousands of thin stabby devices.

"Like this?" I take one and poke it into the soft underarm of the unconscious man.

He groans and turns his head.

"Maybe another?" I slide another skewer into outside of his thigh.

Then the other arm. Through the fatty parts of his belly.

"What are you doing?" Jax grins.

"It's like, shishka-puncture. Right? Acupuncture is the needles?" I tilt my head as I push another poker through the calf of the very awake man.

"Yea, you're correct. But that's usually therapeutic. He looks like a pin cushion," Jax chuckles.

The clown without his makeup groans again. "You're psychotic."

I take one of the sharp tools and carve a star into his chest. "Lara taught me something recently." I move closer so I can talk in a whisper. "She showed me my birth chart. You know, the thing that says the planets and the signs?"

His dark eyes fix on me. "What the hell are you talking about?"

"My sun is Scorpio, and moon Sagittarius." I proclaim loud enough that Jax can hear me too.

Picking up another prod, I shove it between the bones of his wrist until it sticks out the other side. "According to her, I am unhinged. But on the bright side, we can blame your death on the fucking moon. Stop moving, you're getting blood on my shoes."

The spikes sticking out of him make a crinkling sound when he twitches and they hit each other.

"He looks like a porcupine. How many more of those things do you have?" Jax sits on the counter opposite of the clown and uses one of the stainless rods to pick at his teeth.

I glance at the floor. "There's still tons of them. I could make him look like a tin man."

Droplets of blood funnel from the protruding ends and drip down my pants.

Fuck. Onto my new sneakers.

I can fix that.

Kicking them off, the round skewers roll under my feet. "Time for the last round, funny man." I get into the face of the man, pushing his chin up so he can see me.

"Please," he gasps. "Just kill me."

"I can make it fast. Tell me where my Lara is." I curl my finger inside the loop of one of the metal pokers and twist it in a wide circle so it digs into the meat of his chest.

He grits his jaw, sweat dripping down his face and jowls to mix with the seeping fluids at every puncture.

"Fine," he grunts. "She's at the old bottling factory on Nineteenth. Go in through the back," he wheezes.

Jax clicks his tongue piercing. "Whatcha gonna do?" His heels bounce off of the dusty cabinet.

Opening drawers reveals what I'm looking for. A long steak knife is perfect.

Holding it over the pale man's heart, I get close to him again. "You should have stuck with balloon animals, you worthless fuck." Driving it as hard as I can between the ribs, his body jerks back and forth on the ties, spraying me with a thousand droplets of sweat encased blood.

"Dude." Jax leans back with a frown. "You're disgusting." He points vaguely at his own cheek.

I drag my palm over my forehead and look at the crimson sheen covering it.

"I don't care. Let's go find Lara. Can you call Nikolai and Mikhail?" I don't want to touch my phone. I just want to go.

"They're tied up on a weapon's drop. Nikolai said they're on their way, but they're at least an hour out." He hops down and holds the door open for me.

"Um, Alexei?" He stops.

I'm already halfway down the block heading to my motorcycle.

"What? Let's get going!" I stomp my foot onto the scalding sidewalk.

"Your shoes, man." He points down.

My red stained socks stand out on the concrete and I have a wet print trail leading from the restaurant.

"Shit." Running back, I grab my sneakers and carry them. "I'll put them on once I get there."

No I won't. The spikes on my bike are sharp as fuck.

Jax laughs and jogs to his Ducatti parked just past mine.

I don't pay any attention to the traffic. We cut in and out

of the cars, swerving through the intersections at high speed until Jax waves me to a stop just a couple of blocks from where we're going.

He holds his arm out. "We can't just ride through the front doors."

"Why not?" I growl.

Lara is so close. The last thing I want to do is slow down.

"We need a plan. Do you have your pistols?" Jax narrows his eyes at me. "There's only two of us. I got kids, remember?"

"I don't have my guns. Just my knife." I pull it out of the sheath to show him. "We'll be fine. I need to get in there."

Jax grabs my shoulders. "Alexei, if you go in there half-cocked, I'm not going in with you. You might have a death wish, but, well—" He rolls the ball of his tongue piercing between his teeth as he looks away. "—I don't anymore."

"Jax. You don't understand. I can't live without her." I pull away from his grasp and run towards the entrance.

I don't hear him behind me.

Fuck it.

Blowing through the double doors, I sprint through the large room to the only hall in the back.

When I skid around the corner, there's noises coming from the end.

That could be her.

When I peek in, I can see her on a small bed, and there's a man leaning over her.

What is he doing to her?

Her legs spasm, and her hands jerk.

She's *cuffed?*

As loud as I can, I bray like a donkey, holding my own blade up to my own throat.

"Let her go, or the ass gets it!" I scream at the top of my lungs.

Startled, the man turns around and takes a step back, fear,

then confusion warping his expression.

I don't wait, but throw my knife in one motion.

The man stands frozen watching it impale into his chest.

With a grunt, he falls first to his knees, then forward, burying it all the way to the hilt.

Rushing to Lara, I pull the tube out of her mouth that he was putting in her.

As gently as possible, I cradle her as she blinks up at me.

"Alexei?" Her voice is hoarse.

"Yes, pchelka?"

"You found me."

My heart hammers in my chest as I stroke away her hair from her face. As beautiful as ever, even now.

I do everything to suppress the burning rage inside of me as I look at the mark on her face. They will all pay. Painfully.

But for now, I have her in my arms and as I look into her eyes, that is all that matters.

She is the calm to my storm.

"Of course. Nothing could ever stop me."

It's like the room around us crackles as she softly brings her cold hand up and rests it on my cheek. Wiping away the stray tear I didn't even know had fallen.

She's here, she's okay, I remind myself.

She is all I see, all I've ever seen. I willingly gave up my soul to her a long time ago, because she is my person in this world. And I wouldn't have it any other way.

As I look to her lips, this overwhelming urge consumes me to press mine against hers.

"Sladkiy," she whispers.

I smile, leaning closer.

She sucks in a breath, her eyes still burning into my own as my heart feels like it's making an escape through my ribs.

I really, really, want to kiss her.

Fuck it.

One kiss won't ruin what we have.

CHAPTER 21
LARA

Song- Who We Are, Hozier

SOMETHING IN HIS GAZE SHIFTS.

The way he's looking between my eyes and my lips makes me want to scream at him to kiss me.

I am safe, in his arms, exactly where I am meant to be. Tears burn, but I keep my focus on him.

Everything else fades away as he pulls back, focusing on my mouth.

Does he feel this pull too?

I hold my breath. In this moment, nothing else matters.

It's just he and I, together.

"I really want to kiss you," he whispers.

All the pain in my body disappears, replaced by a surge of adrenaline.

"Please, Alexei?"

His features soften as he strokes my cheek gently, bringing me towards him.

The second his lips touch mine, sparks fire through me. I let him take charge, he tastes like cherry sweets and sin.

Like everything I've always dreamed of.

He's gentle, yet full of hunger as his tongue slips in my mouth. Wrapping my arms around his neck, I pull him closer.

I want to get lost in him, I want him to steal my last breath. I feel like I'm dying anyway, I'd gladly let him have it.

He pulls away, and I can't hide the smile on my face, even if it really hurts. Alexei has always had a way of making everything better.

He leans forward, brushing his lips against my cheek and I close my eyes, sinking into the feeling of pure peace. I bet he was frantically searching for me.

"Can we just stay here for a few minutes?" he whispers. I can hear the pain in his voice.

"Y-yes." I manage to croak out.

He rests his head on top of mine, his heart hammering in his chest, beating in my ears.

"I need another." He pulls back and searches my eyes, both hands on my cheeks.

"One more kiss won't ruin everything, right?" I whisper.

It could destroy our friendship. But I'm taking this moment. I'll take any piece he's willing to give me, until he finally realizes what I've known this whole time. We were always destined to be more than friends.

"Nothing could ever tear us apart." He confirms.

A knot forms in my stomach. I really hope he's right.

CHAPTER 22
ALEXEI

Song, Rescue, Lauren Daigle

As MY LIPS press against hers, my entire being is set on fire. This was worth the wait. My first kiss had to be with my pchelka.

I never imagined it would consume me this much. I don't know if I ever want to stop.

And she won't have a clue what this was to me. That she has been the only woman I have had eyes for.

I saw her first kiss, with Vlad. She was seventeen and I followed him home. I wanted to slit his throat. I didn't. Only because he made her smile. But then when he made her cry two weeks later, I made him pay and toasted marshmallows as I burned his corpse.

I pick her up into my arms and she rests her head in the crook of my neck.

She's as light as a mouse.

I need to get her fed and checked by a doctor. I can feel her hip bones protruding out of her skin on my hand.

Fuck. I only have my bike.

Making my way out to the parking lot, I see car lights next to my bike. I know Nikolai's Hellcat anywhere.

The doors swing open and Niki, Mikhail and Jax are striding towards us.

"She's fine, I've got her." I tell them.

Nikolai's firm hand clasps on my shoulder.

"You could have got yourself killed," he hisses under his breath.

"I don't care." I dismiss him.

He doesn't understand, no one does.

I'd die for this woman.

"We'll take her in the car, you follow on the bike," Mikhail says sternly.

I don't want to let her out of my sight.

Mikhail is the boss, I'll listen to him.

I follow him to the car as he opens the passenger side for me. Lara clings tighter.

"I'll be right behind you, I'm not going anywhere."

"I need you," she whispers in my ear, making a shiver run down my spine.

"For eternity," I whisper back and place a discreet kiss on her ear.

As I look up, it's possible Mikhail caught that, but with me and Lara, everyone knows how close we are.

It isn't unusual? Is it?

Shit.

What are they going to say? They know me. They know as well as I do, I'm not good enough for her.

I carefully place her on the seat, my fingers brushing her skin as I secure her belt. She looks up at me through her thick lashes, her blue eyes filled with tears.

I wipe them away.

"I'll see you in a few minutes, pchelka."

She nods and there's a tremble on her bottom lip. I want to kiss it better again. But I don't. Closing the door, I turn to her brothers, but notice Jax is looking at me weird. I slide my hands into my pockets and kick the rock on the floor.

I can't concentrate on anything they're saying. My lips are still hot, and I can taste her on my tongue.

Placing my hand on the metal of the hellcat, I don't know why, but it makes me feel closer to her again.

"I'll have a doctor meet us at her place," Mikhail says, pulling out his phone.

"Jax, you wait for clean up. We need to confirm who those fuckers in there are."

"You got it, boss." Jax takes off back into the building.

Mikhail glances in my direction. "Lara is lucky to have you. You take 'ride or die' pretty damn seriously for her."

Before I get a chance to reply, he's heading towards the Hellcat and I make my way over to my bike.

Ride or die?

She could have died and I nearly didn't get to her in time. I failed her.

A sinking feeling washes over me.

I'll never be enough for her. I can't even protect her. How am I meant to be anything else?

CHAPTER 23
ALEXEI

"WHERE IS SHE?" I scan the room and only see Mikhail and Nikolai.

"Calm down, she's in bed," Nikolai growls at me.

I blow out a breath and run my hands through my hair. Double taking the stairs, I push open her door and come to an abrupt stop.

She's crying.

Each sob makes me feel sick.

I clamber on the bed and pull her into me, letting her tears soak into my shirt.

"No, no, no. When you're upset it breaks my heart, Lara," I whisper into the top of her head.

I wish I could explain how gutting it is to see her this way. It's like every failure of my life beats down on me when I can't make her smile.

"You could never fail me, sladkiy." She sniffles, making me frown.

Shit, I said it out loud.

She pulls herself to sit upright, linking her fingers through mine.

They fit perfectly.

"I'll do better next time, I won't let anyone ever hurt you again."

I try not to look at the angry mark on her face. She's going to hate that, she is always asking me if she looks pretty.

There's never a moment that she isn't the most beautiful woman.

Guilt still riddles me for letting her get caught. "Tell me not to kiss you again."

She grabs both sides of my face, tracing her fingertip along the tattoo down my cheek as she searches my eyes.

"Why the hell would I say something so ridiculous, sladkiy?"

I bite down on my lip as my gaze settles on her plump ones, begging to be kissed again. Leaning forward my nose presses against hers and she sucks in a breath as I run my fingers through her silky hair.

I cannot stand to lose the one person who holds me together, yet all I want to do is claim her and make her mine. Forever.

Is it worth the risk?

"Promise me something, pchelhka," I whisper, my heart hammering against my chest.

"What's that?" Her breath hits against my lips and my cock is pressing against my zipper.

"That this doesn't change what we have. We never lose each other, no matter what."

The way she grins not only explodes my heart, but tells me everything I need to know.

"For eternity." Taking her lips, I tug her closer and lose myself to her.

"You need to get some sleep, Lara," I tell her. And I need to speak to Mikhail. He will knock some sense into me.

Or at least take me skydiving so I can think.

The way everything is battling in my brain, it's a struggle. I have to do right by Lara.

"I'll stay," I reassure her as she snuggles up on the pillow and I hold her close.

I don't want to let go.

I let out a sigh and rest my head against the headboard.

"Are my brothers downstairs?" she whispers.

I swallow the lump in my throat. Not only did I fail Lara, they saved me all those years ago and now I'm kissing their sister.

They might hate me for this. I could never regret anything with Lara, and how can something that feels so damn good be wrong?

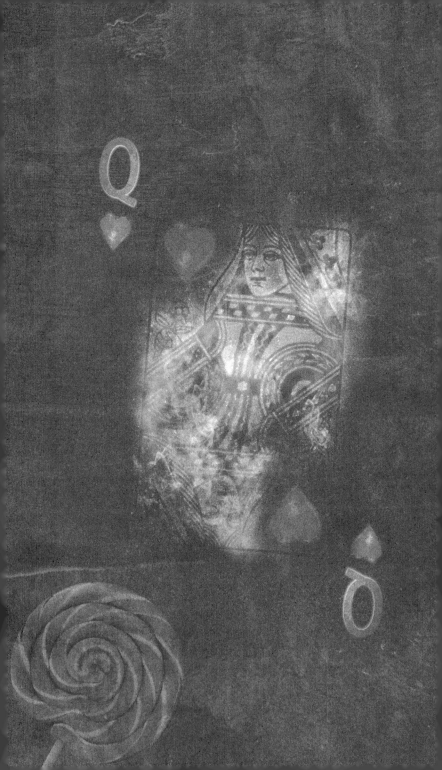

CHAPTER 24

Song- Mistake NF

I CAN HEAR his thoughts ticking. Even as he holds me close, I can feel the shift.

He lets out a long exhale. "Yeah, they are waiting for me."

Silence fills the room. Is he pulling away because he's scared of what they might say? Or because he regrets crossing a line with me?

I'm not good enough for him either. That kiss wasn't what he imagined it would be. I bet he gets any beautiful woman he wants.

"Don't you dare." I try to hide the tremble in my voice as I turn away from him. He might know me better than I know myself sometimes, but it works both ways.

"Dare what?" He responds quietly, very unlike the usual Alexei.

I swallow past the lump in my throat, the butterflies swarming in my stomach. I can still feel his lips on mine.

If it was wrong, why did it feel so right? Perfect even.

"Call that a mistake," I answer honestly.

What I really mean is me.

The damage of never being good enough has broken me over the years, but none of that compares to the pain I'd feel if I were rejected by Alexei.

A life without him?

Impossible.

The second he walks into my space my world goes silent, in the best possible way. The doubt, the self loathing, the pain. It all dissipates, and my mind and body are at peace.

Alexei is the calm I crave in the mayhem of my mind.

I turn to face him, wanting to get a read of his face.

The man who spins my universe. The man whose existence keeps me going. No matter how dark my days become, there is always light when he is beside me.

He shakes his head, swiping his tatted finger along his bottom lip.

I stay rooted in place. Frozen. Waiting for him to shatter me.

He gently tips my chin up to him. His normally wild eyes are softened.

"To me, that kiss could never be. To you? This might be the biggest mistake you've ever made, pchelka."

"What do you mean?"

Never. That's what I meant to say.

"I-I don't know if I can stop. This might have taken my addiction to you a step beyond something we can go back from."

I'm not sure if I should ask. "You don't want to do it again?"

He raises a brow. But there is one thing on his face right now I've never seen before. Fear.

"You need to sleep and I need to go back to protecting you." He presses a kiss to my forehead and pushes himself off the bed, leaving me empty and alone.

That's how I feel whenever he isn't with me.

I didn't expect to wake up alone.

After everything I've been through, and last night, Alexei still left?

Maybe he sent me a message. It's silly to think he would have stayed.

It's not like we're *together.*

But he's all I could think about when I was captured.

Catching a glimpse of myself in the mirror tells me exactly why he left. The fresh stitches in my cheek are a sharp contrast to the red swollen edges that mark where Kirill jabbed that knife through.

Fuck him.

I hope we find him and shred him for what he's done to all of us.

Anger shakes through me.

How dare he? Take me from my family, from the people I love to *ruin* me?

I almost died.

I think a piece of me did.

Still weak, I work my way into the kitchen to find my refrigerator absolutely stuffed with food.

Finger sandwiches, strawberries, and drinks of every variety all stare back at me.

What else is in here?

I bet this was all Alexei. Or, Mikhail. They're both good about taking care of me.

Nikolai doesn't care. If he did, he would have invited me to his wedding.

Maybe I shouldn't still be mad at him. But it's hard not to be.

Where is Alexei? His absence hurts more than anything.

Grabbing a sandwich and a juice, I sit down and check my phone for the thirtieth time to see if he's texted.

The snack fills me up. I went so long while captured without eating, I think my stomach shrank. Probably a good thing.

No one wants me fat and mutilated.

This is for the best. I need to get all of this extra garbage out of the house.

Pausing in front of Alexei's candy bin, it makes me wonder if that needs to go too.

Yes. If he can't be here when I need him, I don't want to keep this here just to beg him for his presence.

Before I know it, tears are flowing down my cheeks, stinging the wound near my mouth.

I don't care.

He left me. They all let me sit forever in that hell hole.

I don't need them. I don't need any of them.

My legs shake as I carry everything outside to the garbage bins. Even the thought of having it all in the house makes me sick.

In fact…

Running to the bathroom, I vomit up the sandwich. The carbonation from the soda burns my nose as it violently leaves my body.

The heart rate on my watch is through the roof.

Stop.

Get a grip.

Maybe they don't all hate me.

I need to find out.

Falling into the tailspin is too easy.

Mikhail told me once that if he's flying and the plane starts to fall, he has to go full throttle before he can pull out.

That's what I should do. I'll go to Nikolai and see if he has a problem with me.

I hate how much looser my clothes are. It takes several outfits before I find something that fits correctly.

Why am I like this?

Nikolai shouldn't care. He's my brother. Shouldn't he love me unconditionally?

Trying to be perfect all of the time is exhausting. But I shouldn't have to try so hard.

When I leave the house and go past the garbage, a twinge of guilt gnaws at me.

Maybe I shouldn't have thrown the food away.

The entire drive I kick myself for doing it.

I'm surprised when Nikolai comes out to meet me at the car.

"Lara! I'm glad you came, Elena has been asking about you." Nikolai wraps me into his arms for a fierce hug. "We've been worried," he whispers against the top of my head.

My phone buzzes in my pocket, so I pull away.

ALEXEI

Where are you? I went for a swim, but when I got back you were gone

ME

I'm at Nikolai's

ALEXEI

On my way

"Is that Alexei?" Nikolai watches me.

"Yea, he's on his way."

He nods. "I wondered. He hasn't gone a second without obsessing over you. I didn't expect to see you without him for a while."

Now I really feel shitty about doubting them.

"Let's go in, I miss my niece." Threading my arm through his, I walk unsteadily up the short steps to the porch.

"Are you sure the doc checked you out? Have you been eating okay?" Nikolai asks as we go in.

I guess I'm leaning too much on him.

"I'm okay." All it's doing is making me more self conscious.

"Auntie Lara!" Elena runs down the stairs from her room towards me with her arms open, but slows when she looks up at my face.

"Oh gosh! What happened to your cheek?" Her little hands fly up and clasp her own jaw in shock.

No, not her too?

The tears return and burn their way down to my lips.

"Auntie Lara is fine," Alexei says from the door. "She's tough as nails and a survivor."

As if soothed by his words, Elena wraps her arms around my waist in a fast hug. "I'm glad to see you."

But she turns just as quickly and runs back upstairs.

It breaks me to watch her go. I know she's only seven, but it hurts to have her shy away from me.

"How are you doing?" Mila brushes her long brown hair away from her face as she steps closer.

Her smile looks genuine, even if it is reserved.

"I needed to go on a diet anyways." I try to return her grin. My lips falter though.

Alexei's arm snakes around my waist, and I lean into him reflexively.

"Oh, don't be silly," Mila laughs. "I think this means we should go out and have cheesecake."

Her athletic build comes from being a trained assassin.

I may work for the mafia, yet it's still a desk job. "I'm not sure. I might take a rain check on that one."

"Come on, it'll be fun!" Mila moves closer to Nikolai, who's gaze never wavers.

I shift uncomfortably. Their new wedding rings seem to glow under the lights.

Maybe this wasn't a good idea.

Usually being this close to Alexei is merely a comfort. But after yesterday, I'm extremely aware of how close he is.

So when he steps away, I notice.

He can come and go as he pleases, and no one seems to judge him for it. There's no pattern with him, just spontaneity.

I'm a little jealous that he can just leave a situation.

Screw it. I almost died. There should be an allowance for that.

Following him outside, I find him leaning against his bike.

He doesn't look at me, or even acknowledge my presence.

"I'll take you home," he says without turning.

"Thank you."

Without another word, I climb on his bike behind him, and we disappear into the night.

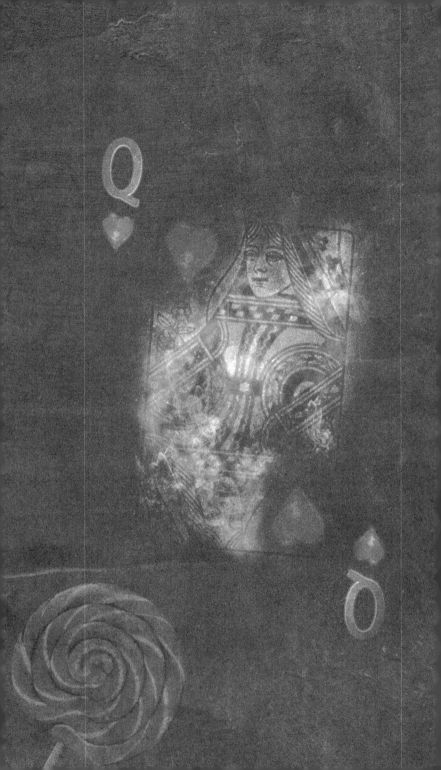

CHAPTER 25
ALEXEI

Song- Silence, Marshmello, Khalid

HAVING her arms wrapped around me is different now.

I know what it's like to hold her close and taste her lips.

It's all I can think about.

The wild part is that this is the first time I've ever held back on anything. I'm too used to giving in to whatever whim strikes me, with no fear of the consequences.

But I know there are very real ones with her.

She's the most important thing in my life. My entire purpose for living.

I don't want to drive her away, or ruin what we have.

I saw her at Nikolai's. The pain that flickered over her face when Elena turned away. How she chewed on her lip and picked at her thumb when she thought no one would notice.

She was wrong. I always see her.

It's as if she's the only light in the room. She's my focus.

I can see how broken she is.

And I fear crossing this boundary will make it worse, for everyone. I left last night because my head is fucked.

I'm not usually one to sit and think, but as soon as Niki

and Miki left, that's what I did. I ignore the voices in my head, yet when it comes to Lara, they're screaming at me.

The fear of losing what we have takes hold.

How is someone as messed up as I am supposed to love or be loved?

I'm crazy, not stupid. I know she deserves better than me. The thought is a stab through my very soul.

As I help her off the bike, and her tiny hand slips into mine, sparks shoot up my arm making my heart hammer.

"Are you coming in?" she whispers.

She's nervous, or sad.

I shake my head. She needs peace, not chaos. I can protect her. Including from myself.

"Can't you see I need you? Now, of all times. Don't pull away from me. You promised me you wouldn't," she sniffles.

I step forward, wrapping my arms around her and she buries her face into my chest.

Tears. They're my fault.

"I can't lose you, Alexei."

I hug her tighter. The thought is my worst nightmare. "You never will, I promised eternity."

What if I can never be the man to give her the type of love she craves? Am I even capable?

Her voice is laced with anger. "Then stop pulling away from me. What is it? Am I not good enough for you? Lara, always on the side lines, never the first choice. Always a fucking maybe."

I pull back and grip her shoulders.

"Stop. That isn't it. Don't ever think that," I say sternly.

Is this what I've done to her? I'm the reason she's never had those second dates. And because of that, I've made her believe she's inadequate. I am the one causing her pain.

All I wanted was her to be happy, yet, I was the one breaking her. Making her think she was a goddamn maybe of this world.

She isn't.

She's the reason I drag myself out of bed each morning. The reason I make sure I don't actually get myself killed.

My first thought of the day and my last is always her. In fact, there probably isn't a minute where she isn't on my mind.

"There is no one on this planet as special nor as beautiful on the inside and out as you, Lara. Your standards should be up in the stars, not in the pits of hell with me."

I swallow the lump in my throat.

"You promised me, Alexei. That kiss wouldn't ruin what we had."

"It won't," I reply quickly. I can't let it.

"Doesn't seem like it." She looks down at the floor. I'm making her sad.

I want to kiss her again. I want to take her to bed and cuddle her. And show her in every single way just how much she means to me.

I want to worship every damn inch of her until she sees what I see.

But I can't. Because if this is what happens after one kiss. A moment that I will replay on loop until the day I die, what happens if we do more?

I will lose the best thing in my life.

"What about an episode of Yellowstone, I eat all your candy and make you laugh?"

She sniffles and looks up at me.

Her eyes burn into me. She wants more, I can see it, sense it. And so do I. But now isn't the time.

Blinking too quickly, she shifts away. "I haven't refilled it for a while."

I link my fingers through hers and my arm tingles. It feels like home, all warm and fuzzy.

Lara's gaze flicks down to our hands and back up to my face.

Damn, she's so beautiful.

Shaking my head, I lead us in through her hall.

"You, sit." I point to the couch.

"I'll get the snacks. I don't want healthy today." I smirk at her and she rolls her eyes, biting back a smile.

Here we go. She's lightening up and honestly, it's a relief.

Tucking the blanket under her chin, making sure she's comfy, I slip from my side of her bed. I can't resist moving the stray hair from her face, and when I do, the softness of her skin makes me stroke her cheek.

I wish she could be mine.

As I step back, my phone lights up on the nightstand. I snatch it and pull myself from her room.

N

> Meet us at Vox. We have a problem. Be
> armed and crazy.

I can't shake the grin on my lips.

Maybe this is what I need, blood on my hands. Maybe that will clear my head, ending lives is where I am my most free.

And, I'm still protecting her by ridding the world of these assholes.

Grabbing a lollipop on my way out, I put the jar back in the cupboard. I need to go and get her some groceries.

All she has is bad stuff, normally it's all healthy crap. But that makes her happy. She needs more.

Okay.

Kill people. Buy strawberries. Check on Sheila. Maybe, Sheila would be good company for Lara while I keep some distance.

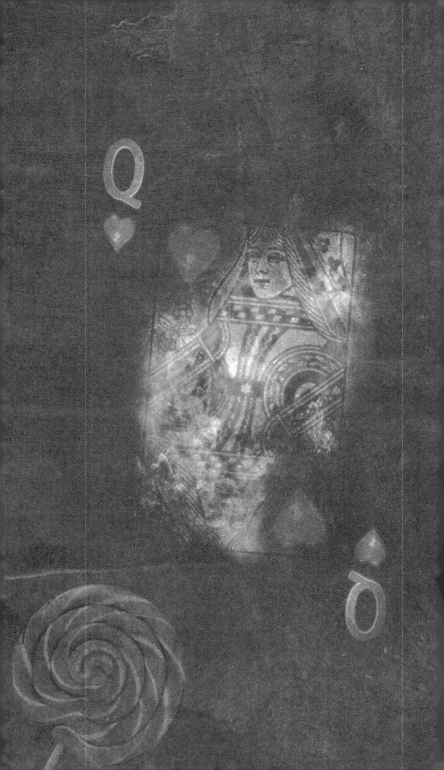

CHAPTER 26
ALEXEI

BY THE TIME we are done at Vox, I'm pleased with myself.

Kill count of at least ten. Although I probably need to throw these sneakers in the trash. I'm pretty sure I have brain matter on the soles after I stamped on a big guy's head.

Ivan can keep sending as many of these goons over as he wants, they all get the same ending.

I'm just waiting for the plan to fall into place where we take out Kirill and Ivan. It's time for this shit to be over.

Vegas is Mikhail's.

And honestly, I think he will take back over in Russia, too.

My job now is protecting Lara.

"You heading home?" Jax calls out as we approach our bikes.

His Ducati is a beaut, I nearly bought one, but Lara liked the all black BMW, so of course I went for that.

"Going to check in on Lara first, then I will."

"You don't want a beer?" Jax points at the bar.

Grabbing my helmet I turn to face him. I didn't like leaving Lara earlier, and knowing Ivan does have more guys than we assumed has kicked my bodyguard instinct into overdrive.

"Not tonight. Fighting makes me sleepy."

He rolls his eyes.

I want to crawl into bed with Lara and cuddle. I can't, but I want to.

"You're a good friend to her." Jax nods.

Friend.

I want to be more than that. That's the problem. Maybe Jax would understand. Or maybe not. No one understands how my brain works.

"I'll see you tomorrow." Shoving on my helmet, I take off on my bike and head to Lara's. As I approach her house, I spot a blacked out Audi parked across the street.

I've never seen that here before. It doesn't belong.

Ditching my bike on the side of the road, I pull out my pocket knife, keeping it behind my back and approach the vehicle, tapping on the driver's side window.

They wind it down slowly, and I'm face to face with a heavy set guy, with slicked black hair in a ponytail.

"You can't park here. Private property," I tell him.

He looks around the empty street.

"I'm not causing any problems." His Russian accent is thick.

My fingers tighten around the blade. It might be small, but it's mighty.

As he turns his head to the console reaching for his phone, I see the mark. The IV of Ivan's mob.

The same ones we all covered up.

Before he has time to turn back to me, I jab the knife tip where the tattoo is.

V marks the spot today.

Blood pours down his shoulder. I caught him good.

"You motherfucker," he croaks out, grasping onto the side of his throat.

Ugh. He needs to die quicker.

I can't shoot. Not here. It's a quiet neighborhood and I don't want to startle Lara.

So, I keep stabbing him.

One through his hand. As he pulls that away and screams out in pain, I shove the short blade right through his eye.

By the time I'm finished adding holes to him, he slumps against the steering wheel, blasting the horn.

"Fuck," I hiss.

Pulling this dead lump back, I push him so he falls towards the passenger side. Wiping my blade on his black t-shirt, I put it back in my pocket and pull out my cell.

I can't type in the numbers, damn blood on my fingers.

Using my nose to press the buttons, I dial Enzo.

"What have you done?" His deep Italian voice booms through.

"Audi parked outside Lara's now has one dead Russian with a lotta stab wounds."

"I'm on it."

"Thanks." I cut the call and head in to Lara's. I know her security code, and I have a key so it's easy.

Sneaking in, I'm careful not to wake her.

She'll be in bed, it's one am. She tends to go to sleep around eleven.

Taking off my shoes by the front door, I don't think she will appreciate the mess. I creep quietly up the stairs, pushing open her door and resting against the frame.

I don't know how long I stand there, listening to the steady rise and fall of her breathing.

It calms me.

CHAPTER 27
LARA

I COULD HAVE SWORN I heard noises last night.

No, not sounds really, more like a *feeling* that there was something moving in my house after I went to bed.

I must be paranoid after everything that went on with Kirill. My sleep was taunted by nightmares of him tackling me to the ground and stabbing me over and over through the face.

A shiver runs up my spine at the memory.

Pulling on my silk robe, I can't help but glance into the corners as I walk to the kitchen. There's just this sense that something is watching me, or was, and the shadows are still lurking.

Stop it. I'm being paranoid.

Or am I? It wouldn't surprise me if Kirill tracked me down. His men managed to find me at Alexei's house, why not here?

Nothing sounds appealing this morning. I don't want to bother with coffee or tea.

Maybe just a glass of warm water. That will fill my belly for a little while.

But when I focus on the carpet near the front door, my cup slips from my fingers and shatters on the cold tiles.

What the fuck is that?

There's a droplet of blood on the white rug.

Oh my god! I wasn't imagining it! Who would come into my house? What did they do?

Shit.

Why would they come in and not take me again?

Or touch me.

I think I'm going to be sick.

This is some kind of fucked up game Kirill has to be playing. That asshole needs to die.

Rushing back into my room, I get dressed in record time. I don't feel comfortable in my own home. Who knows what they're seeing?

Did they put up cameras? *Did they see me change?*

That sends me running to the toilet to lose the warm water that is churning in my stomach.

I need to get the hell out of here.

Grabbing my pistol, I toss it into my purse and jump in my car.

It takes nearly the entire drive before my hands stop shaking.

Why couldn't Alexei stay? He makes me feel safe. And my lips tingle.

Just one kiss ruined everything. I'm a wreck without him.

My heels click on the concrete floor as I stride past the coffee stand on the first level of the casino.

I don't have time today, I need to talk to Mikhail.

After a light tap on his door, I barge in and stand, suddenly speechless in front of his desk.

"Good morning, Lara. What's with the deer in the head-lights look?" He blinks up at me.

My breath comes too quickly, so I move over to the couch and slump into the cushions.

160

When Mikhail stands and towers over me, he blocks out the light briefly before he squats in front of me. "Tell me. Are you okay?"

I nod, trying to form words. "I think, um, that someone broke into my house last night."

He grunts and stands up, his broad fists tightening at his hips. "Who? I'll kill them," he growls.

"I don't know, that's the problem." A knot forms in the back of my throat as I fight the tears that threaten to spill over onto my cheeks. "I was hoping you could have Enzo check into it? Doesn't he still have access to maybe the street cameras at least?"

Enzo has his eyes everywhere. He's the best at finding out anything.

Mikhail pauses. "Yes, that's an excellent idea." He pulls his hand up and cracks his scabbed knuckles.

"Did you get in a fight last night?" I hadn't noticed the wounds when I first came in.

"Yea. Everyone was in on it. Daddy dearest threw a handful at Jax and Nikolai, ambushed them as they were leaving Vox." He shakes his head. "Is there ever going to be any peace as long as Ivan is around?"

"Do you think Dad will come back after me?" I hate asking that question because I'm afraid of the answer.

"We won't be letting that happen. We would all die before it does." He pauses, studying my face. "I can have Alexei move in with you to keep you safe?"

"No." I can see Alexei doesn't want to have anything to do with me, not the way I want.

But Mikhail is looking at me like that isn't enough of an answer.

"I mean, he's more useful to you, we both know that. You need him to fight." There, that should help.

Mikhail's thick eyebrows lower over his nose. "I'd rather you stay protected than put him on the streets. But fine, if you don't want him there, I won't make him." He raises his hand, pointing at me. "Figure out what's going on between you two, though. He's fucking useless right now because of whatever tiff you're having."

My stomach knots. Alexei is messed up too?

I thought he was the one who backed away?

This is even more complicated than I thought.

CHAPTER 28
ALEXEI

"Alexei, did you see someone at Lara's house last night?" Enzo grumbles over the phone. "Mikhail interrupted a very important meeting to find answers, but all I can see is you on the cameras. The guy you dealt with never entered her house."

"Shit, there was an intruder?" Anger boils in me. "I'll kill them! Did they hurt her?"

"She's fine. She's just freaked, and rightfully so. See if you can find anything?" It sounds like he stops to talk to someone else. "I have to go."

Fuck. Was there more than that one guy?

Who was it? I bet it was one of Kirill's men.

All with Ivan behind it.

I hate that man for what he did to my friends, the people I love.

There's a lot of people who call me crazy, but that man is a monster.

A sudden hit to the back of my head knocks me out of my memories.

"Alexei, are you paying attention?" Nikolai's mouth is a thin line as he stares at me.

"Huh? Oh, yea." I forgot we're supposed to be watching that door." I'm squatting in an alley behind a stinky ass dumpster. How'd I lose track of that?

"Pay attention. I have to go back to that corner. Check in on time so I don't have to come back and smack you again." He stalks off into the night, his broad shoulders hunch before he moves into his hiding location.

I wish Jax warned me Nikolai was coming up on my ass. Glancing at my phone shows me he did, several times.

Damn.

I do my best to stay still and focus on the faint outline of the club entrance. The flickering lamplight is giving me a headache.

After what seems like hours, Nikolai finally shifts enough to create a silhouette against the building, then shuffles his way towards me.

"I don't think they're coming. Let's get the fuck out of here. Mila made a dinner tonight that actually tasted amazing," he groans and stretches.

"Pancakes?" Jax teases as he steps closer.

"Funny." Nikolai yawns, leading the way back to the vehicles.

He told us all the story of when Mila was pretending to be someone she wasn't, and attempted to cook for him.

He said that breakfast tasted like hockey pucks.

I guess he must really love her to still keep trying her food.

Why doesn't Lara ever cook? All I see her eat is either really really healthy, or terrible for her.

There's no normal meals with her.

Weird. I hadn't noticed before. Maybe I need to start paying better attention to that.

I'll start now.

Killing the engine on my motorcycle a block away, I push

it the last few hundred feet to her driveway and park it just inside her gate.

The lights are on, so she must be home. I haven't gotten a motion detection alert from the cameras either.

Oh, I better turn them off so I don't trigger it.

Skirting the open lawn in front of the living room, I work my way along the Spanish style villa to the spare bedroom that has her workout equipment.

She's sweating on her treadmill. It almost seems like she's pushing herself to the point of exhaustion.

Why does she do that? She's already thin and fit, I don't understand why she always worries about it.

I see her eyes pinch when she starts talking about clothes. They don't seem to bring her any joy.

Maybe she shouldn't wear any.

My dick begins to throb against my zipper at the thought.

When she finally stops running, she looks like she's about to collapse. Her legs shake as the belt slows, and she nearly stumbles stepping off of it.

It's hard to fight the urge to run in there and scoop her up. She went through so much at the hands of that asshole Kirill, I wish she wouldn't torture herself as well.

I wish there was a camera in her bathroom so I could watch her as she climbs into the shower. If someone was hiding in there, I'd never know.

She isn't safe where I can't see her.

Nerves start to work through me while I stare at her ensuite door.

Relief floods through me when I finally see the handle turn and steam billow out around the cracks until Lara steps out.

In nothing but a thick white towel wrapped around her middle.

But her bare shoulders and legs still glisten from the moisture. It makes me want to glide my palms over her and wipe it away.

To feel her smooth skin and the heat of her burning away the last of the droplets.

Fuck.

I'm only here to protect her, it's my job. It's not because I am obsessed with her or keep dreaming about her.

Okay, she's fine. I can't stand here any more or I'm going to be jacking off in her bushes. And that's probably when the intruder would show up.

Hard to fight one handed.

The lid of her garbage can is off. Did someone rifle through it? I better check.

What is this? It looks like a whole pile of wrappers from the candy that she usually keeps stocked for me.

Did she eat *all* of them?

No wonder she could run so fast.

I've eaten that much sugar at once before, when I was younger.

It made me sick for three days.

Finding a soft spot in the grass, I sit down so I can watch her bedroom. She disappears briefly into the closet, and when she comes back she's wearing a set of silver cami and shorts.

The glow in the soft light of her room before she slides under the covers and then the windows go dark.

She'll be safe, I'll stay out here and make sure of it.

CHAPTER 29
LARA

PICKING at my thumbnail doesn't make my phone give me a notification from Alexei. Neither does the extra three slices of cheese and crackers I had for breakfast.

Why hasn't he come by?

Did I do something to ruin us? All I want is him.

Still no word.

Maybe something happened?

An image of him sky jumping and his parachute not opening shows up in my head, and I can't get it out.

I need to know if he's okay. If he's even alive.

"Nikolai? Good morning," I stammer, pushing another cracker around on my plate.

"Lara. How are you?" He sounds winded. "What's up?"

He's hurrying me.

Why do I always feel inconvenient?

"I was wondering if you've seen Alexei recently? I have, um, his extra charger cord I borrowed." That's probably the lamest excuse I've ever come up with.

Nikolai pants in my ear, but I can hear jostling like he's running. "He's here. With me."

"Oh." Well, at least I know Alexei is alive. "What are you doing?"

"We're chasing down one of Dad's fuckers," he grunts. "I gotta go, I'll let Alexei know about the charger."

I can hear several more muffled words slip out before he hangs up.

Well, now I feel like an idiot.

Alexei isn't hurt, he's just avoiding me.

It's probably for the better. I'm barely able to hold myself together around him. And he's opened up a whole new level of vulnerability.

He's smarter than me sometimes. Maybe he sees something I can't and knows we need some space.

It's time to go to work anyways. I'll worry about him later. Nights are the hardest.

All of my clothes are hideous. They don't fit right.

No matter what I wear, how much effort I put in, I always hate the reflection that stares back at me. I'll never be good enough.

I guess that means it doesn't really matter how I look. Why am I trying so hard?

Ever since getting away from Kirill, I've been fighting the urge to eat anything that tastes good.

Fuck that.

On my way to the casino, I stop at a place I haven't been to in forever.

The doughnut shop.

God, it smells amazing here.

I bet if I get a dozen, Mikhail would want some.

The sweet aroma permeates my car on the drive, and I can't resist pulling one of the sticky glazed ones from the box and sampling.

Absolutely delicious. It's as if I've been starved for months, and this is the first bite.

Licking my fingers, I finish it before I pull into the parking garage.

I'm just reaching the doors when the guilt starts to pour in.

What did I do?

All of that sugar? It's going to make me bloated and fat for the rest of the day.

Pushing into Mikhail's office, I toss the eleven remaining desserts onto his large oak desk.

"What's this?" He looks up from his computer.

"I can't eat any more of them." I'm already half sick thinking about the horrible calories running rampant to my hips.

His dark eyes narrow as he stares at me for a long minute. "Lara…when are you going back to the cabin?"

That irritates me. "What, getting rid of me so soon after escaping being kidnapped and tortured?" I jab my finger towards my face as emphasis.

His brows raise and he takes a deep breath. "No. I know how relaxing your visits are out there, and after everything you went through, I thought maybe you could use some quiet time."

He leans back and laces his hand behind his head. "You know I love you, Lara. I'd do anything to help you. We burned this city down looking for you. But I can't do anything about what's hurting you from the inside. I wish I could."

His chair creaks under his muscular frame as he reaches over and picks up a doughnut. "But I guess if I have to eat these to do my part to save you, I'll suffer in sugar for you." The mask over his cheeks tightens as he smiles at me.

My phone vibrates in my pocket, distracting me from answering him.

"Alexei?" Why does my heartbeat turn into a snare drum?

"Lara! I need a huge favor, please? Life saving! It's an urgent emergency!" He has a lilt of panic in his voice.

"What? Of course," I answer automatically. All of my doubt disappears as he begs.

"It's Sheila," he yells. "She's gone from my cameras. I need you to check on her."

"Your bird?" I glance at Mikhail who shakes his head and rolls his eyes.

"She's more than that. She's important to me."

"Alexei, do you think maybe she just flew away?" I say quietly.

"Lara." He speaks slowly. "Did I just let you go when you disappeared?"

Ouch.

"No, you didn't," I admit. "I'll go check on her."

"Thank you, let me know as soon as you get there." He hangs up with a click.

"What was that all about?" Mikhail grumbles.

"I have to go to Alexei's. Do you want to go with me to check on his pet?" I'll leave the doughnuts here.

Maybe Nikolai or Jax will come by and eat them?

"Um, no. I have a deal to try and figure out for another shipment of guns from Frankie back in New York. You'll have to herd birds without me."

"Understandable. I'll be back soon." Turning on my heel, I head down to my car.

It's strange that Alexei doesn't want anything to do with me, but still wants a favor.

I wish he had never kissed me. I miss how we were.

He's more to me than just some silly fling. I need him like air.

Without him, I feel bitter, alone, and worthless.

Imperfect. Unwanted.

Damn him.

I've never been here without him before, and I realize I

don't have the key to get in. A text from him tells me that the door code is the day he and I met.

Wow, that's sweeter than I expected.

What's funny is I remember exactly what the date was.

My life changed forever when I met him.

Surprisingly, the house is spotless inside. For some reason, I hoped that he was falling apart inside like I am.

Okay, I'm here to look for a giant pink bird. It shouldn't be that hard to spot.

"Sheila? Here girl." I move onto the back veranda and search everywhere that I remember seeing her last time.

Before I was taken.

There's a pool complete with a small sprinkler at the end. Water and food bowls are full.

Where could she be?

I start in the center and start working my way out, but all I can find is the occasional feather. But there aren't enough to make me think that something bad happened.

Maybe she's stuck somewhere?

Not in the shed. Or behind the shelves.

Poking my head into his garage shows that it's nearly empty except for his corvette.

He must have his motorcycle again today.

I even get down on my knees to peer under it.

Did she perhaps sneak in through a window?

Going back into the cool interior, I start going from room to room.

This is starting to feel hopeless, but for Alexei's sake, I keep looking.

I work my way back into his massive master bedroom suite. I've never been in here either.

It feels weird being in here without him knowing it.

No flamingo though.

Shit.

I bet Mikhail has some ideas.

"Yes, Lara? How goes the fowl play?" Of course he chuckles at his own joke.

"Very funny. It's not. I can't find her anywhere. Do you have any suggestions?" I glance down and pause.

The picture by Alexei's nightstand has the two of us in the frame.

When I pick it up to inspect it, we both look so much younger.

Wait. Was that my twenty-first birthday? I can't believe he kept this picture.

I hated that dress. It never fit me right. How can he bear to have this next to his bed?

He looks handsome as ever. His wild hair was tamed and slicked down, and he has that same cocky grin on his face, flashing the silver of his tooth.

I miss that girl in the frame. She was more carefree than I am now.

There's a strange part of me that wants to pitch this in the garbage because of how awful I appear.

But it's Alexei's. I'd never do that to his things.

"I have no idea what to do or where to look for a flamingo in a town that has them everywhere. I bet it flew away to rejoin a flock." He sounds less than enthusiastic to be considering this.

"Please, Miki? For me?" If I find his bird, Alexei would be happy enough he might start coming back over.

"Fine," he growls. "I'll see what I can do. No promises, and you're going to have to start being nicer to Mila."

It's a small price to pay.

CHAPTER 30

ALEXEI

I HAVEN'T HEARD BACK from Lara. She told me her and Mikhail are looking for my baby, Sheila. Why would she want to leave me?

I twist the throttle and weave between the traffic, I have to get home quicker.

That doesn't stop me pulling a few wheelies, the adrenaline takes my mind off it all.

I could lose Sheila and Lara. Both my girls.

My life would end.

By the time I get home, I don't see Mikhail's bike here, only Lara's BMW. With my helmet in one hand, I run towards the door.

"Did you find her?"

Lara stands there biting her nails, her eyes wide.

I take a slow step towards her, damn she's so gorgeous. Those lips. And that tight white dress she has on.

"Ummm,"

I raise a brow as I hear a kind of familiar sound, that same honking Sheila does. But it's different.

I look past Lara at that thing in my house.

Not my Sheila. I know just from glancing. The feathers

aren't the same pink, nor as glossy. I stop right in front of Lara, inhaling that sweet scent of hers.

Distracting.

Looking up at me, she sucks in a breath. I know I am looking directly at her pout.

"Who the fuck is that in my house?" I whisper. "That. Is. Not. My. Sheila."

"I, err." Her voice trails off.

She can't lie to me, same as I can't to her.

"I'm sorry. Mikhail's gone back out to look."

I shake my head and step back, creating the space before I grab her and take her upstairs.

"Why? Why would she do this?" I toss my hands in the air and stomp over to the kitchen, grabbing one of my Gobstoppers from the cupboard.

Leaning back on the counter, Lara watches me warily as I stare at this imposter bird in my dining room.

"The hell do I do with this? I can't look after two of the damn things," I mutter to myself.

"I guess, I can help, it kinda is my fault." She shrugs, sliding her hands into the pockets of her dress.

"No." I push myself upright, making my way over to this new bird, walking around it cautiously. I know Sheila tried to bite me a few times at the start.

"Nope. This one's gotta go."

Striding over to the front door, I open it wide. Lara runs after me, grabbing me by the wrist. That tingly thing happens again and my dick twitches.

"What are you doing, pchelka?"

"You can't just throw the poor thing out? What if Sheila comes home, I bet she would love a best friend. I know I love mine."

That almost knocks the air out of my lungs. What kind of love does she mean? Friend love? Real love like Jax and Sofia?

I'd die for her, I'm obsessed with her, is that love?

I step forward and she takes one back and I slam the door closed. She doesn't flinch until her back is against the wall. There's a thud as I put my hand over her head and the other in my back pocket to stop myself from touching her.

Everything about her, even the way she is staring into my eyes, is making me want her more, in really filthy ways.

"I'm so mad at you right now," I tease.

"I'm mad at you too." She bites her lip and I have to hold in a groan.

"Is that right…"

I lean in, running my nose along her cheek and I hear her sharp intake of breath.

"Tell me for what reason you could possibly be mad at me, when you lost my flamingo?"

"You lost your flamingo. Not me. I'm mad because you've been avoiding me, Alexei. Because you seem to be more interested in the whereabouts of a damn bird than speaking to me."

She crosses her arms over her chest and I pull back.

Her cheeks are burning red.

She's flustered and probably angry. It hurts. Running my hands over my jaw, I sigh.

This is a mess.

"Just go. I'll stay and keep an eye on this one. Maybe keeping your distance is for the best."

The pain in her voice tells me that's a lie.

For some reason, I just nod, bow my head, and leave. Her words replay in my head. I need to find Sheila, then I can calm down and work out what to do.

CHAPTER 31

LARA

I'VE NEVER SEEN Alexei like this. So… flustered.

If anything that gives me hope, he feels this too. He wants more, he just doesn't know what to do. I get it. My brothers, our friendship.

Or I suppose it could be his Sheila is missing.

I jump back when this new flamingo makes a noise, I can't lie, I'm kinda petrified. It's why I waited in the hallway for Alexei to get home the first time.

These damn things are scary close up.

Keeping my distance from the bird, I head upstairs into Alexei's room, except this time, when I look at his bed, I think about him pushing me to my knees and calling me his good girl.

My cheeks heat.

Sitting on the edge of the mattress, I smooth my hand over the silky duvet. Spotting a couple of bloodstained shirts on the floor, I decide to make myself useful and pick them up, tossing them in the laundry.

My phone pings on the counter. I run back over, my heart in my throat hoping it's him.

And my smile shouldn't be as wide when I see his name on the screen, but it is.

A

We found Sheila. Bringing her home with Mikhail now. Don't worry about looking after Bruce.

I frown. Tapping out a reply.

ME

Bruce??

A

That stray you brought into my house. Bruce.

How does he even know that one downstairs is a male? I wouldn't have a clue. I shake my head, it's his problem now anyway and I take it that means he doesn't need me here. Disappointment clouds over me, that glimmer of hope fading again.

Sometimes I want to shake him, but really, I want him to kiss me again.

ME

Okay. I will head home.

Making a dart down the stairs, I snatch the keys from the bowl by the door and jump in my car. I don't know why, I want to cry and drive far, far away.

Maybe if he misses me, he will realize? I can't keep pretending around him.

When I get home, the first thing I do is head to the fridge. Wine might fix my mood. I gasp when I open it.

The whole thing is stacked with fruits, vegetables, and yogurts. All my favorites.

Even now, he's reminding me he's here for me.

By the time I shower and head back into my room, I stop

in the doorway. The security lights in the backyard illuminate through the window. What the hell?

It sends chills down my spine, I almost don't want to move. What if they're back for me?

And no one is here to help me.

I creep over to the window, holding my breath. How long can I live like this? This isn't me. I'm a Volkov. I've been conditioned to be strong like my brothers. Except, whenever it gets tough I run.

And I've had Alexei protecting me my entire life. Maybe I am just weak and useless like my father always told me.

Peeking through the blinds, the light is still on, but as I scan the surroundings I see nothing. Shit. Did I lock the doors?

I jog down the stairs almost skidding on the marble floors.

Phew. It's locked.

Maybe it was an animal or something. Wrapping my arms around my waist, I wish Alexei was here. I'd feel safe and loved, not empty and alone.

I don't want to live in a world without Alexei by my side. It's like our souls are tangled together in this beautiful mess we've created.

I don't notice that the tears are falling until I wipe them away. I need to be stronger on my own.

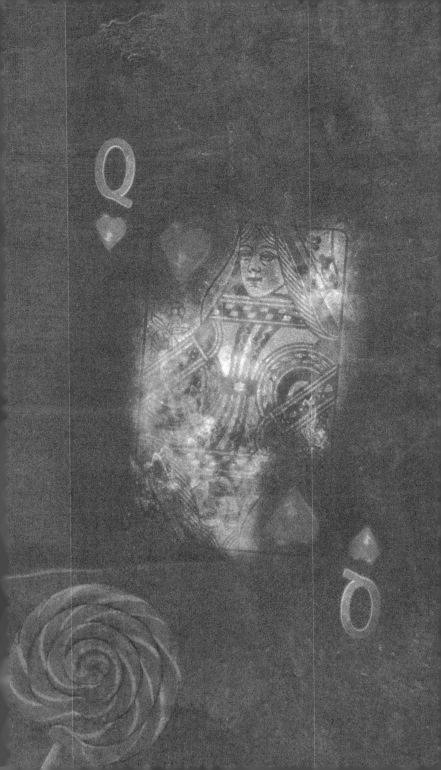

CHAPTER 32
ALEXEI

THREE WHOLE DAYS I haven't been in the same space as Lara. And my heart hurts. Watching her from a distance isn't enough.

Watching her as she sleeps is not enough.

Maybe I need to hear her voice.

"Alexei?" Mikhail clears his throat next to me.

God, I am so distracted. "Sorry, what?"

I clench my fists as Nikolai claps me on the shoulder. I never usually want to swing for him, but everything is irritating me. Even Jax's tongue piercing, I see why Niki gets cranky about it.

"You too busy looking after your birds?" Jax chuckles, tipping back his beer.

"You wouldn't understand. It's hard."

It's not really, but being without the woman who breathes life into me is.

"Lara called," Mikhail says, raising a brow at me.

"Is...is she okay?" I know she is physically. I've been watching her.

"Why aren't you there? I've never seen one without the other. Did you have a falling out?" Jax asks.

I shake my head. "No. We never argue. She's worried someone is watching her house at night."

She never tried to tell me. That hurts. Does she think I'm useless because I didn't save her quickly enough?

I hold up my palm to stop the questions I know they're going to ask. "There isn't, though. I'm still protecting her. Don't worry."

Mikhail nods and Nikolai looks at me quizzically. If they knew how I really felt about their sister and what I wanted to do with her, they would not be okay with me being so close to her.

"I'll go check in on her tonight."

"Good. Ivan is unpredictable and until we find that fucker Kirill, she could be in danger," Mikhail grumbles.

I know that. It's all I think about.

I can't wait to kill that asshole. So fucking painfully.

Dropping a handful of bills to cover my beer, I push out into the hot night and head to my bike. It takes me straight to Lara's, where I wait out on the road until all her lights go out.

I miss laughing with her.

I miss the way she would pout at me pretending to be annoyed.

I miss the way she smells like vanilla.

I miss the way she made me feel all warm inside. Something I've never experienced in my life.

My parents never loved me or cared for me.

Lara does.

Maybe I can give her what she wants. I am a quick learner, especially for her.

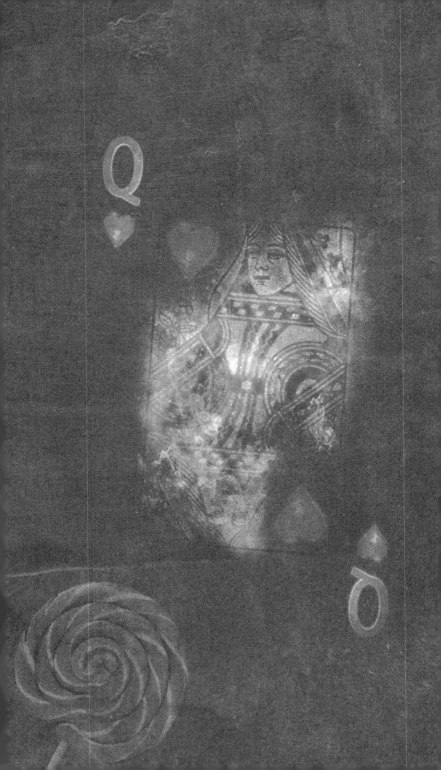

CHAPTER 33

LARA

I SIT on the edge of my bed biting the skin around my nails.

I want to hear his voice. I miss him.

Everynight when it gets dark, I think my mind is playing tricks on me. Hell, the other night I swear it was like someone was looking over me in my sleep.

Except I wasn't scared, at all.

I think my mind is playing tricks on me.

I trust Alexei and my brothers to protect me.

No one can hurt me in my own house.

So I cuddle up under the blanket and close my eyes, trying to ignore my aching heart.

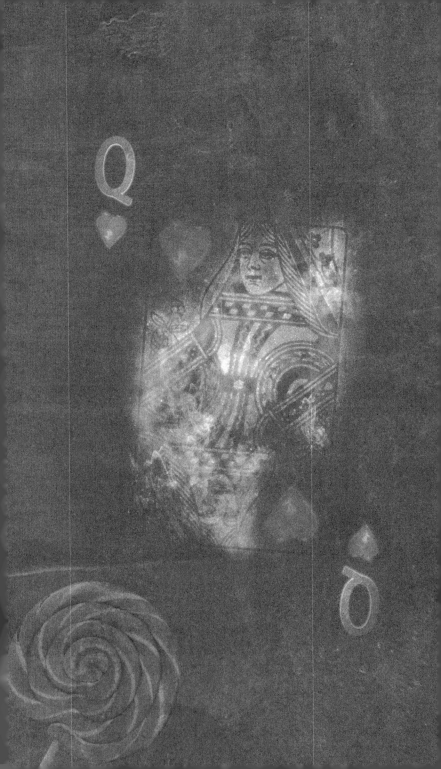

CHAPTER 34
ALEXEI

Song, What If I Told You That I Love You, Ali Gatie.

Taking a spot in my nightly viewing area, I can get glimpses of my girl in the window, and watch out for any intruders.

Once she's asleep, I'll go in and check on her.

It's not enough to stand in the shadows, I need more of her.

Unwrapping a lollipop, I shove the wrapper in my jeans pocket and sit back on the bench. She looks tired today. She's been restless in her sleep, so maybe that's why.

I look on as she empties the dishwasher, but then my phone starts vibrating in my pocket. Digging it out, her name flashes up on the screen and my heart does that jumpy thing.

"I missed your voice," I greet her before she can even say hello. I don't even know why I blurt that out.

She giggles. "Me too."

It's followed by a long sigh which wipes my smile.

"Are you okay?" I press her.

"Yea. Well, no. I don't know. I keep being told I'm wrong, but I thought that you'd understand me. I think someone is watching me. But, I don't know if I'm just a bit fucked up from the kidnapping. Maybe?"

"What do you mean 'watched'?"

I'm always looking out for her, more so recently, I can't risk her being taken again. I would have seen if there was someone lurking around, risking her safety.

"Like, stalked," she says in a hushed tone.

Jumping up from her yard furniture and pace around the front of the house, making sure I'm tight to the hedgerow so I don't trigger the security lights.

The last thing I want to do is to scare her.

"I would know if someone was stalking you, Lara. But, I'll check it out."

As I round the house to the front, I stand and listen, nothing. No movement, no cars.

"Thanks, Alexei." The panic in her voice has subsided.

"Can I kill them if I do find them? You want me to bring you their head, or...?"

She lets out another small laugh and my heart races.

That is all I need to do. Make her smile, make her worries go away. If she's happy, I am too.

"I think it would be more Volkov style to cut the balls off first." she says almost seriously.

I instinctively rub my own through my jeans. Getting my dick pierced hurt enough, having my nuts carved would be worse than death.

"You're one mean woman, Lara. But for you, I will deliver stalker balls." I know she can't see me, but I cover my heart in a solemn oath.

"Is there anything you wouldn't do for me?" she asks softly.

I don't hesitate in my answer. "Nothing, Lara. There is not one single thing you could ask of me that I wouldn't do..." I pause. "Except to not be in your life."

"Neither of us would ever let that happen."

I hear her sigh and want to break the door down and get to her, wrap her in my arms and kiss her again.

It plays in a loop in my head over and over.

The memory makes my dick twinge and that's bad.

Nikolai and Mikhail would kill me if I went there again. Yet, every time I smell her Chanel perfume, or she smiles at me, all I can picture is bending her over and sinking inside her.

I've never done any of that before, but I think about it often with Lara. It's always her.

I bet her pussy tastes even sweeter than her lips, and her moans are as incredible as the sound of her laughter.

Seeing her naked would ruin me.

There will never be another, nor has there ever been. My life is dedicated to one woman only.

"But, Alexei?" Her soft voice pulls me out of the porn scene I have going on in my head that's making my dick piercing hit against my zipper.

"Yes, pchelka?"

"We haven't been the same since the, you know."

"Kiss." I finish her sentence.

"Nothing has changed." I rub my palms against my jeans. Fuck, have I upset her?

"You don't come over anymore, I've barely seen you on your own. I feel like I'm losing you and I can't." She hiccups and that's it.

I knock on her door. "Open up."

I cut the call and shoot a quick and simple message to Enzo.

ME

I need security cameras tomorrow.

He replies instantly.

195

ENZO

Tell me why first.

I roll my eyes. I'm not as stupid as they all think.

ME

Lara thinks she has a stalker, I want to keep watch. The others don't need to know I'm taking care of it.

ENZO

Don't make me regret this, Alexei. I'll have my guys go by tomorrow.

ME

Don't tell Lara.

ENZO

… Continue

I knock again.

ME

I don't want her panicking.

ENZO

Fine.

She opens up with her face glowing, her silky hair wrapped around some weird contraption over her head, and in a white robe.

Shit, I can see her nipples through the material.

I clear my throat and grin at her.

"I, umm, excuse the state of me." She gestures down at her outfit and hair.

"Beautiful always, Lara." I mean it. Like I do every time she asks if she looks okay in her clothes, or if it seems like she's gained a few pounds.

Same answer because it's always true. No matter what, no

woman has ever come close to Lara.

She tips her chin down, making me shake my head.

"Why do you never believe me?" I say, stepping in front of her.

Her breath catches as I grip her chin between my thumb and finger bringing her blue eyes to mine, pushing her back so she is against the wall.

I stare at her lips but drag my eyes away to focus on her.

"You trust me with your life, right? You always have, always will?" I ask sternly.

I never bring this harsher side out in front of her. I try to hide it from her, keep her away from the dark that plagues me.

"You know I do, more than anyone else."

"But you don't trust my words? When I say you're beautiful, I mean it. I may be many things, Lara. A liar is not one of them, especially to you."

She opens her mouth and snaps it shut.

Cute. This is the first time I've had her speechless.

"Come on, say it, I know you want to."

That smile that makes my heart race flashes across her face and I relax slightly.

"You said one kiss wouldn't change anything between us. You lied."

Our noses touch, her lips just a breath away from my own.

As our eyes lock, time stops around us.

And then I get a flash image of Nikolai slicing my head off with a machete. I can't protect her if I'm six feet under.

I close my eyes.

Dammit. I did lie. One kiss did ruin everything. It made me realize the truth that I buried away.

But I can't pull away if it causes her so much pain.

So I do the only thing I know how to do.

"Tell me that you stocked up my sweet jar," I say with a smirk.

I sense her disappointment, I feel it in my bones. Sadly, this is how it has to be.

Releasing my grip on her face I step back.

I'm a fucking idiot. I know I want her.

She keeps her composure, smoothing out her robe, yet her cheeks are bright red, like that time I caught her stealing liquor from her dad's cabinet when she was nineteen.

Her lip rolls between her teeth. "It's half full, I wasn't sure if you were coming back over so I left it."

Guilt riddles me. "I didn't lie. We can make this work." I hold out my hand and she laces her fingers through mine.

"We have to." She tightens her grip.

"So, tell me more about this stalker," I say, leading her into her kitchen. I sit myself up on the counter by the refrigerator and she does the same on the one opposite, snatching the half full sweet jar and opening it.

I catch the gummy worm that she tries to hurl at my head and rip a bite off with my teeth.

That reminds me, I need to get Sheila some more fishies. Well, and Bruce. The damn birds are eating me out of house and home.

Maybe I should get a snake?

They might be easier.

"I might sound mad." She begins.

I look up at her taking another bite of the candy. "Probably. All the best people are, Lara. Nothing wrong with that."

She rolls her eyes. I gesture for another treat, this time she gets her aim right and a hard candy hits me in my eyebrow.

"What? It's true. Now tell me before I get cranky." I put on my best fake angry voice.

"Oh no, I'm so scared." The sarcasm drips from her voice. She holds her palms up in surrender, and then belts me in the head with another sweet and she bursts into a fit of giggles.

There it is, my favorite sound.

CHAPTER 35

UGH. He was so close to giving in.

We both were.

I don't know how much longer I can wait to make him realize that we are an end game. That I am simply madly in love with him.

I want him as more than a friend and I know he feels this too.

Keeping him at arm's length isn't going to cut it, not when I've had a taste.

And damn, that harsh tone he used on me.

Dominant. Possessive.

In the bedroom, I bet he's a beast that will put me in my place and worship the life out of me.

There is no other man for me.

I just need to work out how to get him.

CHAPTER 36
ALEXEI

Song, Circus Psycho, Diggy Graves

I DON'T KNOW how much longer I can take of this.

The urge to touch her, to be near her, it's becoming overwhelming.

I'm not used to holding back when I want something. It's eating me apart from the inside.

Keeping her at arm's length is getting more difficult.

It's like they're shrinking.

I'm a T-Rex, trying to push her away with the world's tiniest limbs, while I want to devour her with the biggest appetite.

Motoring through the dark streets of Vegas, I let my inner dinosaur roar.

The primal side of me that wants to pin her down and ravage her like I'm starving.

Killing the engine and pushing my bike the last two blocks helps take some of the edge off of my antsy energy.

It's easy to slip into her dark house when I already know the code.

She can't hide anything from me. I know her better than I

know myself.

Padding through the kitchen, I reflexively dig my hand into the candy jar she keeps full for me and unfurl one of the shiny wrappers.

Shoving the crinkly foil into my pocket, I push the sugary treat between my teeth and cheek, then sneak towards her room.

The regular breathing tells me she's asleep.

My perfect angel with her blonde hair spread over the pillows.

Tracing the silky locks, I curl my finger around the end and pull it up to my nose to inhale her shampoo.

Even though I didn't tug on her scalp, she shifts in her sleep. A soft sound that ends in a low moan.

"Do you taste as sweet when you're dreaming, pchelka?" I let the tendril fall, then brush my lips across her cheek, letting her hot breath bathe me before I stand.

She makes me drunk on her.

It's like a drug that calms me. Just being near her makes me want to do more for her than myself.

There's never been a time it hasn't been about her.

Shit, she's moving again.

I think she's going to wake up. Backing out slowly, I wind up in the side of the kitchen near the laundry.

Well, the least I can do is fold her clothes for her while I'm here. She'll never know it was me.

The temptation is too much when I discover a sultry red thong.

That's coming home with me.

She won't notice.

Gray begins to fill the windows as dawn approaches. One last handful of candy to tide me over until I get home. Gotta keep my energy up, this watching her all of the time is exhausting work.

Worth it.

CHAPTER 37

LARA

Song, ALWAYS BEEN YOU, Chris Grey

My stomach grumbles and it wakes me up. Checking my phone, it's only seven. I'm just constantly exhausted. Especially being on edge, I just can't help feeling like someone is watching me.

Except that saying it out loud, even to Alexei the other day, I sound crazy.

Shoving on a knitted cardigan over my cami and shorts, I hug it around myself and head into the kitchen. Coffee. That will fix me. Stifling a yawn, I grab a mug from the cabinet, my favorite sunshine one, and jab the button on the machine.

As it buzzes to life, I rest against the counter. When I take a step back, something crinkles under my foot.

What the hell?

Lifting it up, a candy wrapper is stuck to my heel. I peel it off and hold it up to inspect it.

Huh? That wasn't there last night. I haven't touched any and Alexei wasn't here. My heart almost stops. Looking up I spot the jar and rush over, grabbing it from the side. How haven't I noticed how low it's gotten?

Why the hell is he coming over when I'm not here? As I slam the jar down, something jumps behind the container of spaghetti. When I slide the canister out the way, I gasp.

A fucking camera. Squashing the wrapper in my palm, I squeeze it so tightly my nails break through the thin paper. Panic takes over.

Someone *is* watching me.

But reaching to get my phone, I stop. There's something about the sweet wrapper and Alexei's words playing in a loop about protecting me.

The distance between us physically.

The damn sweet jar.

It's him.

Blind rage overtakes me. Swiping up my cell from the counter, I hover over his contact number.

My fingers are shaking, the urge to hurl the phone across the room taking over.

Yet I don't.

A calming feeling settles over me as I picture him watching me.

I don't feel unsafe. No, I feel protected.

I'm just hurt he did this rather than actually be with me. That pains me more. I need him in more ways than just looking out for me.

My heart craves him.

It always has, it always will.

Without him my mind spins out of control.

With him I am calm.

And most of all, I am loved so fiercely. That could never be matched by another.

I just need his crazy ass to get on the same page.

Call me delusional, but the fact he's stalking me means he's obsessed with me. Just like I am with him. I can't be mad about that.

If he wants a show to watch, I'll give him one. In fact, I'll do it so well, hopefully he will be bashing my door off its hinges to get to me. I want him so consumed by me he stops this damn distance thing.

I might not have control over many aspects of my life, but getting the man of my dreams to see me for who I really am is something I can.

I will make Alexei mine.

I wonder what he does when he watches me? I know what I'd be doing. Picking up a red lollipop, I lean against the counter looking directly at the camera.

That kiss was enough to have me turned on every damn night thinking about it. Imagining his lips…elsewhere. His rough hands holding me in place. Letting him own me. Just how I crave from him.

Opening the wrapper, I seductively pop it into my mouth and suck.

It's sweetness bursting on my tongue, I can totally see why he's addicted to these things.

I slide my crop top strap down my shoulder, picking up my phone, I pretend to make a call.

"Oh hi, Dan. I'm bored, and horny. Do you feel like coming over?" I twirl the sugary treat around my tongue.

"Great. See you soon." With a grin, I turn around and flick my long blond locks over my shoulder.

Digging a piece of paper out of the drawer I scribble a note for Alexei, leave my sucker on top, and saunter out of the room.

He's played his cards and now it's my turn. I hope my deal lands with his dick inside me.

If he turns up, that tells me everything I need to know.

He loves me too.

I just hope this doesn't ruin everything. I guess he should have thought about that before kissing me and stalking me.

We're either going to create a storm and demolish everything, or we will dance in the rain together.

Slipping off my shorts, I look at my reflection in the mirror, guiding my hands down my sides. No matter how many times I try this, I never see anything I love about myself.

I see the way my hips bulge out, I see the little bits of cellulite on my ass. In fact, every time I look I find something new I hate.

So, I flick off the lights, keeping my royal blue lace bra and matching thong on, then slip under the covers.

I wonder if he has a camera in here too?

CHAPTER 38
ALEXEI

Slamming the laptop shut, I pick it up and smash it repeatedly against the dining table.

Sheila squawks next to me.

"Shut up," I growl at her.

I much prefer her over Bruce. He's grumpy. Kinda reminds me of Nikolai. Maybe I should rename him.

Fuck. I shake my head. Lara. My brain is on Lara.

I think her little show was for me. Dan? Who the fuck is Dan?

The thought of another man having his hands on my Lara makes me violent. More than that, murderous.

I'm losing her. The one person in my life who keeps me sane, and I'm just about clutching on to the last shred of sanity I have left.

They might call me crazy, they have no idea how far that goes for her.

She is my purpose in life.

I crave her in ways I can't comprehend.

I don't just want her. She's a fucking addiction sweeter than any candy.

213

One taste and I was hooked. I can't let this happen. I can happily lose my mind, but I can't lose my heart.

No, fuck that. One look all those years ago and I was a goner.

Hitting my palm against my forehead over and over as if that will finally be the thing to knock some sense into me.

I'm so damn stupid.

I can't let her go. That would kill me. Game over. My life wouldn't be worth living anymore.

You can't please everyone, sometimes you have to hurt them for the greater good.

Nikolai and Mikhail will forgive me one day, I hope. If not, I died for a worthy cause.

And that is Lara.

The risk that is worth it.

"Ouch!" I pull my hand back before Sheila can peck at it again.

She has that cute look in her eyes, where I don't know if she's going to attack me or rest her head on my arm.

"What are you looking at? Do you have the answers? Do I go get my girl? And risk Nikolai slicing me up and serving me to you?"

Wait, do flamingos eat humans? Would they if they're hungry enough?

I tap my fingers against the table waiting for her answer.

Yes, I ask my flamingo for advice on life altering decisions. She gets me in ways no one else can.

She honks right in my ear. Fuck, I hate that noise.

"Okay. Okay." I hold my hands up. "I'll go get my woman." I point past her towards her food dish. "Only if you eat your fishies today."

I swear she understands me. Or am I really losing the last of my marbles?

Oh well.

I race over to Lara's at lightning speed on my all black BMW S1000 RR, she's a beast. Or as Lara calls it, my death trap.

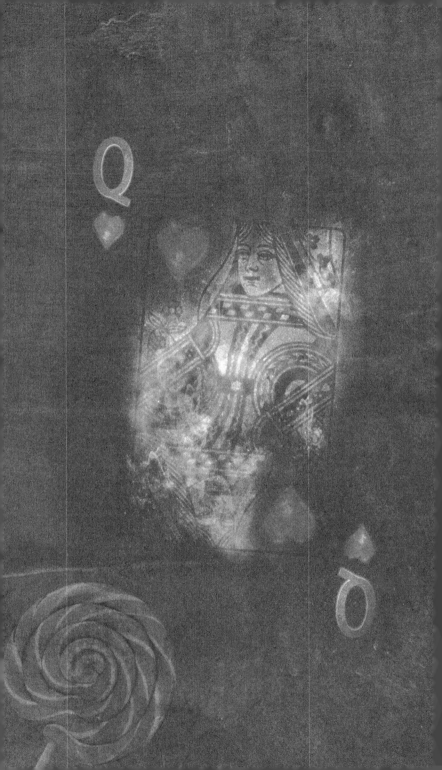

CHAPTER 39

LARA

Song- Joy Ride, Hueston

WITH ONLY SECONDS passing since I hear his bike engine stop, my door abruptly swings open, startling me. He switches on the light, and his face turns red as he runs his hand through his wild hair.

The whites of his eyes flash as he searches the room. I can witness that exact moment of realization when a slight smile forms.

I quickly sit up as he walks in, tilting his head to the side, eating me up with his gaze. Without uttering a single word, he advances towards me, and an electric current crackles in the air.

He stops at the edge of the bed and gently lifts my chin to meet his gaze.

"Tell me what you want. Make it clear for me." His voice is deep and gravelly.

"Y-you," I stutter, but hold eye contact.

Slowly nodding, he examines me intensely, running his thumb along my bottom lip while sensually licking his own.

"Me what? Hmm, give me the details."

Fuck. It's like I've forgotten how to breathe.

I grin at him. It's now or never. "I want you to own me. I want you to fuck me senseless, claim me as yours. I want it all, with you."

With each passing moment, his breaths grow deeper and more audible.

With a tilt of his head, his Adam's apple becomes visible. "No going back after this, pchelka."

"I know."

A rush of adrenaline surges through me, causing my heart to thump loudly and my thighs to clench tightly. God, I want him.

"Hmm." He tips his head to look at me. I squeal as I feel him lifting me up by the arms, and suddenly my back is against the wall.

"You live for destruction and carnage, don't you?"

Despite frowning, he still nods.

"Ruin me, Alexei. Shatter everything we thought we wanted and take what we both need for once."

He runs his fingers through my hair and tugs it back, tipping my face up. His eyes still hold that untamed expression, and his smirk reveals his glinting silver tooth.

"The only way I'll be ruining you is for every other man. You are mine, Lara Volkov."

I sink my teeth into my lip.

"Destroy our friendship then. Make me yours." My breath hitches.

"I can't do this anymore. I can't go another second without tasting you again."

When his lips collide with mine, my heart races out of control. Years of pent-up tension culminate in his commanding the kiss.

In one swift movement, he takes hold of my hip and brings me close, our bodies tightly pressed together. While cupping my jaw with his other hand, he expertly deepens the kiss, eliciting a moan from me.

"More," I pant.

He pulls away, shaking his head before diving towards my throat.

"You taste so sweet," he murmurs while his tongue traces my jawline and his hands slide up my body.

"Fuck, Alexei," I hiss, my eyes closing as he bites and sucks on my sensitive flesh. "Take me, please," I whisper.

As his fingers explore under the lace of panties I inch my legs apart, feeling the tease of his touch so close.

"You know me better than anyone. You'll figure it out. I'm yours to do as you please, Alexei."

"You got it, baby."

As he kisses me urgently, my fingers tangle in his hair and he fumbles with the straps of my dress, sliding them off my arms.

I've never been more soaked in my life. The excitement of having this man worship me is building up.

CHAPTER 40
ALEXEI

THE TASTE of her on my tongue has my dick straining against my jeans. It almost hurts. When the guys talked about the women they've slept with, I never cared.

The only woman ever on my mind for the last twenty years is Lara.

I have been too completely and utterly consumed by her, obsessed with her, to even look at another woman. Let alone touch one.

I wholeheartedly belong to her. *My woman.*

I just want to make her feel good. My purpose in life is to make her happy.

And judging by the way she's looking like she's about to eat me up, the way she's moaning into my mouth, I think I'm succeeding.

The feel of her soft skin under my rough hands almost turns me feral.

"We shouldn't be doing this," I mutter between kisses, hoisting her legs around my waist.

Her hips roll against my cock and I almost lose it.

Not now. This is all about *her*.

No matter how wrong this should be, it doesn't feel it, not one single bit.

"I don't care, I just want you." Her voice is hoarse. Her hands link around my neck and she pulls me closer.

"I could kiss you all day."

She rolls her hips again. I slide my hand along the soft lace of her panties. The wetness soaks through onto my fingers.

All for me.

"God you're so wet for me. I bet you taste so sweet down there, too." I need to find out. I'm desperate, fucking starving. A perfect little gasp comes from her lips as I move the thin fabric to the side and slide my finger along her slit.

It easily slips inside her and she gasps.

"Is that nice?" I whisper on her cheek as I slowly pump her.

"Mmm, yes."

With our lips pressed together, I spin us around, relishing the sensation of her legs wrapping firmly around me. As we make our way back to the bed, I gently place her down in the center.

Resting on my knees, I hook my fingers under her panties, she lifts her hips and I slide them off, and then I move onto the matching royal-blue bra.

Picking up her foot, I stretch out her leg and trail soft kisses along the inside of her calf, savoring every taste of her. When I get to her knee, I lick all the way up, spreading her open. She sucks in a breath when my nose brushes along her pussy.

By the time I repeat this on her other leg, she's writhing on the bed.

"Please, Alexei."

Trailing a finger along her toned stomach, I watch as the goosebumps erupt under my touch and work my way over her full breasts.

"You're beautiful, Lara."

She blushes, resting myself over her, I trail my index finger down her soft cheek.

"Damn baby." I dive into her neck, kissing and sucking, thriving off the moans escaping her lips. Her fingers tangle in my hair as she guides me down her body. Taking her nipple in my mouth, I swirl my tongue. "Teach me how to make you scream for me. Show me exactly how you want it."

I curl my fingers inside her and those moans get louder.

So that's a move she likes.

"Yes, like that."

I kiss my way down her body, watching her face as I do.

"Such a good girl, telling me what feels good." I settle between her thighs, letting my breath tickle against her pussy.

"Please." She rolls her hips closer.

I like it when she begs. When she needs me so much that she's willing to plead with me.

"Like this?" I run the tip of my tongue along her slit. As she arches her back, I slide my hands under and grab her ass. "Spread those legs, baby."

I slide two fingers inside her, focusing on her clit with my tongue, lapping up all her juices. "God, my good fucking girl."

She hooks her knees over my shoulder and uses her hands to push my face deeper into her pussy.

She is so damn sweet.

"I need more, Alexei. More of all of it." There's desperation in her voice, and it's taking all restraint I have not to pick her up, slam her against the mirror and fuck her. There's this animal inside me that wants to come out and play.

But is that what she wants?

"We've waited this long to get naked with each other. Let me enjoy you thoroughly. I want to taste every single inch of you first."

With that, I flip her over onto her belly.

"Up on all fours, baby. I wanna taste you from behind.

Might be even better." I command and slap her ass, tilting my head to admire this fine view, especially the wetness sliding down her thighs.

She liked that?

Spreading her open, I feast on her, this time sliding three fingers in, less gently this time. And fuck, she's soaking my face.

"That's it, be a good girl. I'm not stopping until you come all over my face."

"Keep doing that." Her moans turn into screams, and I do everything I can to make them louder. To the point my dick aches so bad for her, I undo my jeans and shove them down to my knees. One hand is finger fucking Lara, the other is jerking myself off to a similar rhythm.

Her entire body shakes around me. She's screaming out my name. I can't take it anymore. Her walls clamp around my fingers.

Holy fuck.

She's falling apart on my mouth. I'm doing this to her. There isn't a better thrill in life.

I keep going until I lick every ounce of orgasm out of her and she slumps forward. I withdraw my fingers, using her wetness to coat my cock. The most violent climax of my life grips me. I look down at my girl, her perky ass, trying to catch her breath. Her taste on my tongue, dripping down my chin.

"Fuuuuuuck," I let it out, coating her back in my cum.

"Shit, that's hot." she says in a husky voice. My chest heaves. I wonder what it will feel like when I do this inside her.

As I go to get off the bed to grab something to clean her up, she grabs my wrist.

"Where are you going?"

She shakes her head, pushing her ass into the air. "Fuck. Me. Alexei. Please. I am begging you."

Whatever my girl wants, she gets.

I mean, she got off, but she wants more. I must be doing something right?

Spreading my cum over her ass like massage oil, she lets out a content sigh. Running my hand between her thighs, I spread it over her pussy.

A wave of possessiveness comes over me. Seeing me dripping from her has my dick standing at attention.

I want to savor this moment, yet equally, I want to dive into her and never leave. Rubbing the tip of my dick around her entrance, she jumps forward.

"W-what's that? It's cold?"

I chuckle. "I got pierced, remember?"

"What? No. You never mentioned that!"

I'd love to see her expression. Wait. She likes me flipping her around. Now she will get to feel it. Now it makes all that pain of having it done worth it.

I do just that and rest between her legs, letting my pulsing cock hit against her warmth.

"That's better. I can see your pretty face when I take you."

She smiles up at me. "And I get to see your handsome one."

Her palm cups my cheek and I press into it. My heart hammers. This is the moment I didn't realize I was waiting my entire life for.

Pressing my lips against hers and pushing her leg back, it gives me access to push myself against her entrance.

"No going back," I mutter against her lips.

"This is everything I've ever wanted, Alexei."

Guiding myself inside her, it's so fucking warm as she clamps around my dick. I can't help but moan into her mouth. With each inch I push in, she holds onto me tighter, her nails digging into my back.

"Fuck." Her breathless pants turn me on. Biting down on

her bottom lip I push the full length of myself in and wait for her to adjust.

"You fit me perfectly."

"Meant to be." She smiles.

I pull out and push back inside, where I belong.

"Chyort vozmi, ty takaya tugaya, ya hochiu ostatsia v tebe navsegda." **Fucking hell, you're so tight, I want to stay inside you forever.**

CHAPTER 41
LARA

Song- The Best I Ever Had, Limi

With every slow and deep thrust, I edge that bit closer to release. He consumes me. Desperately grabbing his face, I slam my lips over his, letting him have my moans.

"So good," I tell him.

That piercing hits right where I need it, each time sending sparks through me.

He keeps devouring my mouth, threading his hands through my hair. Claiming me as his in every way now.

"Are you going to come on my cock, baby? Show me how good it is for you."

Sweet Jesus.

He rolls us over so he's on his back. I hold myself upright with my hands on his chest. He repays the favor by grabbing my breasts in his hands and pinches my nipples.

"Mmmm." I tip my head back and roll my hips, the pressure on my clit as I do has me tingling all over.

With one of his firm hands on my hip, he thrusts up, holding me in place.

"Fuck," I hiss. Damn, it's even deeper, even more full of him.

"Oh, you like it harder." To emphasize his point, he rams into me.

I can't even respond as a little gasp comes out when he dives in with so much force.

"You look so fucking pretty bouncing on my cock." Our eyes meet, my heart races staring into the pools of pure hunger and lust for me.

Like I truly am the most beautiful woman he's ever seen. For the first time, I kinda feel like it too.

Spurred on by the grunts coming from him, I ride him properly.

"Fuck, Lara. I can't last much longer."

That sends a thrill through me. I'm doing this to him. His fingers dig into my ass and he takes control, lifting me up and down on his dick.

He grabs me by the back of the head and pushes me towards him. The second our lips meet I explode. Tangled in each other, he holds me tight, moaning my name into my mouth, which only makes my orgasm more intense.

Laying on top of him, my face presses against his throat, and his cock twitches inside me as we both try to regain our breath. The smile on my face won't go away.

"Was that… good for you?" I ask him, pushing myself up. He strokes his fingers along my arms and looks up at me.

"Good? Just good? Are you joking?"

I bite back my smug grin. "Best you ever had?"

"Oh, you have no idea, pchelka."

I raise a brow. He didn't say yes though. So, I slowly roll my hips and his eyes go wide in surprise.

"Best for you?" he asks.

Playing along, I shrug.

"Looks like I'll have to keep going, and going, until I am the best." He licks his lips.

"Or maybe you already are, because it's you."

He brings the front of my hand up to his mouth and kisses it gently.

CHAPTER 42
ALEXEI

I CATCH her eyes as I pull my lips away. "I might not be your first, but I'll be your last."

She cuddles closer into me, and I breathe in her sweet scent.

"Same goes for you." She nestles against me.

I take a deep breath. "No."

She pushes herself up on my chest, her eyebrows knitting together in confusion.

I grin and shake my head. "You are my first and last."

Her mouth falls open, so I lean forward and close it for her.

"Shut up. Don't lie to me. You know what you're saying?"

She puckers her lips. I grab her waist, pulling her back into a cuddle.

"Yea. I know what I'm saying. My dick has never been in anyone else. Only you."

"B-but, how? How can you be that damn good, and have a piercing? I don't buy it." She pouts.

Placing both hands on her cheeks, our noses touch. "Have I ever really lied to you about anything important?"

Her nose wrinkles. "No."

"Then trust me. This dick is yours and only yours, got it?"
She nods.

She thinks I was good. I made her happy. Fuck yeah.

"You like what I do to you?"

"More than like."

Rolling over so I'm on top of her, I nudge open her thighs and shift between them, resting my weight on my forearms as I hover over her. "You want me to clean up the mess I made?"

She nods, biting back a small smile.

"Be a good girl and spread them wider for me."

Readjusting my position, so my head is between her legs, I look up and watch her studying me.

Her cheeks are already blushing, and she's rolling her lip between her teeth.

Trailing my fingers along the inside of her thigh, I swipe the liquid and spread it over her pussy.

She has her knees flat to the mattress.

"Mmm, that's it. Look at you."

Leaning forward, pushed by her little moans, I run my tongue along her, just enough to tease and then pull back. "Tell me what you're thinking, baby?"

"I'm just shocked, that—"

I let my mouth glide slowly to her clit and feel her thighs shake. I like watching her build up in frustration almost, knowing I can be the one to set the fireworks when I want. She responds so well to any move I make.

"Because I was made for your pleasure, Lara. It's simple. I'm good at making you come, because I'm obsessed with you. I've spent my life figuring you out. And apparently, this was the real reason." I sink my teeth into her thigh and she cries out. Perfect.

"We are going to have so much fun exploring this." I've waited my life for this and I fully intend to explore every part of it with Lara.

Waking up with her naked in my arms is the best feeling in the world. Except, I have to get up because I have to finish planning her birthday surprise.

Every year I do this for her, except this one is different, it's the first one she's actually all mine.

"Morning, sladkiy."

Her husky morning voice has my cock standing to attention. Is this how it will always be now? Me constantly hard around her?

How am I going to hide this around her family? Now I know what having sex with the woman I love is like, how do I stop thinking about it all day and night?

I'm a man who has discovered sex in his thirties, and now wants to fuck her in every way she desires.

"Morning my beautiful girl." I stroke the tendril of hair away from her cheek and she smiles, that makes my heart race.

"Soooo…" she trails off.

Tugging her closer by her ass, she places her leg over my erection.

"Yes, baby?"

She idly traces the vein on my arm. "That whole, you avoiding me thing, that's not happening anymore, right?"

I chuckle. What a dumb fucking plan that was.

"I'm sorry." I tell her honestly.

"You more than made up for it. But now you've actually had sex." She chews on her lip as she watches me. "What happens if you see another girl you might want to try it with?"

My heart almost stops. The idea repulses me.

"Lara. I've waited all of my life for you. No one would ever compare. And I'm never letting you go. So, I'm more than happy being with you and only you for eternity."

She nuzzles face her into my neck and I rest my head on top of hers.

"I mean it. You always. Okay?" I'll never understand why she doesn't think she's good enough. It makes me sad.

"And only ever you for me."

A moment of silence passes over, as she inches her leg up higher. My dick throbs against her skin.

"Do we tell my brothers?"

Well that's one way to deflate my hard on. "Not yet. Let's enjoy each other for a while before I get my head sliced."

That makes her laugh.

"Don't be silly. They wouldn't." She pauses. "Would they?"

I truly don't know. Nikolai will be more pissed than Mikhail.

"Maybe once we kill the bad guys we come clean?"

"Sounds like you're superheroes."

"We are. I saved you, remember." I tap the tip of her nose.

She rubs her hand over my pecs and it lands on my shoulder. "Always my protector, Alexei. So yes, we can be a secret for now. Can't have them distracted until it's all over."

I kiss her forehead. I just want to be with her, kill all threats against her and maybe run away to a cabin and fuck her senseless for weeks. "I can't believe we waited this long to do this, when this entire time I could have been eating you."

"Jesus." The blush spreading up her throat tells me she's into it.

"What? I like eating you. I like my sweets. Now you're my favorite. But remember, I get addicted quickly. So I'll need your pretty pussy on my face as much as possible to survive."

"Oh, eager for morning sex too?" She teases, trailing her finger down my abs. "You know, you could just wake me up with it one day." She bats her lashes at me.

My eyebrows shoot up. "Is that right? Huh? You want me to have breakfast while you're still sleeping?"

She has no idea what her filthy words are doing to me. Feral. It's the only way to describe it.

A complete fucking mess, but I'll fuck her exactly how she desires.

She bites down on her lip and I can't resist stealing a kiss.

"Hmmm mmm," she hums in my mouth.

"I'd really like that. I want to experience everything with you. And make it dirty, call me your good girl, pull my hair, choke me. I'm yours and I think you'll make a perfect pleasure dom for me."

"A pleasure dom?"

"Yep."

"It's all about control. I hand it willingly to you, in return make me feel good. However you please. You know me, you can learn what makes me tick."

"Sounds like an experiment." I roll on top of her, nudging her legs wider and grabbing her wrists between one of my hands above her head.

I'm starting to see exactly what she wants. Her heart flutters in her throat, so I lean in and suck.

"You're my good girl. You've always been, pchelka. Now it's time to prove it." Running my hand up the inside of her thigh, I swipe the wetness coating her pussy.

"Hmm, I'm learning very fast." Bringing my hand up to my face, I suck my fingers clean.

CHAPTER 43

LARA

WITH A GROAN I roll over and see the onslaught of text messages from my family wishing me a happy birthday.

Even Nikolai sent a cute picture of the three of us as kids.

I open up the one message that has my heart racing.

ALEXEI

> Happy Birthday pchelka. This one will be even more special than the other 28, because this time you are mine. Be ready at 7pm. Wear anything, because you look beautiful always. Love, your Alexei.

Sitting up, my smile burns my cheeks and excitement runs through me. Alexei never fails to make my birthday amazing. Every year I'm showered with gifts, trips out, and parties. But he's right, this year is different. Being with him is my gift. Finally, having the man I've wished for.

As I slide on my robe and make my way downstairs, tears well up in my eyes at the sight of the living room ceiling covered in a sea of pink and red foiled balloons. When I catch sight of the helium flamingo in the middle, a hiccup interrupts my breath.

ME

you really are exceeding yourself already, sladkiy. Thank you for always making me feel special. I don't deserve you sometimes.

Wiping away the stray tear with the back of my hand, I find a mug under my coffee machine with a selfie of me and him plastered on the front. That was taken on my birthday three years ago when we took a trip to New York because I once told him I wanted to go to the Empire State Building.

Opening up the top of the machine to drop in a pod, I can't help but laugh when I see he's already put one in there for me.

This man.

As the machine pours my energy for the day, I spin myself around and rest on the counter.

"Jesus," I mutter, staring at the enormous bouquet of red roses sprinkled with every shade in a crystal glass vase on my dining table.

Next to it is a card in a pink envelope. Ripping it open, I find a picture of a donkey that looks like he's grinning. Typical Alexei.

Lara,

This is just the start of the last year of your twenties.

And this is just the beginning of our new chapter.

I'll see you later for the rest of your gifts.

If you thought you were spoiled as my friend, wait until you see what happens when you're mine completely.

You make me so happy, baby.
Love,
Alexei, Sheila, and Bruce.
(Sheila is still warming up to you)

Despite the burning sensation of my tears, uncontrollable laughter escapes from my lips.

Maybe this will be the best birthday of all time.

Zipping up the last outfit I tried on, I look at the pile of discarded ones on the bed. I need to work out in the morning. Nothing is fitting right again.

I finally settle on a black dress that sits just above the knee, with lace sleeves and a plunging neckline. It hugs me in just about the right places, enough to make it look like I actually have an ass rather than a pancake.

I smooth the sides and twist in the mirror. I wish my hips didn't stick out so much. It would look much sleeker.

I almost jump when the unmistakable sound of Nikolai thudding on the front door echoes through the walls. Grabbing my purse from the table, I straighten the heart diamond necklace Alexei bought me last year, and then I'm ready to go.

Opening up before he beats it down, I find Nikolai with his stunning wife on his arm, smiling at me.

Mikhail is just behind them. I know from the wrinkles near his eyes he's grinning under the black balaclava.

God, I wish I could see his full face again.

"Happy birthday little sis," Mikhail says from beneath his mask.

I run into his arms for one of his bear hugs. He might be

cold to everyone else, but to me, he is always my funny big brother.

Even if what happened to him made his heart full of ice, I know beneath the veil and wall of stone, the real Mikhail is in there.

The sound of frantic beeping has us all looking at each other quizzically. Alexei is missing and I bet that the commotion is his doing.

Which makes my stomach flutter with butterflies.

He strolls into my house twirling a key around his finger with a lollipop stick in his mouth.

"Alexei!" I squeal as he spots me and zooms towards me like a stalker hunting his prey. Before I know it, he picks me up and spins me in the air. I'm almost dizzy when he sets me down on my feet and wraps his muscular arms around me.

"Happy birthday, pchelka."

The moment he releases me and steps away, I feel a fuzzy, tingling sensation wash over me.

Friends. That's what we are right now, even if I want to slam my lips over his.

And I'm sure by the way his gaze is locked on mine, he is thinking the same thing.

"So, where is my present?" I bite back a grin and he raises his eyebrows.

I scan the room. Everyone is mingling amongst themselves while Mikhail pours the champagne. I sense his dark gaze on me from my left. He holds his glass up and nods. I return a sweet smile and return my attention back to Alexei.

"I have many for you tonight, pchelka." He leans in, making a shiver run down my spine.

"Alexei!" Jax shouts and immediately Alexei straightens and moves away from me.

"Yes, wise one?"

"Where is your date tonight, Sheila isn't it?"

Nikolai chuckles, his laughter echoing through the room.

Alexei shoots him a sharp glare. "A flamingo is *not* my date."

Jax grins and clicks his tongue piercing against his teeth. "You sure she isn't your girlfriend? You got trouble picking up women?"

Frowning, Alexei's disapproval is evident. I quickly bite the inside of my mouth to suppress my giggle.

Alexei gestures at me. "I just picked up Lara? You all saw?"

My eyes go wide and I tap his bicep. "Picking up women means like, hooking up, dating, fucking, one of the above," I whisper.

"Oh." He scratches his stubble on his chiseled jaw. "I have no issues collecting the women I want."

My cheeks heat, but a little wave of jealousy runs through me. Even though I know there hasn't been others, the thought still makes me feel like I'm not good enough for him.

Maybe there is someone out there better for him than me.

Mikhail shoves a glass in Jax's hand and whispers something to him, which gets Jax's attention away from Alexei, while Nikolai and Mila dance tongues in the living room. I want to roll my eyes, but I get it. He's in love and the more I see them together, the more I can look past her hurting him and see they truly care about each other.

Alexei clears his throat and leans in, touching my arm. I sneak a glance at him.

"Any women you want, hey, big shot?" I nudge him and his jaw clenches before his mischievous smirk appears.

He bends down a little and discreetly brushes my hand.

"Yep. I caught the one woman I've always wanted, didn't I?"

I swallow. He laces our fingers together and my arm tingles with electricity.

"Fair point, sladkiy," I whisper back.

"Nice dress." He pauses. "It will look even better on my floor later."

Fuck, I am internally on fire and he knows it. "Don't rip this one. It's my favorite."

"I like you bossy. Depends how much you want my dick tonight, doesn't it? Whatever the birthday girl wants, she gets."

"Alexei, stop." My cheeks are burning. I'm sure someone is going to notice the change between us.

He's circling his finger on my wrist, his touch so soft it's making me clench my thighs. I know what he can do with those fingers and I want it right this second.

"I bet you're soaking for me." He moves his touch up my forearm. I take a deep breath, staring at the happy faces in the room.

"Fuck. You are, aren't you?" He coughs and fixes his zipper on the sly.

"Looks like this became an issue for both of us." I tease.

"I need you, Lara. Really fucking bad. It's becoming a problem."

"I can't, not today, I'm on my period." I am irregular at best, that's if I have one at all. Not that it will be heavy, it never is. Mine only last a day or two.

"I don't care. You think a bit of blood bothers me? I'm so damn desperate for you I can't see straight." His fingers tremble as they slide along my hip and circle my waist.

My heart's pounding, his hand glides on my lower back, just above my ass and damn, I almost moan.

"I could say I'm sick?"

He shakes his head. "I'll think of something. You can't miss out on the surprise I have planned."

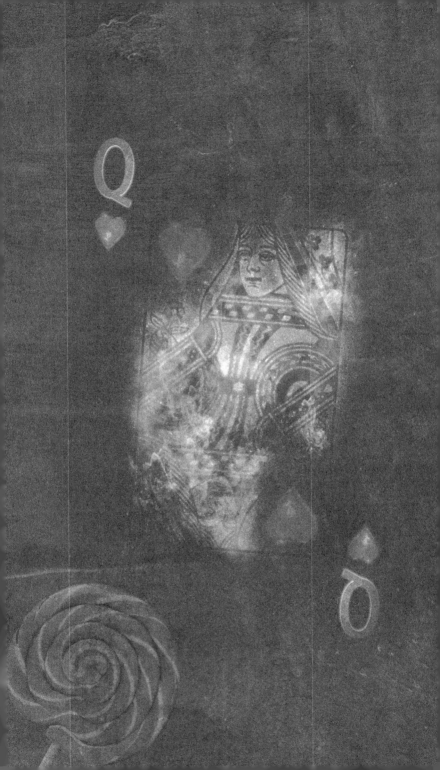

CHAPTER 44
ALEXEI

"Who the fuck let Jax drive this thing?" Mikhail grunts out.

"He's a good driver," I reply.

"Yeah in a Lambo or on a bike. I'm going to end up with a concussion if he takes another corner like that!" Mikhail's arm shoots out and grabs the headrest in front of him.

Just as expected, I brace myself as he suddenly turns left. Lara's body slams into mine and I quickly put my arm around her to protect her.

"Jax. We have women in here, including your wife. One more and I'll drag you out myself and leave you on the side of the road," Nikolai seethes.

"Stop being so miserable, Niki. We haven't died." Lara scowls at him.

"Yet," I say, pointing a finger. "I can always drive." I suggest.

"No." Both Nikolai and Lara reply at the same time.

"There's nothing wrong with my driving." I let out a pouting sigh.

"Limos don't do wheelies," Niki replies deadpan. I can feel Lara's hard stare in the side of my head.

"You better not be doing stupid shit with that bike again," Lara hisses next to me.

I only smashed up one motorcycle. Oh, and her car.

I look at her, cross my heart, and give Niki a glare to shut the hell up.

"You know me. Responsible. Never trying to die," I say with a grin.

When she bites down on her glossy lip, I can't stop imagining not only my cock, but my entire body covered in her marks. God, she's gorgeous tonight with that tight black dress, those matching heels with the red soles. I wonder what she has on underneath. I hope it's dark and lacy. Against her cream skin will send me wild.

It is taking every bit of self-restraint I have not to grab her and sit her on my lap. She's all I can think about.

She runs her fingers through silky curls, and I almost lose my breath. If it was just us tonight, she would be naked and at my mercy by now.

Her Chanel perfume wafts up my nose and I nudge myself closer to her, pulling out the little box in my jacket pocket and placing it on her lap.

"What's this?" she asks sweetly.

"Open it and find out."

Confusion is written all over her pretty face as she looks at the single key inside. "I have one to your house already?"

"Yea, I know that."

Her big blue eyes blink slowly as she stares at me. "Okay, do you want to tell me what this one unlocks?"

"Your new house." Well, I am hoping it will be ours.

A furrow forms in her forehead. "You've lost me."

"I haven't. You aren't going anywhere." I grin.

She laughs, my favorite sound, and the limo goes quiet for a second.

Tapping my fingers on my knee to distract myself from my heart pounding.

"The house you had your heart set on when we first came to Vegas," I proclaim proudly.

"That one that sold before Mikhail could buy it and the new buyers we're adamant not to sell?"

I nod.

It crossed my mind a couple of years ago just to kill them in their sleep and then buy it, but I was too busy to pull that off.

"Well, turns out recently they wanted to move."

Her eyebrow raises, as if she read my mind.

Yes, I may have put in place some circumstances where they may not have felt safe anymore.

"And I bought it." I pause, tugging on my now seemingly tight collar. "For you, or for us?" I whisper in her ear.

She looks down at the key and I can see her eyes start to water.

Fuck, did I mess this up?

"It doesn't have to be for me, too," I say quietly.

She shakes her head. "I want to live there with you. When?"

I glance over and Nikolai and Mikhail, both deep in conversation and I swallow. After all these years, I still don't know how they would react.

I expect Nikolai will be mad at me. Mikhail not so much.

Lara can't lose her relationship with them and neither can I. I can't let that happen.

"Soon," I reply. "It needs some work. We will make it perfect."

It's all I can give her for now.

I squeeze her knee, knowing she needs the reassurance. Her mind is racing. I can sense it.

"I'm all in, baby. Never question that."

She doesn't look at me as she puts the key in her purse.

"Me too," she whispers back, placing her hand over mine.

"Are you going to tell me where we are going?" She bats her lashes at me for full effect.

My leg is bouncing with excitement. I can't wait to see her face when she walks in and sees what I've done.

"Nope."

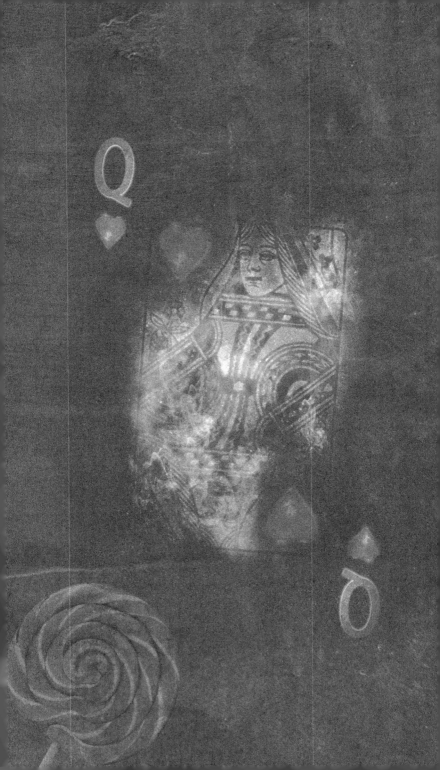

CHAPTER 45
LARA

Song, DIE FOR ME, Chase Atlantic

With Alexei's hand on the small of my back, he guides me into the vast building, separating us from the rest of the group. Every time I look back, he has a mischievous grin on his face.

Ushers guide us into the main room. Looking up, I am in awe as butterflies, trees, and the night sky are all beautifully projected on the ceiling, leaving me breathless.

With each step, we move forward, and the security guard acknowledges Mikhail's presence with a nod. The red rope is untied, revealing our private bar area, nestled upstairs, offering an unparalleled view of the stage.

The booth has pink balloons and roses all scattered around and a "Happy Birthday Lara" banner with a flamingo on the side.

"This is so cute." I want to squeal and jump up and down, but I stay reserved.

He rests his chin on my shoulder. "Cute, like me?"

I don't even need to look to know he's pouting.

When the back of his hand brushes against mine, I shiver. I want more.

It's like we are the only two people in this room.

Sofia rushes over with two champagne glasses in hand and Alexei backs away, running his fingers through his loose curls. I miss the contact already.

"For the birthday girl." She hands me a drink and then Alexei's.

"Na zdorov'ye. *For Health.*" Alexei holds up his flute.

"Thank you." I smile sweetly, with one sip my cheeks are on fire.

Holding onto the railing of our private balcony, I look out onto the stage and a buzz of excitement runs through me.

The room gets louder as everyone settles into their seats below.

"You like this band? The screamy ones you blast in the morning?" Alexei settles behind me, his musky aftershave filling my nose.

"I absolutely love them."

He grabs the bars on either side of me, caging me in. "I've noticed. Jax seems obsessed, too. I can't get away from them."

"Sacred is one of the best bands in history. It's more than just screaming. Listen to the lyrics, they speak to the soul." There's something that hits so hard when I listen to them. It's as if they understand the pain I feel that I can't express.

He sneaks a look behind him and then turns his attention back to me. As he smirks, his warm breath tickles my ear and he leans in, gently brushing my hair over my shoulder.

I let out a soft moan as his teeth graze the sensitive skin just behind my ear, sending waves of pleasure coursing through my body.

"Did you just bite me?"

"Yep. Leaving my mark on you. Don't worry, I'll leave more in places only we can see."

"Mmm, that's hot. I want more of them." I am internally scorching right now.

"I know you do. I have a plan. I want you to be sitting there, still feeling what I did to you. Knowing it means you're mine and I'll kiss every single one better later."

"You play cruel games, Alexei."

"How so? You think I'm going to be able to keep my hands off you for an entire night? Not a chance."

He gently releases my hair, allowing it to cascade back into its natural position. With his hand firmly on my hip, I can feel the heat radiating from our bodies as they press together.

When I rest my hands on his black suit jacket, I notice the faint scent of cologne lingering on the fabric.

"You look damn fine in a suit, sladkiy."

He looks good in anything. But this? Damn. I'm wet just looking at him.

"Thank you, baby. I'm only wearing it for you. I can take it off anytime." He winks for full effect.

"I'm so wet for you. This isn't fair." I even sound like a needy slut. I guess I am for him.

With a grin, I cup his hard dick through his trousers.

"Come with me," he says sternly. His fingers circle my wrist and he leads me out of the balcony down the side steps away from our suite.

"Where are we—" I don't pull away, but follow in the hope I get what I want most.

"I need you. I need you so fucking bad."

I close my mouth and let him lead.

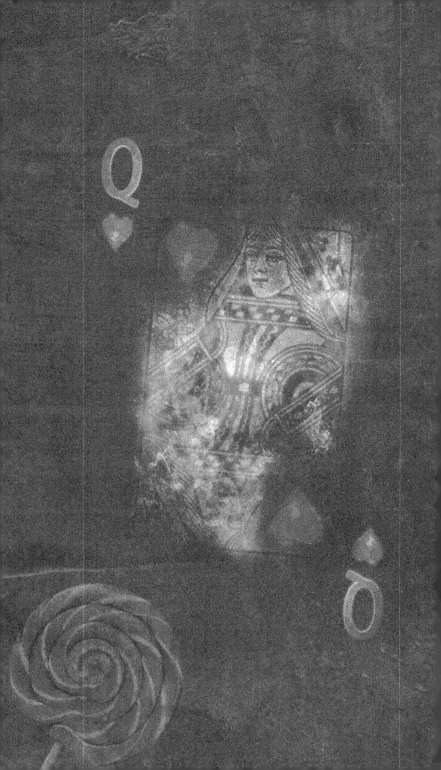

CHAPTER 46
ALEXEI

Song, DARK, WesGhost

As soon as the closet door clicks behind me, I pounce on her. Pinning her hands above her head, I press her back tightly against the wall.

With a gentle tug, I unzip the side of her dress, and it effortlessly falls to the floor, leaving her standing there in nothing but her lingerie.

"I told you I'm on my period," she whispers. Her breath hitches as I run my finger along her panties.

"And I told you, I don't care. Blood on my hands? That's a normal day for me."

"Not the same." She rolls her eyes, so I grip her cheeks.

"Are you giving me sass? Hmm?"

She tries to hide her grin, the darkness flashing across her normally blue eyes tells me everything I need to know.

She loves this side of me.

Nudging her legs open with my knee, I tilt her head to the side, exposing her slender neck.

And lick, so slowly, all the way up to her ear.

"Looks like I'll have to fuck that attitude right out of you, baby. Question is, with my fingers, tongue or cock?"

Leaning down, I pepper kisses over her breasts, and suck hard enough to leave a mark.

One just for me.

"Oh, shit," she hisses.

Should we be doing this here? With everyone only a few footsteps away?

No. But do I care? Also, no. I'm too wrapped up in her to give a shit.

"Such a good girl for me. I think you'd look beautiful down on your knees for me."

She blushes and it makes my heart race.

"Anything for you."

I let out a groan, slipping my hand under her black panties.

"Fuck, Lara. The thrill of getting caught really gets you wet, hmm?"

She nods again.

"Words. I like to hear them," I whisper in her ear.

"Yes."

"Listen to you soak my fingers, baby. How bad do you want to come for me?"

Her eyes flutter closed as I circle her clit, letting her hands above her head go. I wrap her hair around my fist and pull her head back.

Her moans get louder as I kiss and suck on her throat.

I slick up her wetness and pull my hand out. "Just a little taste to keep your mind occupied," I tell her.

Stepping back, I unbuckle my belt to release my aching cock.

"But you can have a treat." I stroke my dick with my other hand, waggling it for her.

"You're a filthy man, sweets."

She flicks her hair over her shoulder and drops to her

knees, keeping her eyes locked on me as she takes my shaft in her mouth.

I'm mesmerized by her.

Tears spill down her cheeks as she takes all of me. Running her tongue along my piercing has my legs tensing.

"So good, baby. Fuck."

Gripping onto the back of her head, my fingers tangle in her hair. This is a dream.

I almost jump when she tickles my balls.

I can't last long like this.

Holding her head in place, I take over the rhythm, fucking her mouth and she moans around my cock.

Goddamn.

With a few final thrusts, I spill into her mouth and she takes every drop.

"Don't swallow," I say breathlessly.

I stroke her cheek, carefully removing myself and help her up.

"Mmm, I can't wait to hear what sounds I can get you to make for me tonight."

I lean in, kissing her jaw.

"But right now, I need you to be good for me and open up. Show me how good you've been."

A red blush spreads up her throat. I trace my fingers along her neck as she opens her mouth for me to see the cum coating her tongue.

What a sight.

"Mmm. You've been such a good girl for me. You may swallow now."

She does as she's told. The second her throat bobs, I grab her face and kiss the life out of her.

Picking up her dress from the floor, I tap her foot so she steps in, dragging it up her slender figure. I'm almost hard again pulling the zipper up on the side.

"How do I look?" she asks, brushing her hair out with her fingers.

"Freshly fucked and absolutely perfect."

With a wink, I gently interlock my fingers with hers, creating an instant connection.

"Now let's go listen to them sing and then I'll make you scream for me at home."

CHAPTER 47
LARA

Song- i know (faded) Ex Habit

"That was the best night ever," I tell him between kisses as we stumble through his front door. I fumble with his jacket, trying to get it off him as he deepens the kiss, pushing me back against the wall.

"Anything for you."

I let out a squeal when he bends down and picks me up, throwing me over his shoulder.

"Now for your next birthday treat," he says and slaps my ass.

I bounce with each fast step he takes up the stairs.

He places me down on unsteady feet, and raw hunger fills his eyes as he unbuttons his shirt.

"Strip," he commands.

I do as he says, as sexy as I can. Until both of us are naked and exposed to each other.

When he looks at me, like he's ready to pounce, I don't feel so ashamed of my body. But it's always a nagging thought in my head. He's just so damn good at distracting me from it.

My breath hitches as he steps forward.

I tip my head back letting his tongue explore my neck. I inch open my thighs and he smiles against my skin, gently tugging on the tampon.

"This has gotta go," he whispers, pulling away and heads to the bathroom.

As soon as he's back, he tugs me close by the waist, kissing my throat again and thrusts his fingers inside of me. Spreading my legs wider across his thighs, I straddle him.

He groans against my throat. "Greedy girl." He nips at my skin.

"Yes," I pant out as he slides in another finger and skillfully circles my clit with his thumb.

His hand glides over my breasts and up towards my throat.

"Now tell me. What else can I do to make you scream? I want to know everything that gets you going, Lara."

He pulls back and bites his lip.

"I think it's about time you gave me a hand necklace," I whisper and lick my lips as I watch his reaction.

His brows furrow in a look of confusion. "Explain, is this another English term?"

"Choke me, Alexei. Your hands become my necklace." I can feel my cheeks get hot.

He gives me a little smirk and dives his fingers in deeper.

"Why do you wanna be choked, pchelka? You trust my hands around your throat? Not many people would."

I lean in and roll my hips against his palm.

"It will make me come so fucking hard for you, sladkiy." I suck in a breath as he curls his fingers deep inside me.

"I trust you with my life. Do you want to learn?"

Leaning back, I guide his hand up to my throat. "You've strangled people to death before, right?"

He grins. "A few, yes."

My eyes go wide as he grips my neck too hard, for a split second, then releases.

"Yeah, not like that," I cough.

He gives me a lopsided grin. "Just testing."

"Here." I guide his fingers to the right point on one side of my throat and his thumb to the other.

"Now squeeze here, avoid my windpipe."

Keeping the pace going in my pussy, his fingers tighten around my neck in the perfect position, and he peppers kisses along my jaw.

That fuzzy feeling in my head appears, and all I can focus on is him. How he makes me feel. My mind is free of anything other than this man.

"You like this, I can feel your pussy tightening around my fingers."

"Hmm, mmm."

As my eyes flutter closed, I grip onto his hard shoulder as my climax builds from my core.

"Fuck," I pant.

He releases his grip, sucking on the tender skin instead.

"Feels like you need more, baby."

"Oh, we can take it even further. Are you ready to learn how to make me come so hard I nearly pass out?"

He pulls back and assesses my face. When he bites down on his bottom lip, I can't resist leaning forward and sucking on it.

"If you cover my nose and mouth with the other hand, choke me with this one and fuck me at the same time."

"You better not pass out on me,"

I giggle and shake my head. "Then pay attention to my reactions, sweets."

A growl erupts from his chest, his hand squeezing my throat as he pushes me onto my back on the mattress.

Spreading my thighs wide open, I hear him pull down his boxers.

"The birthday girl wants my cock, I can't ever say no to that request. Pull your knees up, I wanna sink deep inside my pretty pussy."

Oh fuck.

"Tighter. I want to be able to see your fingerprints tomorrow."

He does as I say, and a strangled cry escapes my lips as he pushes himself inside me, inch by inch. The groans that come from him only push me further.

"Such a good girl for me, yet so fucking naughty."

When he pulls out and drives back into me, my eyes nearly roll into the back of my head.

"Deep breath, baby," he growls into my ear.

Filling my lungs with air, I lock eyes with him and I know he's on the final straw of restraint. That crazed look is in his eyes and damn, it's hot.

His palm clamps over my mouth and nose and his fingers tighten around my throat. As the blood pounds in my ears, almost matching the intense rhythm Alexei is fucking me to.

"So beautiful, Lara." He praises.

At the point my head starts to spin, he moves his hand allowing me to take in more air before clamping it over again.

My legs shake against him, I close my eyes.

"Look at me, Lara. I need to see you," he demands.

As I open them, my back arches and his piercing hits the spot.

"Such a good girl." His deep voice, and his dirty words have me on the edge of exploding.

"I'm about to fill you up, baby, you better come with me."

He removes his hand and I gasp for air.

"Holy shit," I pant.

"Give it to me. Come for me." His words send thrills through me.

With one final thrust and his hand back in place on my neck, I fall apart for him.

He rolls us over, so I'm on top cuddled against him as he strokes my cheek.

"Still alive, that's good." There's amusement in his tone.

"God. So good. You're a natural." My breath slows as my limbs relax.

"Only for you."

I stifle a yawn, and he pokes his finger in my mouth, almost making me heave.

"Alexei. That is so annoying."

His chest vibrates beneath me as he laughs. "I know. Funny though."

I shuffle on my side and snuggle up against him.

"What's the plan for tomorrow? I'm not working."

I trace my finger idly over his six pack.

"Then we go have some fun. I will think of something."

CHAPTER 48
ALEXEI

"I THOUGHT you liked this place? You order from here all of the time." I shove a fork full of pasta into my mouth.

I'm not picky about food, it all tastes good to me.

But watching Lara poke at hers makes me wonder if I'm missing something. "Is it *der'mo*?"

She shakes her head. "No, Alexei, it doesn't taste like *shit*. I'm just not very hungry."

"How can you not be starving after all of that screaming I made you do this morning?" I grin at her before biting the end of a shrimp off.

The corner of her lip sinks into a frown. "I just don't eat much."

I stab a piece of steak and hold it out for her. "You don't eat enough. You almost fainted on the way to the car. I mean I know I'm sexy—" I run my palm down my chest and circle my shirt with my finger where my nipple sits beneath. "—but I don't have a habit of making women pass out because of it."

"I always overdo it," she scoffs, and takes a bite of spinach for emphasis.

My hand finds the inside of her thigh and my fingers tickle the hem of her panties. "If I asked you to get on top of me and ride my like a bumpy motorcycle, how long before your tank runs dry?" I pick up a sprig of alfalfa sprout and roll it against my thumb. "Three of these wouldn't last very long. I'm a cross country bike, pchelka."

Her blue eyes widen before she smiles. "Oh, really? Is that a promise?" Her voice takes on a sultry rasp as she moves her lips closer to my ear. "You think you can go all night?"

"I'm the Enterprise Bunny." I whisper.

She laughs much louder than the joke warrants. "Don't you mean "Energizer" Bunny?" she giggles.

I'm confused. "What is the difference?"

"One goes to other planets, the other just keeps going." She smiles and ruffles her fingers through my hair.

"Then yes, both of those. Next time I get you alone." I pick up a morsel of chicken from her plate and hold it up to her lips. "Let's get those engines going."

The flicker in her eyes tells me she's switched to doubt.

What is that about? I know her well enough to stop pushing.

"Did you want to come with me to pick up the girls?" I lean back, giving her room to avoid the bite. Instead, I pop it into my own mouth.

"Can you pick them up? I have to get their movie night stuff ready. Then maybe tomorrow night you can show me all your rabbit moves." Her grin returns.

That's better.

"Deal. Do you want me to pick up some snacks—"

"No." She cuts me off. "I mean, I'll take care of them." The worried look pinches the corners of her eyes again.

Why haven't I noticed this reaction before?

It's bugging me all the rest of the way through dinner, not that it lasts much longer.

Even all the way home, any time I even mention food she bristles.

After I drop her off, I head to Jax's first.

Maeve may be younger than Elena, but the two girls love spending time with each other. They bring so much joy to Lara when they visit, but I know they're also tiring for her.

It's why I help. I can keep them playing until they're too exhausted to wear Lara down.

"Hi, Alexei, come on in." Sofia answers the door. Her maroon hair is almost a light shade of pink tonight.

"Maeve has been excited all day. It's been a few weeks since Lara's had the girls over. Since before the…" Her voice trails off.

"Kidnapping?" I finish for her. Why is it hard for people to talk about? It's over.

"Yes. Anyways, Maeve's had dinner, but she said she was saving room for popcorn." Sofia turns and touches my wrist. "Please, for the love of God, Alexei, don't give her candy right before bedtime." Her eyebrows bunch in the middle of her forehead.

"You girls, so picky about your food. What is the big deal? I eat it, and I'm fine." I smack my palm across my chest as a testament to my strength.

She rolls her eyes before handing me a small duffel bag. "It's important to instill good eating habits when they're little. Then they don't have to fight food issues when they're older." She pats her belly for emphasis.

"You just had a baby and look fine. Do you do that thing that Lara does? Where she goes days without eating and then eats a huge meal but gets sick after?" I watch her pause.

Did I say the wrong thing?

"What are you talking about, Alexei? Starving and binging isn't healthy either." She chews on her lip. "Did that start after the, you know." She waves her hand.

My face scrunches as I concentrate. "Um. I don't think so? She's always been weird about eating. But I know when she's stressed out she can eat three big bacon cheeseburgers."

Which is why I think it's even stranger when she only wanted a few leaves of spinach tonight for dinner.

"Alexei. I have a hard question for you." Sofia takes both of my shoulders just as Jax comes down the stairs.

"Everything okay?" he asks as he steps past, raising the eyebrow with the piercing.

"Yep. Alexei and I are having an important conversation." She keeps her gaze fixed on me.

"Gotcha." He smiles at his wife before disappearing again.

"Alexei. When Lara eats a lot, does she get sick afterward, or does she *make* herself sick after?" Her dark eyes flick back and forth between mine.

This feels serious. "Um, I'm not sure. I don't watch her. I do hear her sometimes, though."

Sofia's fingers dig into my biceps. "Alexei," she asks quietly. "Is Lara talking to anyone?"

"That's a stupid question. She talks all the time to everyone." I shrug, pulling out of her grip.

"Not what I meant, Alexei." Sofia crosses her arms and glares at me. "She needs to get help. Does she have a therapist?"

"No." I glower back. "There's nothing wrong with Lara. She's perfect." I sling the duffel over my back. "Just funny eating habits." I turn to find Maeve working her way down the stairs. "I promise not to mess hers up."

"'Lexi!" Maeve runs and jumps into my arms.

Hoisting her up onto my hip, I give her a broad smile. "Ready for movies with Elena and Aunty Lara?"

Maeve bobs her round head, the dark curls bounce with her enthusiasm. "Yes!" Her chubby palms smack together in an excited clap.

"You have fun. And, Alexei? Think about what I said. I've wondered about it myself watching Lara." Sofia reaches up and kisses Maeve's cheek before backing away. "I worry about Lara, especially after everything she's been through."

That makes me pause. Is there something more that I'm not catching?

I want Lara forever. If she's hurting herself, I need to help her to stop.

"Thank you. I'll watch her." I turn and head down the steps to the car.

Is what Sofia said true? What's wrong with Lara?

CHAPTER 49

LARA

"Shut the fuck up, look." Alexei tugs on my hand and points towards the Hook-a-Duck stand at the carnival.

"What?" I chuckle.

We've been at this fair for hours. I haven't laughed this much in a long time. I get the sense he is bottling something up. But then today he's back to his usual self.

He leans against a low counter. "The flamingo stuffed toy! Do you think Sheila might like it? Maybe it will be like a baby trial for her and Bruce."

"We don't need more flamingos, those two are quite enough."

"Everyone needs more flamingos, Lara."

I shake my head but I smile. I can't help it. Being around this goofy ball of happiness makes my day.

He distracts me from my own head.

Following his lead, he rolls up the sleeves of his white shirt. I almost drool when I look at those veiny, tattooed fore-arms. And so does the woman behind the kiosk.

I clear my throat and shoot her a look. He's mine.

"Hi, handsome. You here to hook up?" The girl tucks her

black hair behind her ear and bats her lashes. I clench my fist and take a deep breath.

Alexei is completely oblivious to her flirting, he gets out his wallet from his back pocket and stuffs a twenty in her hand.

He turns his attention to me with a grin. "Do you want to go first or should I?"

I step forward, and he strokes my hair away from my face.

"If I win, do I get a reward when we're home?" I whisper in his ear.

"Who said anything about waiting till then?"

When he pulls back, I feel the death stare in the side of my head from that girl.

He steps out of the way letting me stand in front of the little pool with the floating yellow ducks. Reluctantly, she hands me the hook.

"You've got four tries," she says flatly, then pops the gum in her mouth before dropping onto a short stool behind her.

A fuzzy feeling washes over me when Alexei snakes his arms around my waist and rests his chin on my shoulder.

Leaning forward slightly I aim for the first duck, and my ass presses against his crotch.

"I want my duck to be that wet," he mumbles in my ear, just loud enough for me to hear.

Bursting into a fit of laughter, I completely miss the floating toy.

I'm wheezing and tears are burning my eyes.

I can barely see Alexei watching me with an amused grin through my blurry vision. Every time I go to speak or pick the hook back up, I double back over.

"Y-you. Do. It," I manage to say before returning to my giggle fit.

I watch from the side, trying to regain some composure, yet every time he glances at me I have to hold my hand over my mouth to stop laughing.

On the second to last try, he hooks a duck.

"YES!" He jumps up, throws the hook in the water and launches himself at me, twirling me round in the air like he's just won some sort of championship prize.

"You did it." I hold onto his firm shoulders as he lowers me to the ground.

Stealing a quick kiss, he points to the flamingo hanging up.

"I'll take that."

The woman frowns, pointing up at the big sign next to her.

"No. That's for the small ducks. You hooked a big one." Her jaw works with a bored expression.

I hold back rolling my eyes. Alexei flashes me a grin, pulling me closer by my waist.

"You have a big *duck*." I say under my breath, just loud enough for him to hear.

This time it's his turn to laugh. Except he holds it together better than me.

"Fine. Fine." He pulls out his wallet and slams more money on the wooden top.

"Now, I'll have my baby flamingo."

"Please." I add with a fake smile.

"Ergh. Fine." She rolls her eyes and begrudgingly yanks the stuffed animal from the hook.

"Careful. It's only a baby." Alexei shakes his head.

He's serious.

With his prize secured under his arm and his other linked through mine, we wander between the games and food booths.

"Cotton candy?" he asks, gesturing towards the spinning sugar.

My stomach grumbles. The doughnuts smell amazing. But I forgot to update my calorie app after breakfast. I'm not sure I have enough available to have any more treats. If I indulge, I can't get rid of it, not while Alexei is around. I don't want a confrontation. I have it under control at the moment. He doesn't need to see that side of me.

I'm fine.

Now in front of the stand, I pull my arm out and look at the brightly colored bags.

All of them would make me fatter.

Alexei is busy pointing through the glass at all the different sweets for his order.

He comes back showing his purple and blue candy. "Do you want anything, baby?"

I twirl the ring on my index finger. Trying to do the math.

I had oatmeal and a banana. Maybe if I do an hour in the gym I could have some.

And a salad for dinner?

I shake my head. This is too much.

"I can just have a bite of yours?" I give him a small smile.

"You can have a bite of mine anytime." He winks and rips off a chuck of the candy and stuffs it in his mouth.

His hand cups my cheek, then he leans down and kisses me. I can taste the sweetness of the dissolving candy still on his tongue as he deepens the kiss.

"Tasty, right?" he says as he pulls back.

I'm hot and flustered. "Very."

"Let me show you my seat on the ferris wheel."

I stop him as we walk. "Your what?"

He nods, stuffing another mouthful of candy.

"I know the owner. I like that car. So I have it when I want it. I think better when I'm above the earth. That's why I skydive."

"Makes sense. You chasing a high clears your mind. It's very you."

And that's what I love about him. He is unapologetically him. He doesn't give a single shit what the world thinks of him. He does what he wants, when he wants, and doesn't take life for granted.

He's a free spirit. He's refreshing to be around.

CHAPTER 50
ALEXEI

FINALLY MY SEAT comes around and Keith opens up the door.

"Thanks boss." I salute him.

No one else ever goes in my seat. I pay good money to make sure.

It's basically my office, and a bit of gun storage. You never know when you might need a random supply of weapons here.

I lead Lara in and she sits next to me, wrapping my arm over her shoulder. I pull her snug against me as she rests her head on my pec.

Her hand rubs up and down on my jeans and my dick is twitching with need.

"Last bite. You want it?" I hold the cotton candy in front of her.

"Nope, go for it."

Hmm. She's hardly eaten today. Since Sofia made the comment about her eating habits, I did a lot of research. Well, I've hyper fixated on it while she sleeps.

I just don't know the best way to approach it with her. I don't want to push her away. She's a runner, she always has been.

And every time I try to talk to her, she seems to go back to eating. I haven't heard her throw up since we've been staying with each other every night.

But I think Sofia is right. Lara's face dropped when I mentioned candy. It's like I could hear her brain trying to work out whether she should eat it or not.

I'm struggling to wrap my own head around it. She's so perfect as she is. No matter what her weight is. I've never looked at her any different, to me she is always my beautiful girl.

The one who stole my heart.

"So this is your thinking spot?" she asks, looking up at me.

Damn, I love that smile.

"Yep. I could change the world from up here."

"What was the last big thinking thing you did up here?"

I tap the side of my head.

"Most recently. Well, now. I was thinking about how much I love Lara Volkov. And how beautiful and perfect she is in every single way. Far far too good for a brute like me. Except, I could never let her go so she's stuck with me loving her... for eternity."

She sits herself up, the shock on her face as her mouth drops open.

"Did Jax punch you again? You can't have many more brain cells to lose."

"Hey!" I dive at her, tickling her sides as I lift her effortlessly, so she straddles my lap.

Bad move. Dick engaged.

"I love you, pchelka. It's you. It's always been you. It will always be you."

It feels right saying it out loud. I've always known she was mine. I never imagined it would be this good.

Twirling a tendril of hair around my finger, her eyes start to water but a smile erupts on her face.

"I've been in love with you for a long, long time, Alexei. Please never stop being you. Never stop making me laugh, or being your crazy self. I love you for everything you are. And I'll love you until I take my last breath."

She places her hand over my rapid heart.

"Trust me. You won't be taking your last breath before me."

I can't even think about anything happening to her. I still wake up in the night seeing how I found her.

Never again.

"Does that make me your girlfriend?"

Picking up her hand, I press a kiss on each of her fingers.

"I've never had one of those. I want everything with you, baby. Question is, what if I can't give you that picture perfect life you used to talk about years ago?"

She pulls back and tilts her head.

"No. That's a life that's created for everyone else to watch. We've never fit in with society's standards, why would we start now? My perfect life is simply just being with you. Nothing more, nothing less. You are my happy place and we can do whatever the hell we want with our future."

Her answer makes my chest hurt. I'm her happy place.

"You wanna go skydiving with me? Steal more flamingos? Wash the blood out of my hair? Hide the bodies with me? Let me eat you out on my bike whenever I need to?"

She bites down on her lip.

"Yes. All of it. All of your crazy, Alexei. I don't love you despite it, I love you for it."

Lacing my fingers around her throat, I drag her closer and kiss her so damn hard.

She pulls away breathless and traces her nail along my throat. "Now, did you say something about eating me out on your bike?"

I lick my lips.

"Damn right."

CHAPTER 51
LARA

UGH. I pinch the flab on my belly as I stare into the mirror. I ate too much with the girls last night. Adding more time to my treadmill might not cut it.

It's so hard to watch my calories now that Alexei is here all the time. My only option is to run.

Or to find excuses to go to the bathroom.

What is wrong with me? Why is it so easy for other people to eat whatever they want, and never gain a pound?

Sofia looks amazing so soon after having her baby.

What's my excuse?

I have this flabby layer on my hips. Floppy skin under my arms.

Is that a double chin?

Tears well in my eyes as I inspect myself.

My reflection is awful. Do I always look like this?

I back up until my legs hit the rails of the bed and collapse backwards. The ceiling blurs as the droplets smear down my cheeks.

This isn't fair. I try so hard just to be hideous.

How can Alexei want me? I'm not good enough for him.

He's always been there for me. Am I the one taking advantage of our friendship?

"Lara? Have you seen my—" He stops at the doorway of my room as I sit up quickly, wiping the tears streaking my face.

Before my hand leaves my skin, he's on me.

Leaping onto the bed, he pins me against the mattress, arms and knees straddling me.

"What's wrong?" His nose almost touches mine. "You were fine just a few minutes ago, what happened?"

There's some things I just can't put into words.

"Nothing. I'm having a hormonal moment." I let my eyes close. I don't think I can watch him when I lie to him.

"Lara, I know better." His thumbs rub lightly over my lids before he forces them open to see his grinning face. "There's my girl. Come on, let's get up. Enzo needs us at the club. Top secret super spy stuff." He flashes his silver tooth before bouncing off of me.

His rough palms tug at my wrists and he pulls me until I'm sitting.

"You can just go without me." I don't feel like being around people today.

Alexei clenches his jaw as he stares at me. "Lara, I don't go anywhere without you if I can help it. You're my person."

Even when I'm hardest on myself, he's there to do his best to guide me out of that darkness.

I hope that never changes.

"What do you think he wants?" I follow close, letting Alexei tug me along with him.

He shrugs. "Enzo always works in mystery. A fog of intrigue. In the shadows of darkness."

I giggle and tug down my tight skirt.

Alexei had insisted I looked amazing in it, but my nervousness is getting the better of me.

"Where did you get those lines from? They sound like tags from a mystery movie."

"I like those old black and white ones. You know, from when we were kids and that's all that would play from America?" He smiles before we reach the main doors.

I'm nervous about being in public with him. It's like a million eyes are watching us now that we are more than friends.

I still haven't told my brothers. The thought makes my stomach twist into knots.

Mikhail may be okay with it, but Nikolai might not be.

Stepping up onto the curb, I let my fingers slip from his grasp under the guise of adjusting my hem again.

He comes to a full stop and sticks out his palm.

I hesitate.

Enzo tells Mikhail everything.

Especially something this big.

"What's wrong?" he whispers.

We're both standing on the sidewalk. It may be dark, but the heat from the Vegas sun radiates back from the concrete beneath our feet.

When I don't answer, he tilts his head to look over his shoulder at me with one eye. "Are you embarrassed?"

"What the hell? No. I don't want you to die."

"You think Enzo wouldn't already know? The man is a god. He sees everything, hears everything. He knows." He shakes his hand, beckoning me to take it.

I slip my fingers around his thumb and walk next to him.

The cool rush of air pours over us when he opens the door.

"Alexei." He nods at the girl at the desk inside.

She gives him a stiff smile and presses a hidden buzzer to open the second entryway.

"She doesn't like you?" I whisper as we make our way into the huge foyer. The low pump of music is almost too deep to hear easily, but I can feel it in my chest.

"We had a miscommunication." He winks at me, then leads me to the bar. "What do you want?"

"Um, how about some Prosecco?" I haven't had anything bubbly in a while, and it isn't overly sweet.

Alexei gestures for the bartender and orders.

"So, if Enzo already knows, does that mean we can have some fun here?" I lean against the wall and look out over the diagram showing all of the different rooms and their themes.

Before I take another breath, he pins me to the brick with his hand laced around my throat.

His knee pushes my tight skirt to its limits when he shoves it between my thighs.

"If you're wearing panties, no. If you aren't, then yes, we can play." His hot breath tickles along my neck, then he tilts my head to suck my earlobe between his teeth.

"You'll have to find out." My nails dig into his shoulders and pull him closer.

His fingers move down my hip and dance under the end of my dress, tracing a hot path up my leg to my—

"Alexei? This way please." Enzo calls out from the hall.

Alexei growls against my skin. "I'll discover your secret before the day is done." He peels himself away from me and whisks me with him to Enzo's office.

"Sit." Enzo points at the two leather chairs framing his long black desk.

He leans back in his executive seat and leans back, swiveling to point at a large bank of monitors on the wall next to him.

"Alexei, I want you to explain this." He clicks a button and pulls up a screen of text messages. "Who is Max and how did he contact you with Tatiana? That number has been scrubbed since you got a hold of him." Enzo turns back with his brows knotted.

Alexei shrugs, still firmly holding my hand. "I've known him since we were kids."

Enzo runs his palm over his face, then smooths back his dark curly hair. "But *how* did you find him to get her information?"

Alexei blinks slowly. "I told you."

I don't understand what's going on. "Alexei." I pat his knuckles. "Just tell him." I don't remember anyone by that name, but I know Alexei had a lot of friends through the years.

He has a way of charming people without even trying.

Alexei glances at me, his lips pursed. "It isn't a mystery. He was my dealer when I was younger."

Now I'm really confused. He hasn't done real drugs as long as I've known him. Said it reminded him too much of his father.

"What did he deal?" Enzo threads his fingers on the pile of papers in front of him.

He looks like he's almost at his limit.

"Jawbreakers." Alexei grins, showing his silver tooth and chomps his teeth.

Enzo shakes his head. "You have got to be fucking kidding me." With a sigh, he slumps into his chair. "I need you to find her again. I can't get a good picture on her. Anywhere. And then I find out you met with her? Face to face?"

"No, that isn't how it went. She was in disguise." Alexei stops him. "I only saw a partial side shot of her in Russia when I went to get Niki. So, I'm not even sure it was really her I talked to here."

Enzo sputters. "*Here?*"

Alexei nods, nonchalantly.

"She was here, in Vegas? Shit! When?" Enzo's fingers fly to his keyboard and he starts bringing up camera feeds.

"Um, it was how I found Lara. So that day." Alexei squeezes my hand before throwing me a wink.

"Wait, I didn't know that. Did you make a deal with her to find me?" I know how dangerous that woman is.

Her reputation precedes her. I know how much Mila worries about her.

Being in her debt is terrifying.

And Alexei put himself there.

"Shh. It's okay." He blows me a kiss.

"No, it's not," Enzo grumbles from his computer. He points to the screen above him where two Reapers are walking towards my Alexei on a corner.

After a few words which we can't hear, Alexei jumps a man and drags him into the building behind.

The image scratches as Enzo fast forwards past Jax going inside.

Alexei steps into the street, covered in blood.

I barely remember that day, but I wondered why.

Now I know.

I think I'm going to be sick.

"Which one of those Reapers was her?" Enzo rewinds to show a tall and short bearded man talking to Alexei.

He zooms in the grainy image, but it's almost like they knew the camera was there, never turning their faces for a better angle.

"Motherfucker," Enzo mutters as he tries several other tricks to try and improve the resolution.

I tug on Alexei's arm to draw his attention. "What did you promise her?"

He lets go and cups my cheek with his palm, this thumb smoothing over the scar on the corner of my mouth. "For you? Anything. I'd promise the world and the moon. I'd have dived to the center of the earth or floated out to the middle of the ocean to have one more chance with you."

My throat tightens. I had no idea.

"Oh." What do I say to that?

"Fuck!" Enzo flips his keyboard hard enough it lands on the floor near my foot.

"What's the big deal?" Alexei still has his eyes on me, acting completely unfazed by Enzo's outburst.

"She's a chameleon. I've been chasing down leads on someone very important, and I know that—" He points angrily at the frozen image. "—monster is the key to finding them. But I can't get to her."

"Who?" Alexei reaches down and picks up the computer piece from the tile and slides it across the desk.

Enzo stops and looks at him with wide eyes and flared nostrils.

He pants heavily before flattening his palms on his thighs. "It's a story for another time," he grunts.

I don't think I've ever seen him worked up. Even in the most hectic and dangerous situations, Enzo has always been the pinnacle of calm, cool, and collected.

Today, he's acting…bizarre.

"Are you okay?" I ask him quietly.

"It's frustrating as hell to get so close, and still can't get the answers I'm looking for." He wipes his face with his hand before shifting to rub his temples. "It's been years."

As if a switch has been flipped, he straightens his spine and neutralizes his features. "Thank you both, that's everything I need."

Alexei jumps up and reaches for my fingers. "Come on, we need to go."

"What's the hurry?" I close the office behind me, leaving Enzo with his blurry nemesis.

"I have my own obsessive mystery to solve." He pulls me

down the hall at a brisk pace, past a row of blacked out windows.

Spinning me into his arms, he presses his body against me, pinning me to a dark door.

"Now, tell me." His lips hover over mine, making heat race though me.

"I have no panties on," I whisper just as he crashes his mouth against me.

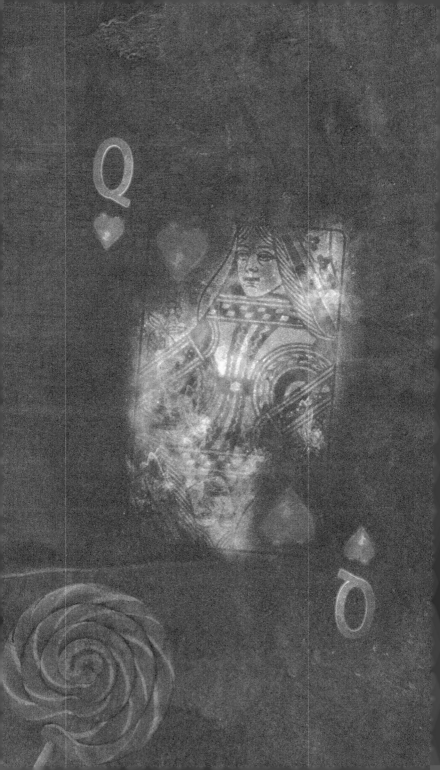

CHAPTER 52
ALEXEI

"HOLD STILL, ALEXEI," Jax growls from behind me.

The buzz of the tattoo gun tickles against my ribs as he traces the scratch marks that Lara put there last night.

"It feels weird." I drop my forehead onto my arm and try to do what he asked.

"Probably doesn't hurt as much as the original, stop whining," he laughs. "I'm almost done."

"I just want to show her. She'll love it." I want to prove to her how I feel, maybe this will do it.

My phone vibrates and Lara's moans fill the room.

Fuck. I didn't think about anyone else hearing her when I made that my ringtone.

Jax throws up his gloved hands and curses at me as I scramble to get my cell quieted. "Hey, Lara, can I call you back?"

"This is someone much more important than your little girlfriend." A sultry voice croons into my ear.

Shit.

"Who is this?" I wave Jax back as he points to the machine in his fist.

"Oh, Alexei. I thought we were better friends than that? You are so very special to me." She draws out the end huskily. "I have something you want, you have something I *need*."

I let my legs drop over the side of the table and sit up.

Jax shakes his head and puts down the tattoo gun, crossing his arms over his wide chest to watch me.

"First you need to tell me what's going on?" There's only one woman for me, and it isn't the one on the other end of the phone.

"I'm fulfilling the second half of your request. You wanted to find your Lara, and kill who took her. Correct?" The sexy lilt to her words fades as she slips into all business.

Tatiana.

"Yes, that's right."

"I'll send you to him, and make sure you cross paths. Once you're finished with him, I'm calling in my debt. Tidy up your loose ends, you're coming to visit my homeland." With a click, she hangs up.

A surge of energy courses through me. I can finally put an end to the man who hurt Lara.

"Everything okay?" Jax raises his pierced eyebrow.

"Better. I'll finally get Kirill." Sliding off the table, I grab my shirt and helmet and race for the door.

"I'm not done yet," he shouts after me.

Pushing out into the hot street, I jump on my bike, ignoring the burning seat from the Vegas sun.

I should tell Lara.

But I need to talk to Mikhail first.

Dodging through the traffic has me pulling into the casino parking garage in minutes. I run through the main entrance and don't even turn toward the elevator.

It takes too long.

Two flights of stairs barely have me winded, then I'm skidding to a stop in front of Mikhail's office door.

I guess I could have darted into hers. Too late.

Without knocking, I push into Mikhail's space and rush to his desk.

"Alexei? What the—"

"She called me." I blurt out. "Tatiana. She knows where Kirill is."

"How do you know it isn't a trick?" Nikolai asks from the couch.

I didn't see him there. "She's come through every time so far."

Mikhail takes a deep breath, fluttering the fabric of his balaclava when he exhales. "We can't trust her. What did she tell you?"

"She said I'm going to Russia. Who's going with me?" I twist my head back and forth between them.

"What about your, um, obligations here?" Mikhail's eyes widen as his forehead furrows.

"It's because of those I have to go." I don't *want* to leave.

But I need to make sure that Lara is safe. She's the most important thing to me. Taking away the man who kidnapped her will help her to ease her fears.

She might not like me leaving, yet I can't bear another day seeing her in pain.

I catch her crying, or running herself to exhaustion, and I know it's because she's worried she's still being chased.

"If I die protecting her, it's worth it that she can sleep again." All those nights standing and watching her toss and turn, the cries that would wake her up, it's too gut wrenching to continue.

That monster Kirill has already made things harder for her.

I've seen her obsessing over the scar on her cheek.

She doesn't listen to me when I tell her I love it. It's a badge to me of just how damn tough she is.

Her mark proves that she fought back. My Lara wouldn't give in.

"I think you're making a mistake. Let's wait until we can catch him here, with our numbers. We can take him out." Nikolai leans back and his lips thin.

"Who went with you to get Mila? You were willing to die to chase her down, and you left Elena here. Do you love your daughter?" I ask him angrily.

"Of fucking course I do." His fists bunch on his thigh. "That was a different situation. She was in imminent danger."

"You didn't know that when you left!" My voice raises and I slam my palm down on Mikhail's desk. "You chased her down for revenge. It isn't much different than what I'm doing. Except I see Lara suffering every single day because that guy is still out there." I jut my finger towards the wind for emphasis.

"She's our sister." Nikolai points to Mikhail. "Don't you think we want to protect her, too? What's gotten into you?"

Do I tell him it's because I love her? What would he do if he knew? How can he not want to protect her? Kirill was just as fucked up to Mila, why isn't Nikolai more worked up over that?

Mikhail stands up abruptly and moves between us. "He's doing what's right." His heavy hand lands on my shoulder. "I'll make sure you get there. Tell me what you need." He turns me so I'm no longer facing Nikolai.

"He has a family, too," he says quietly. "We all want what's best for the people we love." He gives me a slow, meaningful nod. "Go talk to Lara. Fill her in. See what she wants you to do."

As I make it back to my bike, I kick a stone on the ground.

Maybe they are right?

Leaving Lara now, when things are so good? Doesn't feel right.

Yet, this overwhelming need to protect her rages inside me.

I need to actually think this one through rather than acting on my impulse.

Lara is calming me.

CHAPTER 53

ALEXEI

MY STOMACH GRUMBLES as I stroke Lara's hair. Her head rests on a pillow on my lap.

We've nearly finished Yellowstone. I'm gunna miss those cowboys.

I need to eat.

And then discuss with her my next job. Not that I know much about it. But the more I think, the more in love with her I fall, the more clear it becomes I have to do it.

"Hey, baby. Shall we go grab some food? I'm so hungry I could eat a crocodile."

Her body vibrates as she laughs.

"People normally say horse. And I'm not really hungry. I'll come with you though, shall we walk somewhere?"

How is she not starving? She eats way less than me.

Sofia's words whirl in my head. Lara sits up and scoots away.

"You need to have something, you can't go to bed on an empty stomach. Not for what I have planned for you."

Reluctantly she nods.

"Burger?"

Her face drops. Almost in a look of panic. But she quickly covers it with a smile.

But it's a fake one. I know her.

"Let me go get changed." She stands and pats down on her dress.

"You look perfect as you are." I pin her with a stare. There is more behind my words than what's there on the surface. I hope she realizes.

She jogs up the stairs and I tip my head back on the couch, running my hands over my face.

How do I help her?

How do I get her to see what I see?

I've read some horror stories online about how people die from this.

I can't lose her.

CHAPTER 54

LARA

Closing the bathroom door, I run the cold tap and splash water over my face.

Shit.

It's almost like he knows.

I shouldn't be shocked. That man knows me better than I know myself sometimes.

I don't want to talk about it, let alone confront my demons.

How do I put into words that I hate myself? That everyday I find something new to despise?

I'm used to it.

I deal with it.

As long as I am in control, I survive.

Picking up my phone I notice my hands are shaking.

I open up my calorie log for the day and frantically jab in the food I've consumed.

Maybe, if I have the burger and no fries and work out first thing, it won't make a difference?

After one bite, I'd just want more until I was sick. But I can't do that in front of Alexei. He can't save me from this. I don't want him to see me broken, he already rescues me enough.

I want to smash my head against the wall. Why am I like this?

There's a soft knock. I look in the mirror and I'm crying. I didn't even realize it.

Tears over a simple dinner.

Pathetic.

"Are you okay, baby?" His voice is muffled through the wood.

I quickly wipe my face and lock my cell before opening the door.

"What's wrong?" He stops me before I can walk past him with his hands on my shoulders.

"You can talk to me about anything, you know that right? No matter what, I love you and I am here for you."

I swallow the lump forming in my throat.

Silence fills the air.

What if he thinks I'm too damaged? A lost cause?

How can he love me when I can't stand any part of myself?

"Why don't you want to eat? What were you doing in there?" He chews on his lip.

I want to throw up. I want to run. Especially seeing the worry on his face, I can't be a burden to him.

"Just using the toilet."

He nods.

"So I was speaking to Sofia, and she said she thinks that you may have an eating disorder."

My stomach drops. The blood rushes out of my face. I want the floor to swallow me whole.

"Y-you spoke to her about me? Why?" I stumble back.

I can't deal with this.

They all probably think I'm crazy.

I can't even see through the tears erupting. It's like the walls are closing in on me as my chest heaves.

"Lara?"

I push him out the way and run as fast as I can down the stairs, grabbing my keys and jumping in my BMW.

Slamming my foot on the gas, I peel out of the driveway. Letting the tears fall down my cheek, the road is blurry, the lights make my eyes sting.

I hate myself. They all deserve better.

I need to clear my head. I need space. I need control back.

But I always need Alexei.

CHAPTER 55
ALEXEI

"FUCK!" I slam my fist into my front door as her tires screech down the street.

The pain on her face.

I fucked it all up.

I knew I would. I have to make this right.

Grabbing my helmet and keys, I hop on my bike.

She won't be far, I can catch her.

Filtering through the traffic, cars honk at me, but I don't care.

I have to get to her.

Up at the next block, I see her white car. Checking left and right, my traffic signal is red, but to hell with it. I hit the throttle and go.

It would be exhilarating if I wasn't in such a panic.

As I approach her, her light turns green and she zooms off.

Shaking my head, I speed up, enough so I'm even with her.

"Pull over!" I shout, pointing to the wide spot up ahead.

She shakes her head, looking back at the road.

I can't let her leave.

Edging my bike closer to her, I keep going. I'm dangerously close.

She swerves to the right away from me, and slams on her brakes to pull into the parking spot.

I kick down my stand, and pull off my helmet while stomping over to the driver's side.

"Open." I yank on the door.

"Go away." She mouths.

I shake my head. "You know me better than that. Open the damn door."

I step back.

"I'm not going anywhere, Lara. I'll stand here and wait all night and day if I have to. I am never leaving your side. Eternity remember? It's a long fucking time."

I hop up on the hood and take a seat.

Fuck it's warm.

Tapping on her windshield, I wave. I can see she's trying not to grin.

So I keep doing it, and turn it into the tune to that song she always listens to.

That gets her.

She winds down the window.

"I don't need saving, Alexei," she shouts.

Sliding off the front, I approach her window and place my hand on her cheek, wiping away a tear.

I'm going for a new technique. She's right. She is strong and brave. This isn't about that.

And she likes my dominant side. So I lean on that.

"I'm not rescuing you. I'm loving you. There's a difference. Now turn around, get that fine ass back to the house and we can talk there if you want to. Regardless, you are coming home to me. Okay?"

She sniffles and nods.

Poking my head through the window, I kiss her. "I love you, pchelka. Always remember that. No matter what."

Resting my forehead against hers, I kiss her one last time on the temple. "Please, baby. No more running, only back home to me. I need you too."

When she nods, I walk back to my bike. Her blinker leads her back onto the freeway, and turns left towards our street.

Good girl.

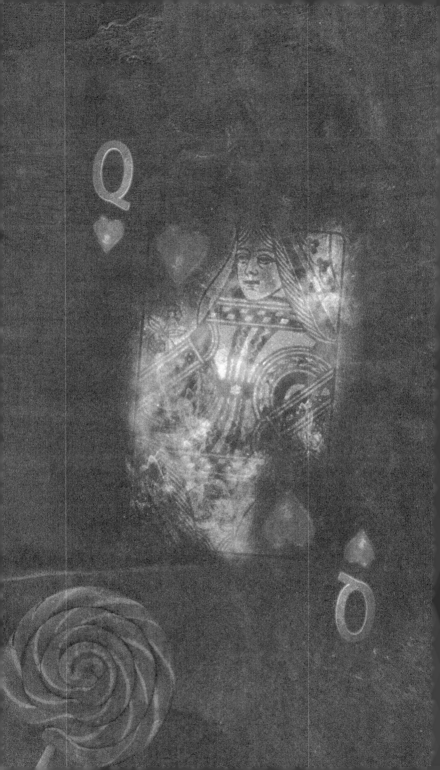

CHAPTER 56

Song- Sleep token- Fall For Me.

I GET BACK HOME before he does. But he isn't far behind, so I fill up two glasses of water.

He stalks towards me and cups my face in his hands.

"Let me get those damn birds outside and then we can talk, okay?"

All I can do is nod, I don't know what to say.

"I love you, baby," he whispers.

I close my eyes as he kisses the top of my head.

After he causes a commotion outside herding his flamingos into the yard, he wipes the sweat from his forehead and grabs his water before joining me on the couch.

"Come here." He holds his arm out and I scoot over into his comforting touch.

"I never went behind your back to speak to Sofia. It was an off hand comment she took and—"

"Stop." I cut him off. "I don't really think you two are conspiring against me. Your hearts are both in the right place, I know that. This is my fault. It's on me."

He strokes my shoulder.

"From what I've researched, this is *not* your fault."

I shrug, holding back the tears.

Wait, he's been studying to try and help me?

"It's my brain I can't fix. My insecurities."

"You aren't on your own, not anymore," he whispers.

"How can I help you? What can I do to help you?"

"Y-you can't, some things just can't be undone."

"How long?"

I take a deep breath, ready to let it all spill out. I trust him. I love him. Maybe he can fix me.

"Since I turned eighteen, on and off. It started off with dad forcing me to count calories and work out to stay in shape so I was in his words a 'good choice for a wife'."

He holds me tight.

"And then when I realized there was no getting out of that, it was the one thing I had control over. If I threw it back up, I could eat what I wanted. I could still find joy in life. But then once we came here, it became my lifeline."

The words are tumbling out so I let them. Alexei is my safe space.

"I hate how I look, whether I'm lighter, heavier, dressed my best or in my sweats. No matter what I do, I look in the mirror and despise the woman staring back at me."

"And I look at you in all of those times and see perfection, Lara," he says quietly.

With a shaky breath, I continue.

"Mikhail risked his life, was left permanently scarred, saving us. For what, Alexei? I can't do anything. I'm basically a prisoner in my own house. No real job, no qualifications. I'm just Lara, a mafia princess waiting to be stolen or married off. Never good enough to be picked."

"Stop."

I don't listen. "Everything around me always falls apart and you know what I do? I starve myself to feel some sense of normalcy. Sometimes I don't eat for days and work out until the room spins, but all I can hear is my father telling me I don't look good enough for a man to marry. Every first date never turns into a second and now, I'm so in love with the one man I can't openly be with, why? Because my brothers control my damn life. Maybe it's for the best we just go back to being friends. I ruin everything."

He pulls back and grips my shoulders, looking right into my soul as the tears spill down my cheeks.

"Lara Volkov. I've been in love with you for what feels like my whole life. My loyalty may be with your brothers, my heart, that's all yours, baby. And that comes first, even before my own life. That will never change. What we have, it's forever. There is no end. We don't hide. I would be nothing more than honored to be your man to everyone in the outside world, your brothers included. But it's a risk."

"Yet, one not worth taking." I chew on the inside of my cheek to try and bite back the tears.

He tips my chin back up.

"Look at me Lara. You are worth every risk. For you I'll take the chance on my life and I will fight with everything I have to make this right so we can be together. I only want you, in all your imperfections."

"And what if this is all too much to deal with, Alexei?"

"I'm asking you to fall with me, Lara. If we crash and burn, so be it, at least we know we tried everything we could for our love. So please baby, I'm begging you, take the chance on us."

"You really want this? All this broken, all this mess to deal with? I'm not an obligation."

"Never. My love for you is my fuel, one spark and I can set the world on fire. Our love is forever. No beginning, no end. Infinite."

"I'll take the fall with you. It's all I've ever wanted, sladkiy. I've only ever wanted you. I just don't know if I will ever be fixed."

He wipes away my tears with his thumb and presses his nose to mine.

"Maybe we don't need fixing, maybe we were always meant to be broken together, pchelka."

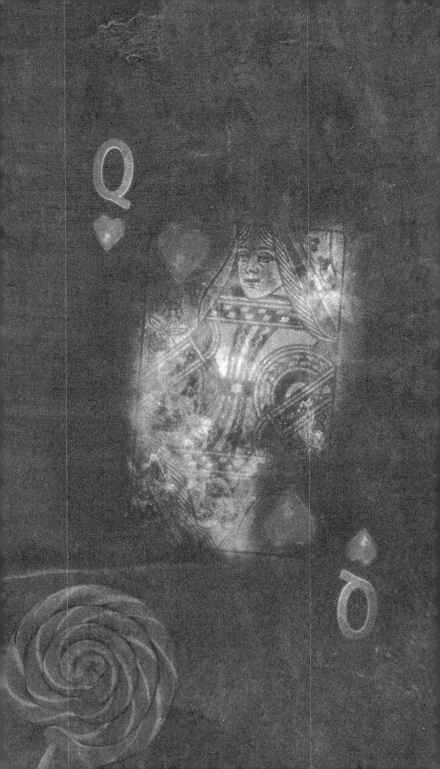

CHAPTER 57
ALEXEI

ALL THIS TIME I have been protecting her and this was happening inside her head?

Those doubts, those thoughts, I could have shown her a long time ago how wrong they are.

That she is the essence of beauty, not just on the outside, but on the inside, too.

I fight my own urge to cry, for the pain she's been living with. This heartache I never saw. The nights of online searching has scared me, the thought of losing her to this is like a stab in the chest.

"You know, all these years, the only reason I'm still standing is because of you, Alexei. Without you, I'd be in pieces."

"Don't give me too much credit."

"I mean it. You are my crazy sparkle of light, Alexei. No matter how dark it gets, you are always there to brighten my life. If I didn't have that, I would have given up a long time ago. Your love keeps me alive."

Her words pain me. I don't want her trapped in the dark.

"So how does this link into food, to throwing it up? What makes you do that?"

It's the part I can't wrap my head around.

"When everything around me crumbles, my calorie counting, exercise, purging, it's something I can take back control and maybe obsess over. Distracting me from the chaos outside. And when I hate what I see in the mirror, it drives me to do it more."

I nod in understanding.

"I want to help you. I want to make sure you're healthy. I just want you to be happy, pchelka."

"You do make me happy. I promise."

"So what about we start with a meal plan? I will do it with you, we can prep together, work out. You aren't alone in this."

Her brows furrow. "That could work."

"What about speaking to Sofia?"

She shakes her head and goes to pull away. "I'm not ready to talk to anyone else yet."

She looks down, but I tip her chin back up.

"Whatever you want, it's on your terms."

"Thank you. That wasn't as bad as I thought it might be, you know, talking about it."

I am her safe space and I will protect her, even from the demons in her head.

Except, how the hell do I do that when I'm leaving for Russia?

CHAPTER 58

ALEXEI

"Come in." Mikhail's deep voice booms through his office door. I didn't even need to knock.

As I step inside, he leans back in his chair, and I take the seat opposite his desk.

I don't say a word. I know why he's called me in.

He pours me a vodka and slides it towards me. His dark eyes pin me with a stare.

"We talked about this, you are going through with it. Yet, you're delaying. Why?"

Knocking back the contents of my glass, I debate my answer. I can't tell him the whole truth. That's Lara's story to share when she's ready.

But a half truth, that means he might keep an extra eye on her. That could work.

"I'm worried about leaving Lara."

He frowns, pouring himself a glass.

"You're always worried about her. We have extra protection in place. Nothing will happen to her while you're away. Me and Nikolai can look out for our sister too. It's not always just on you."

I swallow hard.

None of us knew how dark it was for her. So really, did any of us do a good enough job?

"I'll tell her tonight and then I'll get it done. Okay?"

He nods, swirling the clear liquid.

"We will do everything we can to keep track of you. I don't trust Tatiana. But for some reason, I trust your judgment. Don't give me a reason to change my mind on that." He pauses. "Donkey."

I'll never live Nikolai's nickname down.

I bite back telling him to shut up. He is the boss after all.

"I'll get it done. You look after—" I rub my jaw, stopping myself from saying my girl.

"She's lucky to have you, Alexei. You know, you don't have to do this much for her. You have more than repaid your debt to us years ago. You aren't just her bodyguard."

"It's more than that. She's special to me."

He flicks his gaze to the picture of the three of them on his desk from when he showed his face.

Back when he smiled.

Fuck. Did I say too much?

"I know. I appreciate your love for her. She needs you to come back in one piece. Remember that."

He jabs his finger towards me. "No pulling stupid shit. You hear me? Behave. Use the brain I know is in there."

I salute him with a smirk. "Me? Reckless? How dare you?"

An unease settles in my gut. Before I never realized what I had to lose if it goes wrong. All those times I risked my life, I didn't think.

Now I know what it would do to Lara.

He gestures towards the door. "She's in her office. Do it now."

Heading down the hall I stop outside. The quicker I get this over with, the faster I can come home.

I don't knock, I just walk in. She's deep in conversation, her brows furrowed as she looks at her screen.

But as soon as she sees me, she smiles and gives me a little wave.

"Hi, baby." I mouth, taking a seat opposite her.

She looks magnificent.

And now I'm picturing bending her over the desk.

Jesus Christ, Alexei. Not now.

What's a few more hours anyway?

CHAPTER 59
LARA

Song, Fire Up The Night, New Medicine

IF HE CLICKS that pen one more time I will scream. I know he has something to get off his chest. I wish he would just say it.

"You're distracting me." I flick him a stern look, but have to bite back my smile when he wiggles his eyebrows at me.

"That was my master plan."

With one final click, he tosses it at the wall and it bounces off into the trash can.

"What am I going to do with you, Alexei?"

He reclines back in the chair and lets out a dramatic sigh.

"Me. You're going to do me. Right here, right now, and that door—" He pauses and points behind him. "—stays unlocked."

"Oh, you want me?" I tease, twirling a blond curl around my finger.

"Want? No. Need, yes. I want you every second of the day." He winks at me.

A blush spreads on my cheeks.

"You know we can't do it here. Just wait until we get home."

I nearly jump when my phone rings and the floor manager's name stares back at me.

I've just about had enough of that man's useless number crunching for today.

Glancing up at Alexei he has a smug grin on his face. It's like he knows.

Probably because I'm on fire right now. Squirming in my seat, I hit accept and bring it to my ear, motioning Alexei to be quiet with a finger over my lips.

Not that it's even unusual for him to be here, but since we've started dating, I'm almost paranoid my brothers could ruin this for me. Once it's out in the open, this will be a lot easier.

"Bill." I greet the manager and Alexei shifts in his seat.

"I'm sending you a spreadsheet now. I think it's all done." The gruff voice echoes from the speaker.

I clench my fist in annoyance.

"You think?"

Resting my forehead on my hand I sigh. Bill's excuses almost become background noise when I hear the unmistakable sound of Alexei's zipper.

"One second." I rush the words into the phone, then mouth to Alexei "don't you dare".

He runs his tongue along his teeth. I swear to God I'm soaking my panties by the time his dick is in his hands.

His eyes are fixed on mine as he swirls the pre-cum over the tip.

"You want?" He mouths.

I bite down on my lip and nod.

"Are you there?" Bill startles me from my cell.

"Uh, yes. I'll take a look and get back to you." I clear my throat, the heat spreading up my neck.

I fidget in my seat. Holy fuck. Alexei is going to kill me.

Bill continues. "Did you want me to come to your office and talk you through it—"

"No." I cut him off quickly. "It's fine. I'll catch up with you later."

Alexei's veiny, tatted hand strokes his cock and his wild eyes burn into mine.

I cut the call and toss it down on the desk. His master plan worked, I'm going to ride his dick and have him be the one begging me for more this time. I know this man would drop to his knees for me in a second.

But after the stunt he's just pulled, he can stay down there and earn forgiveness with his tongue.

"You have my full attention. Now what are you going to do with me?" I rest my chin on my hand and bat my lashes at him, squeezing my thighs together.

"Come sit on my lap." He taps his thick thigh but I stay rooted in my seat.

"Say please?" I say sweetly, chewing on the inside of my cheek.

"You have to earn me begging for you." He continues to stroke himself. "I have exactly what you need right here. Ready and waiting for your tight pussy. I can take all that stress away. All you have to do is get your ass here."

I pout, pretending to think. I can't say no to that.

Rounding the desk, his eyes light up as I ruffle my skirt over my hips and straddle him.

His hands skim over my shirt and he grips my throat.

"Good girl." He pushes my panties to one side. "Just how I expected. Soaking for me." He groans as his finger slides along my pussy.

I lift my hips, letting the tip of his dick press against my entrance.

He circles it and guides it in, pushing me down slowly by my neck.

My mouth falls open as I stretch around him, taking every inch.

He steals my breath away with a kiss.

"Ride me like you mean it, baby," he whispers and slaps my ass.

Using his shoulders to lift myself, I bounce on his dick and he squeezes my throat between our frantic kisses.

Our moans fill the room, his louder than mine, which is so fucking hot.

"As much as it turns me the fuck on hearing you moan for me, Alexei. I need you to shhh." I press my finger against his lips just as he thrusts up deep inside of me, digging his fingers in my waist to hold me firmly in place.

"Holy shit." I want to scream, but I can't. Not here.

Tightening his grip, he draws me closer.

"Hard isn't it?" His hot breath hits against my cheek.

"Your dick? Yes, very." I wiggle my hips and my god, that feels so good.

"Well, yea, that. I mean keeping quiet. When all I want to do is let every motherfucker in this building hear you're mine, and how good you ride me in your office like the naughty girl you are."

"Only for you, sladkiy."

"Ugh, fuck. I love it when you talk like that," he grits out.

With his hold on my ass he guides me up and down on his cock.

"I'm so close, Alexei. So close." It's almost a whimper.

He flicks my clit and my body trembles.

"Fuck," I cry out.

"Now beg like a good girl. Beg me to come inside you."

I suck in a breath.

"Alexei." I struggle to even form words as he releases his grip on my neck.

I'm on fire.

"Might be easier now. Let me hear it, baby. Tell me how bad you need to come," he grunts into my ear.

"You were meant to be the one begging."

He chuckles, and runs his tongue along my throat. "How's

that going for you, baby? Seeing how you're the one shaking, needy and desperate?"

Biting the inside of my mouth, I try to stop myself from coming.

"How's this, say the words, 'Alexei please let me come' and I'll allow it. As your reward I'll give you what you wanted...Me on my knees and I'll clean you up ready to go back to work."

I squeeze my eyes shut as my climax builds, I'm so damn close I can't think straight.

I also can't hold my breath much longer either. "Please, Alexei. I am begging you. Let me come for you."

He thrusts up hard, holding me in place by my waist.

"Okay. You may come now," he mumbles in my ear.

I bite down on his neck as my orgasm crashes through every nerve in my body. I'm shaking around him, pure ecstasy running through my veins.

He consumes every part of me.

Pulling me by my hair, he brings my face to his and slams his lips over mine. Taking everything from me.

And I'll always give it to him willingly.

As I ride it out, I bury myself against his jaw and cuddle him while his strong arms wrap around me.

"That was so hot, Lara. Office sex is epic."

I chuckle, despite not having any breath left. "Yeah. Come by whenever you want."

He remains silent, which is strange.

"Let me clean you up. Then you can get back to work and I'll make us dinner tonight, sound good?"

I pull back and search his eyes.

"You okay?" I ask.

He nods, kissing my cheek. "Of course."

CHAPTER 60
ALEXEI

Song- The Fray, I'll Look After You.

I can't watch her pick at her dinner any longer. I hate seeing her like this, I wish I could understand what's going on inside that pretty head of hers.

To me she's perfect. She's smart, she's brave, she is my entire life and soul. I can't comprehend why she looks at herself and hates the woman that stares back at her in the mirror.

When I look at her, all I see is my future.

I'm doing everything I can. I read through every damn bit of information Sofia shoved at me. The one word that keeps sticking out is control.

And it makes sense when I look back over the years.

Something bad happens, she runs. That's why I bought the cabin.

I scratch my head then she looks up at me, returning a sad smile.

That hurts worse than my dick piercing.

I need to be comfortable that she is okay before I go on this job. And I am running out of ideas.

"Alexei, stop analyzing me."

"Never."

My life is always out of control, it's how I thrive. It's who I am. The only time I have my shit together in my head is when I'm on my motorcycle.

My bike.

Control.

Freedom.

Standing up so fast I knock over my chair, I hold my hand out to her. Her blue eyes flick between my face and hand.

"What just happened in your brain that I missed the memo on."

I bite down on my lip and that earns me a real smile from her.

"Do you trust me?" I ask.

She places her dainty hand in mine and stands. That fuzzy feeling in my chest is almost making me dizzy.

She has always had this effect on me, and now I know why. Because I love her so damn much I have to do everything in my power to help her.

Because I can't, and I won't, live without her.

"That is never a question you have to ask, Alexei. I trust you, for eternity."

I swallow the lump in my throat.

I know she means it, I know my Lara doesn't mean to hurt herself the way she does.

But she could die if she carries on this way.

"Why didn't you ever tell me?"

As she goes to take a step back, I take one forward and wrap my arms around her, hugging her so tight.

"You were holding me together without even realizing it. You already spent your life protecting me, emotions aren't your thing, Alexei."

Resting my chin on the top of her head, I let out a deep sigh.

She's right, for the most part. I've had to learn to read emotions.

"Other peoples aren't. Yours, Lara, are more important to me than anything. Actually, yours are the only ones I care about, well, and Sheila's I suppose."

She nuzzles her face against my shirt.

"I could have done more, pchelka." The irritation in my tone is purely at myself. I mean, she never once, in all these years, touched a single sweet in the jar she keeps for me.

Everyone loves candy. It's addictive. Why didn't I spot it sooner?

"Alexei, stop. It's going to be okay. I'm not going anywhere."

I might be able to read her, but it's as if she reads my mind.

I am the one that has to go and it's killing me, but I can't delay it any more.

Pulling back, I frame her face with my hands, staring into her tear filled eyes.

"I love you enough to know that I have to go first. I'm not living a single second on this earth without you. So yes, it will be okay, there is no other option. We will get you through this, together. Whatever it takes."

She nods but her bottom lip starts to quiver, so I lean down and press my nose to hers.

"You are Lara fucking Volkov. The beauty, the brains and the heart of the family. I have loved you for a long time and I will love you for eternity. I'd love you if you became a flamingo, I'll love you when you're gray and wrinkly. I love you even now when you wake up and breathe on my face with your hair piled up on the top of your head. You can't see you're perfect, I probably will never truly understand why, but I will spend the rest of my life showing you just how magnificent you are to me. That I promise you."

Our love has never been about her appearance, it's built on the fact I simply cannot survive a day without her in it.

Before she can respond, I softly brush my lips over hers.

I've learned that a kiss can speak a thousand words.

One single kiss changed our entire future.

And I will give her as many as she needs to make her feel safe, loved and in control.

Because my Lara deserves the world and I will be the man she needs to bring it to her.

"I don't know what I'd do without you, *moya liubov'*." Lara whispers against my lips.

Ugh, just hearing her speak in Russian has my dick twitching. There is something about the way she speaks in our home tongue that gets to me.

"You'll never have to find that out."

"*Ya budu liubit tebyai i vse tvoi sumashestviya, vechno.*" **I will love you and all your crazy, for eternity.**

My smile is so big it almost hurts my cheeks. I am home, right here, with this woman and my Sheila. I never need anything else.

"*Vechnosti ne dostatochno.*" **Eternity is not enough.**

She pulls back and laughs.

"Well, that's the most infinite way to describe time, so it will have to do."

"Fine," I gruff, stealing one more sweet kiss.

Later will be the time for more. I'm addicted to her in every way and need my fill.

And I want to show her something.

Maybe teach her a little bit of my crazy.

And give me the ride I need to work out how I break the news, I've let it eat at me for too long now.

One last ride.

CHAPTER 61
LARA

Song- breathe, mxze

ALEXEI JUMPS off the couch holding out his hand. "Come with me. I want to show you something."

Intrigue getting the better of me, I place my palm in his and he helps me up.

I know better than to ask what he's doing, so I tag along to the garage where he switches on the light.

He grabs a black helmet with a red stripe, and flashes me a smile.

"That new?" I ask.

Excitement dances in his eyes as he nods.

"Yep. Yours." He holds it out, almost proud of himself.

"You want me to get on the back of that?" I point to his black BMW. Or also known as his baby.

I've seen the way he rides, like a maniac, is the best way to describe it.

He steps towards me; holding the gift out in front of him.

"You said you trusted me." He wiggles his eyebrows in amusement.

"With my life," I reply. I hold up my finger, so he doesn't get too excited. "But I've seen how you ride that thing."

As he hovers the helmet over my head, I can feel the weight of it pressing down slightly on my scalp.

"I never have precious cargo on the back. I'd never put you in danger. So, you in?"

My heart flutters, the excitement on his face solidifies my answer. "Yes. No wheelies though."

He rolls his eyes and secures the strap under my chin.

"Just hold on tight and let your mind be free. When I open her up, the wind crashes against you and all you can hear is the sound of the machine, those nagging voices in here—" He taps on the side of his head. "—they shut up. It's just you and the road."

"That sounds peaceful."

He snaps my visor down and grabs a leather jacket, sliding my arms in before he zips it up.

"It is. And I want you to experience my one calm place. Maybe, it could be our place."

God my eyes are stinging. He's adorable. So thoughtful without even realizing it.

I watch him secure his own black helmet. He helps me onto the back of the bike and presses the button to open the garage door. Once he is on, I hold his waist as tight as possible.

"Relax," he tells me, giving my hand a reassuring squeeze.

The roaring engine filled the air, intensifying the blend of nerves and excitement within me. Starting off slowly, he navigates his way from the driveway and merges onto the road, the scent of hot asphalt filling the air.

I'm holding my breath for the first few minutes, but he behaves, staying with the traffic.

I know this man. It won't be long before he pushes it to the extreme, because that is his calm.

After the next set of lights, he tugs my arms tighter around him. As we jolt off, I squeeze my eyes shut and mentally brace myself for the ride.

The air beats against me. I squeeze him and eventually open my eyes as the world whizzes by me.

He weaves in and out of the cars with skill and finally, I remember what he told me.

Relax. Clear my mind. Focus on the ride.

So I do.

With my helmet resting against his back, the desert stretches out before us as he moves away from the Strip, and the sun begins its descent, painting the sky to my left.

It's breathtaking.

And he's right. There are no other distractions. I'm totally in the moment with him.

I don't know how long we ride until he pulls over on a dirt track.

As he cuts the engine, I cast a quick glance over his shoulder, and am immediately struck by the serene beauty of the sunset unfolding on the horizon.

While he disembarks, I stay seated, expecting him to lend a hand in helping me off, but he doesn't. Instead, he removes my helmet, gently sliding it off my head and placing it on the gravel beside him.

Brushing out my hair that now feels stuck to my scalp, he flicks up his visor so I can see his eyes.

I know that look.

The feral one that turns me on in all kinds of crazy ways.

"You look gorgeous on my bike. Fuck, the things I was thinking about doing to you, that's why I had to pull over."

Moving closer, he places his firm hand on my thigh.

"Oh yeah? Tell me more. Did it involve me bent over the bike and you taking me from behind, wearing your helmet? Cause that would be so hot."

"Fuck," he mutters. His eyes squint so I know he's smiling

under there. "Is that what my girl needs? Hmm?" He twirls my hair around his finger.

"I'll even beg for it if you want," I tell him, running my tongue along my bottom lip.

"No begging today. Today you're going to earn your reward like a good girl."

That makes my pulse race.

The way he's devouring me with his eyes is driving me wild.

I take a sharp breath as his hand suddenly grabs my neck and forces me to make eye contact.

In a quick motion, he flips his head and drops his visor. "You can see yourself, right?" His voice is muffled, but I can hear him.

"Yes."

He tightens his grip on my throat, and I squirm in my seat.

"Lay back on the bike and put on a show for me. Come undone and watch yourself fall apart in the reflection. See how beautiful you are. See what I see for once."

He releases his grip, and I am already breathless and needy for him.

"Can you help?" I make a pouting face while he shakes his head.

"All by yourself, pchelka. I'm just here to watch you come for me." His hands trail down my sides and he stops at the button on my pants.

"I'll help you take these off, how's that?" There's amusement in his tone. He's loving this as much as me.

Looking around, not a single car has driven past. We're off track enough to not be seen. Honestly, I don't care. I just want to earn my reward.

Carefully maneuvering my body, I position myself over the gas tank, surrendering to his touch as he gently removes my jeans and panties. The warm air kisses my skin as Alexei mounts the bike on the opposite side, my heels finding a comfortable resting place on his thigh.

His fingers dig into my calf and he massages his thumbs in circles.

Resting my head back, I take a breath and trail my nails down my body and let them travel south to my pussy. Slowly sliding my index finger along my slit, I let out a little gasp at how wet I am.

"Eyes don't leave the visor, baby. You be a good girl and do that for me, and I'll give you exactly what you need."

I snap my head up and catch a glimpse of my reflection in his dark mirrored visor. I can see everything and it's hot. I just wish I could see his eyes to know what this does to him.

Working in small circular motions on my clit, I move my other hand down and tease my entrance, putting on a show for him. Spreading my thighs further apart, he holds my ankles to secure me.

My mouth falls open as I slide in a finger. The rush of doing this here makes every feeling more intense.

"Shit," I hiss, keeping my eyes on him.

"One more, Lara. I know how much you like feeling full. Just imagine how good it will be when I spread your ass apart and sink inside you. Inch. By. Inch. And once I'm all the way in, I'll twist your hair around my fist and pull your head back as I slowly pull almost all the way out. You'll be panting, almost aching for more. Begging me to hit it harder. And when you're trembling against me, that's when I'll thrust so deep, you won't be able to stop the screams. And I won't stop, baby, until I take what's mine and give me everything you have. Now that's my good fucking girl. See how wet you are? Look."

Holy fucking shit. His words almost make me come on the spot. I add the second finger and my juices drip down my hand. I've never felt myself this wet. Ever.

"Alexei," I plead with him.

"I know you can take more. I know your body better than you do. Trust me. One more."

I suck in a breath before adding the third finger. This time, his hand covers mine that's working my clit and he takes control of my motions, speeding it up.

Seeing both of our hands, my legs shaking, the blush spreading up my throat, all in the reflection. My hair falling over my shoulder. Lust in my eyes. He's right, I look hot like this.

"I-I can't take anymore." I struggle to get my words out.

My body is trembling. It feels so good. I up the pace of my hand. Hearing how wet I am for him is driving me crazy. I bet it's driving him crazy, too.

As he leans in, I can feel the hard metal of the bike against my back, and his body pressing me tightly.

"You've been so good for me, Lara. I'm proud of you." He strokes along my cheek before his fingers lace around my throat. My pulse races against his palm.

"Please let me come," I whisper.

"Come as hard as you need, but watch every second."

I lock on the visor as his finger finds my clit, and he pinches. I scream out. The second my eyes close, his hand tightens and I open them back up.

And I watch myself fall apart for him.

One of the most empowering moments of my life.

CHAPTER 62

ALEXEI

Holy fucking shit.

I'm about to come just watching her.

I hope she sees how pretty she looks when she loses control.

As she reaches the end of her climax, gasping for breath, I release my grip on her throat and sit back.

Running my hand on my leather seat that is coated in her release.

"Look at the pretty mess you made on my bike, pchelka."

I flip up my visor so she can see the hunger in my eyes.

I need her. Right this damn second.

Without wasting another breath, I push myself up off the bike and grab her by the waist, lifting her into my arms and positioning her over the seat.

Releasing my throbbing cock, I run my hands over her ass cheeks. She cries out as I slap my right hand hard over her pale skin. The red mark forms almost instantly and damn it's beautiful.

Staying true to my word, I spread her wide.

"How bad do you want it?" I ask, biting the inside of my mouth as my cock presses against her pussy.

She wiggles her hips, backing into me.

"So bad, sweets."

She looks over her shoulder. Her lust filled gaze has my heart racing. I take my time, gliding my cock along her soaking cunt, covering my shaft in her. I press the tip against her and a little moan falls from her lips.

I work my way inside her, inch by inch, gripping onto her ass until I am balls deep. She immediately clamps around me, strangling my dick.

"You feel so fucking good, Lara."

I pull out almost all the way and drive back inside. She cries out in pleasure, so I do it again. Over and over.

Fucking her, how she needs to be taken.

Raw and rough. Just how I've learned my girl likes it.

I'm sweating in this helmet, almost fucking suffocating.

She buries her face in her forearms and I push my hands through her hair and yank her head up.

"Look at the sunset. It's so gorgeous. Almost as good as my view," I tell her, keeping her looking at the sky while I watch myself thrust in and out of her.

"You going to come on my cock, baby? Are you going to give me what I need?" I slap her ass making her screams rip through the air.

It only makes me go harder.

My entire body is tense, I can't focus on anything other than how good this feels.

"Fuck, Lara." I can't take it anymore.

I tip up my chin, chanting her name as I spill inside her, and she crumbles around me.

My cock twitches inside her. I never want to leave. Reluctantly, I pull out, watching as my cum spills down her thighs. Without thinking, I drop to my knees and swipe up the excess, pushing it back inside her.

She looks behind, her face flushed, and a smile spreads across her lips.

"What are you doing?" she asks, her voice husky, and that makes me hard again.

"Why waste it? It belongs inside you. You are mine, Lara Volkov." I stand and lift her spent body into my arms and sit her upright on the bike, facing me.

"Now you're going to have me spilling out of you all over my seat as I ride us home. You're full of me, and that makes you all mine."

CHAPTER 63
ALEXEI

I'M PACING around the bedroom like a caged bear.

I don't want to leave her. I don't even want to utter the words. But Tatiana's threats are loud in my head.

If I don't do this, Lara isn't safe. In reality, this is the worst of the evils I am protecting her from.

A billow of steam comes from the ensuite as Lara dries her hair. She stops when she spots me.

"What's up? I could hear you stomping around even with the water going."

She tosses the towel in the laundry basket and tightens the one around her breasts.

"Words, Alexei. I'm a grown woman, I can handle it." She frowns and looks at me.

"Unless you've cheated. Then we have a serious problem and Mikhail will have to hide your body."

I shake my head.

Is this worse? No. I don't think so.

"God, no. Can you umm, sit down?"

"You're worrying me. Spill."

Oh no. Her hand is on her hip. She's getting mad.

"I have to go away for a little while. I promise, once I'm home, we tell the truth and we have our forever. Together."

She sighs, sitting on the bed, I take a spot next to her, placing my hand on her knee.

"Tell me you're not going to Russia."

She won't look at me.

"I vowed to keep you safe, pchelka. That never stops, I can't stop until the ones who took you are buried. The threat against you has to die. No matter what it takes. This is the only way."

"You aren't going on your own."

"Mikhail will come with me. Now in the meantime, I need you to stay with Niki. Take Sheila and Bruce."

I don't need to add more worry by telling her that Mikhail is simply dropping me off.

"How long?"

I shrug my shoulders. "I don't have the answer to that."

I hear her sniffle and wrap my arm around her, tugging her into my side.

"I need you, sweets. I don't want to be without you."

Fuck.

Turning to face her, I kneel on the bed and take her face in my hands.

"There isn't anything you can't do. You never needed me, not really. You need to let me go, and I need you to be fierce. Be the girl that stole my heart all those years ago, pchelka."

I see fear in her eyes, I can feel it.

"We will find our way back to each other, I promise. I simply cannot exist without you."

Resting my forehead against hers, I inhale her scent, like coconuts from her shampoo.

"Our love isn't just inevitable, it's destined. I'm going to need to you fight for us, pchelka. More than anything, look after yourself, fight those demons until I'm back to help you. I need you to be okay while I'm away. Please try for me, baby."

I kiss her and then wrap my arms around her holding her as close as I possibly can.

"I will try my best, Alexei. Don't worry, just come home to me."

I always will, it's my purpose.

"When do you leave?"

"Tomorrow." I hold my breath, waiting to see her reaction.

Her jaw tightens. "I can do this. I'll be strong for us."

"I love you, Lara."

"I love you, all of it."

I kiss her, like it's possibly the last time. I will fight my damn hardest to make it back to her so we can finally live our lives how we were meant to, together.

"I'd never spend a single second away from you if I had a choice. I'd glue you to me if it was safe to do."

We snuggle up under the covers and she settles in my arms.

I hold her tight. I don't want to ever let her go.

I'm going to be empty without her by my side.

There is no me without her.

And feeling her body shudder from her silent cries is enough fuel for me to make sure I kill whichever motherfucker I'm sent there for.

Song- Sleep Token, Sugar

I can't fucking sleep. The voices plaguing my mind won't shut up. Usually, I don't care, I welcome them.

Now, I know what I have to do and I feel like I'm about to rip my only source of happiness away from myself.

A sacrifice I'm not ready for and I know Lara isn't either. But it's the only way.

Brushing her hair away from her face as she sleeps

soundly with her head resting on my chest. I wonder if she can feel my heart pounding.

"Alexei." Her voice is almost a whimper. That raises my brow and sends blood rushing to my cock.

Gently, I run my index finger along her scarred cheek, but her eyes stay closed, her breathing is still heavy.

Interesting.

I do wonder how she'd taste when she's dreaming.

Sliding my arm from under her, she rolls onto her back. Jesus, fuck, she's beautiful. I can't resist. Leaning in, I start peppering wet kisses along her jaw, as she tips her head to the side, I work my way down the column of her neck.

So responsive to me, even in her dreams.

"Do you need some help waking up, pchelka?" I whisper in her ear.

Her body shivers against me.

Just tracing the tip of my finger between her breasts makes her back arch slightly off the bed and her lips part.

So I keep going, lightly brushing the skin all the way down, and as I reach her hips, her legs spread for me.

'Mmmm." She breathes out.

I reposition myself, being careful to keep quiet as I do, my hands grab the inside of her thighs and push them wider as I sink lower. Running the tip of my tongue along her pussy, she's already wet for me. I watch as her hands float up and land by her head on the pillow. So, I slide mine along her stomach and grab a handful of her breast, rolling her perky nipple between two fingers as I suck on her clit.

I keep it slow and sweet, sweet just like she is on my tongue.

Her hips start to roll in rhythm with me, I slide a finger inside her tight cunt.

"Shit." She sucks in a breath, turning her head into the pillow.

I don't want her awake yet. I don't want that until my dick is being strangled by her. That's the perfect wake up call, being fucked into consciousness.

And what a way to say goodbye.

"Such a good girl for me, aren't you?"

"Hmmm."

A little sleepy smile plays over her lips as she stretches, pushing her pussy back into my face.

I give her what she needs, eating her out until I notice her legs quivering next to my head.

Before she can fully wake, I sit up, licking the taste of her from my lips then lining my cock up with her entrance. Leaning over her, holding my weight on my forearm, I slide in, inch by inch.

Her mouth opens and I can't help it, I thrust inside her and slam my lips over hers.

"Morning, baby," I whisper against her.

"Morning," she says lazily, dragging her nails up my sides sending shivers down my spine.

Maybe I should get those tatted too. Or her name.

"More, Alexei."

She bats her lashes at me, with another thrust as deep as I can go, I grip the sides of her neck, just like how she taught me.

Giving light pressure, that sleepy look in her eyes replaced by a pure feral desire for me.

"Like this?"

She tries to nod and I squeeze tighter. As I up the pace, I kiss along her cheek, those strangled moans coming from her are like music to my ears.

I'm careful to make sure I don't clamp too hard, and I almost lose it when she digs into my back.

"Fuck, you're perfect," I grit out, pushing her knee to her chest so I can hit that spot she desperately needs.

As her moans grow louder, the harder it is to control myself.

I need her screaming my name loud enough the entire street gets woken up too.

CHAPTER 64
LARA

I LET OUT a shriek as he flips me onto my stomach, my head is fuzzy as I suck in a breath. With my head buried in the pillow, I'm soaked for him, I can feel it dripping down my thighs as he caresses my ass cheeks.

"Fuck me, Alexei." I hardly recognize my own voice. It's full of need like the little slut I am for this man.

I wiggle my hips and am rewarded with a slap that has me stifling a moan into the soft satin.

Anticipation builds in my core, I'm so close to the edge, ready to explode.

He works his hands up both my sides, his fingers dig into my skin.

"Please?"

I am so desperate for more, I could cry. My entire body is on fire and blood is pounding in my ears.

"Is this how you like waking up? Begging for my cock?" His deep Russian accent is thick with lust and it turns me on more.

"Every day if you want," I reply.

I wish he wasn't leaving me.

"Is that right? You were so fucking wet for me, were you dreaming about me?"

He pushes the tip in and it's almost a relief.

"Always,"

This right here is all I've ever wanted, just waking up next to him, calling him mine. Letting him love me the way we both crave.

He wraps my hair around his fist, yanking my head back. I swear everything is so much more heightened when you've just woken up.

"I need to hear you come for me." He sinks inside and I swear my eyes nearly roll to the back of my head.

"Gimme your wrists," he demands.

So I push my chest more into the mattress and do as he says, placing them together behind my back for him. He grabs both in one hand, pulling on my hair so my head is back up and the pain sears through my skull, but it's completely dulled by the fact he's fucking me to the point I could forget my name.

And forget what he told me last night.

With every thrust, his groans fill the room, echoed with my own moans that I can't even control.

"I said I need to hear you. I can feel your tight cunt strangling my cock, so come for me and make it loud, baby."

I'm a complete hoe for anything he tells me to do and I wouldn't have it any other way.

And I let go.

Just like he tells me to. Because with him, I am free.

My body jolts forward on the bed as he fucks me from behind, I let the violent orgasm ripple through every fiber of me. I can't see straight as my body trembles around him. But he doesn't stop, instead riding me through it leaving me gasping for air.

As he flips me onto my back, our eyes lock as he sits on

his heels and strokes his huge cock. I don't take my eyes off him, licking my lips waiting for him to tip over the edge.

I gasp as he leans forward, grabs me by the throat to sit me up, the tip of his dick between my breasts.

He tilts his head, roaring my name as the warm liquid spills all over my chest, running over my tingling nipples.

"Fuck, Lara," he groans, loosening his grip on me, bringing his face back to mine with a satisfied smirk on his lips.

Damn, he's fine.

He glimpses down at my breasts, tipping my chin up to him.

"Like a piece of fucking art,"

He softly wipes some of his cum with two fingers and hovers them in front of my lips.

"Open, taste what you do to me."

His salty flavor is on my tongue, closing my mouth around his fingers I suck him clean and swallow.

When he leans in and kisses me, the realization that this will be our last time for a while sinks in.

"Let's have a shower, get cleaned up and then have some breakfast together?" he asks, running his thumb along my jaw.

"Sounds good." I'm not hungry. I'll eat so he doesn't worry. I can't have him losing concentration because of my damn issues.

"Good girl." He drops another kiss on my lips making me melt against him.

"I'm going to miss this," I whisper.

"Me too. I'll be back before you know it, I'm sure of it."

That's the worst part.

We are all left in the dark, we have no control over this. Only that bitch, Tatiana, does.

And if she hurts my Alexei, I'll hunt her down myself.

CHAPTER 65

ALEXEI

I'VE NEVER BEEN nervous flying before. I don't think it's the being in the air part, it's the getting farther from Lara bit that's really fucking with me.

This is the first job I've ever had my doubts about. But I'm determined to get to Kirill, kill that asshole, and get the hell out of Russia in no time.

"You remember the coordinates I'll pick you up?" Mikhail's calm voice cuts into the headphones.

Nodding, I pull the door open, filling the cabin with the violent rush of freezing air.

"Alexei? Did you hear me?" Mikhail points his finger at his earpiece.

Shit, I always forget. "Yes. I got it. Death and destruction, then escape. I'll be there."

"I'll check back at eleven pm every night for three days. If you don't make it back, I can't stay any longer. We'll have to figure out something else." His deep grumble echoes into my ears.

There's no chance that will happen. It's too important that I get back home. Whatever little errand Tatiana has for me won't take long.

I'll make sure of it.

But just in case I don't make it, I need to ask him a favor. "Tell Lara, I love her and I'll be back for her."

"Excuse me?" His head whips around, then back to his instruments.

"I'm doing this for her. Don't ask questions, don't give her shit, just look after my girl."

"Alexei, are you high? You never worry about failure." His hand waves out to emphasize his point.

My chest hurts knowing I may never see her again. "No. I'm in love with her, Mikhail. Obsessively, deeply, madly, I'll die for her. Fuck, I might not make it out of here."

There's a pause before he replies. "What aren't you telling me? What did you do?"

I chew on my lip watching the ground move so far beneath us. "What I had to. I have to keep her safe."

"What is Tatiana making you do?" Anger seeps out of Mikhail's mic.

"Not a clue." I laugh. "But I'll figure this shit out."

"Motherfucker."

"Just go, Ivan can't get to you. Keep Lara safe. Trust me for once? I'm not as dumb as you think. Not when it comes to her." I pull off the headset, hang it on the hook by the door, and jump.

A series of cryptic texts have led me to this tiny town on the edge of a forest. Frost eats into the edges of the windshield on this piece of shit car I stole.

Why can't they have a decent heater? Who owns a vehicle in Russia without a way to stay warm?

I did them a favor. Maybe now they will get something better.

What does that flimsy plastic sign say? Carnival?

Sure. Might as well find something sweet to eat while I wait on the next message telling me where to go.

I pull this crappy sedan onto a grassy field where everyone else is parked. The plants have a thin layer of frost on them that's been trampled away by the many footsteps leading towards the festivities.

But the smell of pastries and fried foods draws me. It makes me miss Lara.

She should be here with me to experience the fair. The sights and sounds.

To eat all of the delicious treats that there are to indulge in.

If she would.

Winding my way through the bundled crowds, I dodge kids weaving between legs and young couples kissing by the game booths.

I'm jealous. It should be us darting behind the action.

When I'm standing in line for a pile of cookies, my phone vibrates in my pocket.

UNKNOWN

He's wearing a blue parka carrying a pink butterfly

What?

Kirill is here?

I'm still getting my snack. I've been waiting for almost ten minutes for those snickerdoodles.

Pictures are the only way I know what he looks like, I've never actually crossed paths with this guy before.

So tonight will be fun.

There's a pink toy. Oh, it's some sort of princess.

Maybe I should get one for Elena and Maeve after I'm done here? Depends on what Tatiana has planned for me next.

Blue jacket?

No beard. He always has a trimmed one in all of the shots I've seen.

Wait.

I think that's him.

He's standing near the line for the Ferris wheel.

Every plan has led to this moment.

How many months have we been tracking him, only to have him slip through our fingers?

All this time, I just needed Tatiana. I thought Enzo was a god for being able to locate people.

But she's the queen at it.

Empress?

Devil. She barters for the soul in exchange.

What did I sell to get put here with him? This won't be a light payment.

I move next to him and grip my pistol in my jacket. "Next?"

His distracted gaze lands on me. "Um, no. Go ahead."

"Here, have a cookie." I hold out one of them and watch the look of confusion flush across his face.

Crumbling it into my fist, I snap my knuckles forward and hit him right between the eyes.

His pink butterfly falls to the ground as he stumbles backwards, but I grab him before he takes another step.

"I'm Alexei, and I'm here because of Lara Volkov. You fucked up my friend." I drag him close and jab the barrel of my pistol into his ribs.

The people gathered nearby don't seem to have noticed the small scuffle.

Good.

"Let's go for a little ride, eh?" I tug on his elbow and direct him to the loading area of the Ferris wheel.

"Two?" asks the bored attendant.

"Go on, pay the nice man." I encourage Kirill with another poke from my pistol.

Sweat beads on his temple as he hands over a few bills before letting me push him into the rocking carriage.

"Hey, buddy? I'll give you ten thousand Ruble if you let us stop at the top for a while?" I whisper to the short operator.

His squinty eyes narrow. "Prove it."

"Five thousand now." I slap the money into his palm and watch a smile pull up his pimply cheek.

"Deal." He grins, stuffing the cash into his shirt pocket.

"Shit," Kirill mutters.

He moves where I push him, folding himself into the metal seat. "What do you want?" He tries to hold himself as far away from me as possible.

"To eat dessert. And go for a ride." I gesture at the massive machine we're sitting in. "Enjoy yourself. You've earned this."

"Who was the stuffed bug for?" I ask as I push another bite into my mouth.

"My daughter, you fuck," he growls, just as the ride begins to move.

We rock in rhythm to the jerky movements of the archaic motor.

"Isn't this beautiful?" I spill crumbs on my shirt as we slowly climb into the sky. The last of the evening sun glistens over the treetops, catching the frost already spreading over their branches. "You know what I'd rather be doing?" I reach my arm around his shoulders, snugging him against me.

He shakes his head.

"I'd rather be holding my girl and kissing her unscarred cheek." I press the nail of my finger into the matching spot on his face. "Don't get me wrong, I love her with all of the things that make her unique. But you see, she didn't have a very good time when you did that to her."

She nearly died. I would have too, without her.

Kirill just grunts.

"Oh, you don't have anything nice to say about that? How about my best friend's wife, the one you sliced and diced her brother apart? Remember? Do you?" I pull back the firing pin on my gun, making sure he hears it.

His Adam's apple bobs as he swallows hard. "Of course."

"You deserve much worse," I say quietly and pull out another cookie. "I don't even want to share these with you. That's how shitty you are." I let the sugar melt over my tongue as our swinging seat reaches the top.

"You'd have done nothing different in my position." He stares out over the forest, clasping his hands on his lap.

"Wrong. I tie up loose ends. That's where you messed up. You let me hold her when she cried, and let the fury of hell soak into my shirt with her tears." I dig my fingers into the back of his neck and lean in until my lips almost brush his ear. "So now you have a choice. Sit here like a dog and take a bullet to the face, or take a leap of faith that you'll live with only a broken leg."

Before he makes a sound, he pushes himself up into the chair and steps off the edge.

But as his foot clears the lip, I grab his ankle, twisting him in his fall so his head plummets towards the earth first.

The scream echoes through the park making people look.

His blue coat billows around him while his arms churn trying to right himself.

I've jumped out of a lot of planes, and fallen a million miles.

That won't work.

There's a dull thud when he lands, followed by more shrieks of terror from the crowd.

People splinter off in every direction from him, and I take the chance and climb out of the seat too.

Gripping the steel bar, I let myself slide down until I land on the giant sprocket in the center of the great wheel, then shimmy onto a horizontal one.

It's only a short drop to the next, and within seconds I'm hopping down onto the platform at the bottom.

Everyone is so distracted by the growing pool of blood around Kirill's splintered skull, no one seems to notice me slipping through the crowd.

"Hey. You promised."

Well, one person caught me. The attendant stands in front of me with his palm out, the same bored look still dulling his features.

"Here's a little extra to forget what I look like." I wink and hand him a wad of bills.

Would I have liked to have Kirill tied to a frame to torture for days?

Sure.

But I want to get back to Lara and be the one to tell her I killed her boogeyman.

Now it's time to find that piece of shit sedan and go to the airfield where Mikhail is meeting me.

Except my phone dings with a text.

CHAPTER 66

LARA

WHY HAVEN'T I heard from him?

I can't think, I can't even function without knowing he's safe.

The first night isn't awful. Nikolai is letting me stay here with him, so at least there's Elena to keep me occupied.

Him and Mila are busy with preparing for their newborn. I've been so wrapped up in my own head and Alexei, it was almost a shock when I got called to look after Elena.

Mila has the cutest little baby bump i've ever seen, you'd hardly know she was pregnant.

"Aunt Lara? Will you color with me?" She tugs on my hand before I've barely opened my eyes.

"Yes, sweetie. What time is it?" Groggily, I lean over and pick up my phone.

No messages and it's six am.

I fucking hate this.

"I dunno. Daddy and Mila are still sleeping. I don't want to go in their room." She smiles and holds up a finger to her lips. "So we can be quiet and draw princesses?"

"That sounds like so much fun. Can you give me just a

few minutes to get up and dressed? Do you want any cereal?"
I fling back my comforter and swing my legs over the edge of
the bed.

It feels strange to wake up without Alexei. I've gotten
used to him being there.

What if he doesn't come back?

Pain digs through my chest at the thought. No. I can't
always imagine the worst.

But it's hard not to.

"Oh, the chocolate kind?" Her eyes widen excitedly.

My father's words echo in my ears from when he caught
me with a candy bar when I was barely her age.

I won't be that person for her.

"Sure, the little pink bowl? Maybe you can split some
strawberries with me too? I love those in the morning." I try
to give her a grin as I lie to her.

I never want to eat early.

That's when I do my best on the treadmill.

And hopefully suggesting the tiniest container for her will
limit the sugary stuff.

I wish someone had taught me better habits when I was
younger. Life would have been so much easier.

She carries her breakfast and I have the berries to head to
her room.

I don't know what time my brother and his wife normally
get up, but I'm certainly not disturbing them.

"Aunt Lara? Are you gonna have any kids for me to play
with?" Elena asks as she colors a purple butterfly.

I wasn't expecting that.

"I'm not sure. It's a very important decision that Alexei
and I would have to talk about." I'm working on a blue
dragon sitting on a castle.

I don't think it would be good for me to be pregnant, I
don't know if I would cope well. It's not fair on any of us to
go through that.

Elena giggles. "You and Alexei? That would make funny looking babies."

My stomach rolls. She thinks I'm ugly?

"Why would you think that?" I try to downplay it, but it hurts.

"They might have a silver tooth when they're born like him." She grins widely, pointing to her missing front one. "Maybe when mine grows in it will be gold?"

Dropping her crayon, she digs through her box for a bright yellow one. "Like this." She scribbles over the face of the sun.

That isn't nearly as bad as what I thought she meant.

"That's very pretty, I love it!" Why do I always think the worst?

A light knock on the door frame startles me.

Nikolai stands there, crossing his arms over his chest. "Mikhail called."

I think my heart triples its rate. "Yes?"

"He said he got Alexei dropped in, and will be heading to the pickup zone tonight." He shrugs his shoulders. "Sounded like everything went as planned."

Except I still haven't heard from him. "Is he out of cell range?"

Nikolai wipes his hand over his face. "I have no idea. Alexei doesn't tell me shi—" He glances down at his daughter. "—anything anymore." He shakes his head. "I'm making coffee, want some?"

"No thanks." I don't want to tell him I've already passed my calories for this morning with the three strawberries I ate.

Wait. Alexei's diet plan says that I can. It allows for both.

I like not having to worry. "Actually, that sounds nice, thank you."

Nikolai nods and disappears down the hall.

"I wish your daddy knew more about what Alexei is doing." I try to focus back on the outline in front of me.

"What is he doing?" Elena doesn't look up as she reaches over and pops a berry in her mouth.

"He's paying for saving me." And risking everything to do it.

CHAPTER 67

ALEXEI

"Why did I have to drive all of the way out here? A phone call would have worked." It took an entire tank of fuel in that shitty car with no heater.

I'm freezing.

Tatiana is bundled so completely, I can only see her eyes through the thick ruff of fur framing her face. "I know you got what you came for, crazy man. Now it's time you pay up."

I hold out my palms. "What is it, money? I have that."

The heat of her laughter makes a fog around her head. "Funny man. No. I want to introduce you to your new lawyer." Her black gloved finger points to a beast of a man who is leaning against the door of her SUV.

When he straightens, I'm almost positive he's bigger than even Mikhail.

Fuck.

"What do I need a lawyer for? I did nothing wrong." Well, except one or two teensy tiny killings.

But they deserved it.

Especially those jerks who treated Lara bad on their dates. It's like they were begging to die. Eh. A few of them did by the time I was done with them.

"Oh, Alexei. You're so adorable." Tatiana reaches forward and reaches up like she's going to stroke my cheek.

But then her fingers wrap around my chin and squeeze. "You're going to prison for murder. And Drago here is going to make sure that you get put into the maximum security wing."

I jerk my head out of her grasp. "The fuck I am. Absolutely not." I can't leave Lara.

Russian jails are death camps.

"Tisk, tisk. It would be a shame if your little girlfriend ended up captured all over again. Do you think she could handle it?" Tatiana pulls out a cigarette and places it through a slit in her mask before lighting it.

The smoke hangs in the cold air in a languid dance.

It's like time freezes.

I don't want Lara to ever experience that trauma again. I know she struggled before, but that has made her wake up with nightmares that even I have a hard time consoling her from.

Damn this world.

"Fine." My exhale swirls the steady smoke.

"See? You may be crazy, but I know you're smart. That's what I need once you're in there." She takes a long drag of her cigarette. "You're going to kill an untouchable man. And it will take everything you have to survive long enough to do it."

Her eyes narrow as she points to me with the burning ember. "Fail? Your girl belongs to me."

Son of a bitch. I'm so fucked.

"Fine. I'll do it. Then we're even?" I need to get Mikhail to get me the hell out of here.

Her head tips back in a full laugh. "You're hysterical. Of course we'll be even. I'm sorry this will be the last time we'll get to see each other." She twirls her fingers in the air.

Three men swarm me before I can pull my pistol, pinning my arms to my sides.

Drago steps closer as Tatiana crawls into the heat of her car.

I'm jealous. I'm freezing.

At least these brutes are warming me up a little as they almost break my elbows forcing my hands out.

Heavy handcuffs fall over my wrists before I get pushed into the back of his SUV.

"Don't worry, Alexei," Drago says as he gets behind the wheel. "I'll make sure to use a fake name so your friends won't know about your tarnished reputation."

I try to shift my weight enough to feel if my phone is still in my back pocket. I have to get a message to Mikhail.

"Useless," one of the heavily jowled men next to me mutters. "I have your cell already. I'll be jacking off to your girlfriend's pictures tonight." His grin reveals a wall of silver teeth.

I slam my forehead into his mouth as hard as I can in the short space.

The scream and rush of blood spraying down my face is worth the backhand from the other guard.

"At least the whole time your throbbing nose will remind you of me." I try to reach for my device in his flailing hands, but I can't reach with the other asshole pinning my arms.

Fuck.

Drago turns around with a scowl. "Just drug him. He doesn't need to enjoy the scenery."

"No! No! No—" A needle pierces my neck.

I try to fight it, but the world fades into black.

My head hurts.

So does my back.

Where the hell am I? There's so many voices, they turn into a low hum.

Shit. I remember.

I'm afraid to open my eyes. It stinks like body odor and onions.

Fucking Tatiana. I don't even know who I'm supposed to kill here.

Maybe it was all a trick just to get me caught.

Rubbing my temples doesn't help the pain to fade, but I open my eyes anyways.

Well, at least I'm alone. There's a bunk above me with the mattress folded over so I can see the ceiling.

The bed is hard as nails. I miss mine already. No, I miss Lara's. That's where I'd rather be. Snuggling her on the downy pillows, pressing my naked body against her.

Not here in this frigid cell in a fucking gulag.

I know the stories. I've been lucky enough to avoid jail. Mikhail helped keep me out.

There may have been once or twice I should have gone.

Looking through the bars, a row of men stare back from the other side of the corridor. One grins without teeth, his bare gums smacking wetly.

How do I find out who the target is?

I have to at least pretend that is my purpose.

This sucks so incredibly much.

Then my door slides open with a loud buzzer.

"Mess number three." A staticy voice blares over a speaker.

I watch two rows of cells open on both sides of the hall.

Food?

Everyone shuffles out forming lines towards a big set of double barriers. I fall behind a short hunched man with a wave of matted gray hair.

A fist drives between my shoulder blades, nearly crumpling me to the concrete.

Maybe that is the man I'm supposed to end?

As I fall, I sweep my leg behind me and take him out at the ankles.

With a grunt, he falls backwards, bouncing his head on the hard floor.

Before anyone stops me, I leap onto his chest and gouge my thumbs into his eyes until they give.

With a scream, he bucks his hips and throws me off, his palms covering his empty sockets as he rolls back and forth.

"That's what you get for getting me when I didn't see it." I step over his leg and fall back into place behind the old prisoner.

I'm nearly into the cafeteria when two guards trot by with a stretcher carried between them.

One gives me a subtle glare, but they don't say a word.

I didn't do anything wrong. Just fought back.

Soundlessly, the old man picks up a metal tray and then points at the stack, his wrinkled face turning to glance at me.

Following his cue, I pick one up and slide it onto the rails like him.

His gnarled finger jabs at the array of questionable foods behind the plexiglass screen and tucks his dish under the narrow gap at the bottom.

Green, purple, and brown slop get dropped in the cavities of my tray before I pull it back.

What the shit is this?

Is this edible?

There's a bin of round wooden spoons near the end that the old hunched figure grabs out of.

Monkey see. I get one too.

He seems nice enough, so I follow along behind him, passing the glares of the other prisoners.

Not sure what the fuck I did to make them mad.

I don't really care.

The age-spotted hand reaches out again and points to a spot on one of the long benches by the table.

There's a large empty circle around us, like everyone is too afraid to sit close.

Is it me, or the old man?

"Are you going to shank me over this dog food?" I ask him quietly once I'm facing him.

I don't know if I can even swallow this shit.

He squints dark eyes watching me drip the runny stuff off my spoon. "You don't want to waste that." His voice is as torn and ragged as the collar of his outfit.

With a shaking hand, he pulls some to his own lips, then nods at my tray.

"Why isn't anyone messing with you?" I whisper before choking down the first bite.

It tastes like rat piss.

The tattered sweater around his shoulders raises and lowers as he shrugs. "They know me."

By the third or fourth mouthful, the expectation of flavor is less.

He's right, I'll need the nutrition. I wish I had something sweet.

What I'd give to have Lara's candy jar here.

No, I'd rather have her. But sure as hell nowhere close to this place.

Damn. I have to figure out how to get out of here.

"Why are you helping me?" I ask him as I look past and see a hulking figure glaring.

His spoon stops halfway to his chin, but he doesn't raise his head.

After a long pause, he slurps the gruel from the narrow curve before it lowers back to his plate. "I was young once, and knew many people. There was a particularly cruel one that I remember well." He takes a slow nibble before his dark eyes meet mine. "He looked an awful lot like you."

CHAPTER 68

LARA

The smell of fresh espresso fills the foyer when the double doors slide open. Cool air blows over me as I push out of the Vegas heat.

I'm tempted to stop and get one of the sweet drinks to help soothe my nerves, but it isn't on the diet plan Alexei and I came up with.

Pain rips through me at the thought of him.

I haven't heard a word, and it's been days.

The ride up to Mikhail's office is the longest it's ever taken. It has me almost running down the hall once I'm on the fourth floor.

Bursting into his office, I can barely contain my irritation. "Why didn't you reply to my texts? Why didn't you call?"

I've been hanging on every update hoping to hear how Alexei is doing. Well, Mikhail too, but I know Alexei is the one in the most danger.

My brother looks up from his desk with sadness tinging his eyes. "I wish I had something to tell you. I couldn't tell you I had nothing."

Digging my nails into my palms doesn't lessen the stabbing ache that pierces my chest. "I need to know…anything?"

This hollow emptiness inside of me, the not knowing, it's killing me.

Mikhail hangs his head and slowly shakes it. "I dropped him off five days ago. I even went back to the rendezvous another night, hoping he'd show."

Anger tries to replace the agony. "Why didn't you wait longer? He could be there right now, maybe hurt, needing you." Before I realize it, I've stepped across the room and am pounding my fist on his desk. "Please? This hurts too bad."

My knees give, leaving me hanging on the edge of the oak surface.

Mikhail jumps up and wraps his arms around me. "I know, Lara. I have Enzo working his entire team trying to find him." Gently, he turns me towards the couch and sits me next to him.

The tears finally fall, but it doesn't help. "I miss him."

That isn't anywhere close to the mark. I don't know if I'll be able to live without him.

He keeps me steady. His patience supports me when I stumble without wavering.

I'm going to shatter without him.

"Can't you go back? Look again?" I sniffle.

"You know Ivan keeps a close watch. Would you want me to be captured also? Let Enzo do what he does best, find things out." Mikhail's broad hand pulls me in for another hug before he stands. "You don't need to come to work, Lara. I know this is hard on you."

"It's the only thing keeping me sane. I would be going crazy at home." I'd probably hit thirty miles on my treadmill a day if I was left to my own devices.

He nods. "I get it. Okay, want to help me go over some surveillance? I want to see if Kirill came back into the country or if he's still here. I'm worried that Tatiana fed Alexei bad intel." He gestures at his computer. "It'll keep us busy. There's at least a month's worth here to check."

CHAPTER 69
ALEXEI

THE THIN PASTE gets stuck in my throat, making me choke. "What?" I cough. "That's why you're helping me?"

With narrowed eyes, the old man peers at me. "Let's just say, finding out he was killed was one of the best days." He drops his spoon and stands with his empty tray, carrying it to a table near the locked door to the kitchen.

His crooked finger points to a forming line near the exit where he stands silently.

How did he know my father? Were they friends? It didn't seem like it.

Who is he?

So many questions that I know better to ask close enough to all of these other prisoners.

At least I made it through my first meal. I wasn't sure that would happen.

I watch him raise his arm and gesture at a pair of men moving towards the line.

They both nod and separate. One takes his place in front of the old man, the other moves behind me.

Is this a trap?

"Are you tricking me?" I growl in his ear.

A heavy palm flattens on my shoulder. "Any friend of the Butcher of Buresk is a friend of ours."

The words send an icy chill down my spine.

Everyone knows the stories. It happened before I left Russia almost ten years ago.

This is him?

No wonder everyone avoids him.

The carnage he caused was the stuff of legends. He wiped an entire town off the map.

What the fuck?

I'm going to roll with it. His reputation might keep me alive.

A gust of cool wind billows over us, but we start to move forward.

Heavily armored guards flank us from above while we trudge outside into the frosty exercise yard.

Everyone splits into smaller groups veering off to different locations. Some move towards heavy rocks where they start lifting them, others jog the perimeter of the fence.

I'm sticking close to my new lucky charm, and pull my shirt tighter around my chest.

It's too damn cold out here, so I start bouncing from side to side to stay warm.

I can get a better look at the two men who guard the Butcher. They look eerily alike.

"Are you brothers?" I think they could even be twins.

They both nod.

One with his head shaved stabs his thumb to his chest. "I'm Sven. That's Ben." He points to the other who has his greasy brown hair tucked behind his ears.

"You work for him?" I jut my chin towards the grizzled man sitting on one of the wood benches bolted to the ground.

"No," replies Ben. "We owe him our lives." He crosses his arms over his massive chest.

They remind me of Niki and Miki in size.

"That's a twist." I find it hard to believe that small old man could be their hero.

I guess I shouldn't underestimate him.

"Did you really take out that whole town?" I ask the question that's weighing heaviest. I have a million more, though.

The Butcher nods. "They killed my daughter. It was the least I could do," he says quietly.

Oh shit.

"They caught you after that?" I can't even fathom how.

He shakes his head. "No, I let myself be caught a few years ago. Ivan fucking took my youngest, and sent an army after me." He sweeps his arm in a slow circle at the exercise yard. "At least in here, he can't touch me."

"Volkov?" I swallow hard.

It seems we have a common enemy.

The Butcher's whiskered lips thin. "That son of a bitch is almost as bad as your father."

I catch myself unconsciously touching my mouth, remembering all the times Papa split it open in his anger.

"You know, I almost killed him once." He leans back and stares at the gray sky. "You were very young. I had the barrel of my gun pressed against his head because he slaughtered one of my best whores." His tongue runs across his teeth and his eyes unfocus.

"You should have," I grumble.

All these memories come stirring back. The pain, the fear. The hatred.

He runs his fingers through his silver hair. "You had no one else."

All I had was a monster.

Until Nikolai and Mikhail took pity on me, and gave me Lara.

I have to get out of here.

The time in the yard is signaled to an end by a loud siren. Everyone lines up, our personal bouncers included.

It's a long walk back to my cell where I go in to huddle alone.

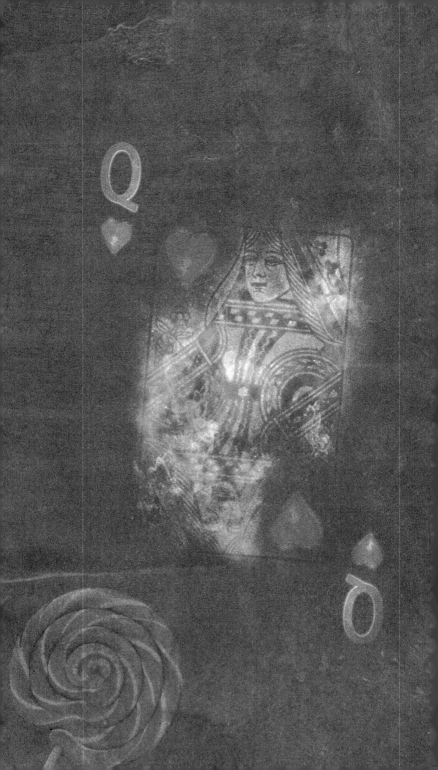

CHAPTER 70
LARA

"I CAN'T BE HERE ANYMORE." Seeing my brother so happy with Mila is killing me with a thousand tiny cuts.

"I know something will turn up." Nikolai runs his fingers through his hair as his jaw ticks. "We'll find him, Lara."

The rage that has festered in me since Alexei first disappeared wells up and explodes from me. "Stop lying to me!" I scream.

It feels like my heart is going to burst in pain. There's a knot that tightens around my chest and doesn't let me breathe.

"Lara," he says quietly. "You really think we'd just let him go?"

That knocks the wind out of me, and I slump to the bed with my half-filled bag clutched in my hands. "I can't."

I've never felt this much ache before.

Hollow.

Lost.

Why is it so different now? This isn't the first time Alexei has been missing.

But it's never been like this between us before.

With him, I felt whole, complete.

Now, I'm shattered all over.

How do I live without him?

"We won't. Enzo is searching for him. Mikhail thinks they might have found where he was at his last contact." Nikolai stands at the door, leaning against the frame.

That's all it will be known as.

Last contact.

It's how we'll all remember Alexei.

"It's been ten days, Nikolai. He would have found a way by now." I stuff the last of my clothes into my small duffel and zip it. "I just want to go. I'll be at Alexei's house if you need me. I'm getting tired of going back and forth to check on his birds."

At least Sheila and Bruce won't ask me constantly how I feel.

Numb.

"I get it. But are you sure? You know you're always welcome here." Nikolai's voice trails off.

"I know. Thank you. Really. It was fun to hang out with Elena. I'm just ready for some quiet time." Slinging the strap to my satchel over my shoulder, I brush past him and down the stairs.

This will be better. Space away from everyone.

Alexei will come back, right?

I'll get his house cleaned up for him. It's been a chore to make it over to check on the flamingos, but if I'm there it will be easier.

But will I be able to be there, with his things all over, and not shut down?

Only one way to find out.

CHAPTER 71

ALEXEI

HOW MANY DAYS? Fourteen? Twenty? I've lost track.

All I know is that if I kill everyone in here, I'll be able to get out.

But who do I start with?

The Volenski gang would rip me to shreds. And there's probably thirty of them.

Cell block D has their own little group going, I won't start there either.

Maybe the outcasts in A wing. I can off them one at a time and hope I get lucky and get who Tatiana wanted.

I doubt that deal is real. She tricked me to get me sent away.

I can't remember what Lara's perfume smells like any more. The scents of body odor and shit fill my nose every day, blocking out any good memories I have.

This is where I'll die.

I'll never see her again. If I do, I'm not letting her go.

I'm in hell, and I want out.

Rubbing the spoon I stole against the rough concrete, I manage to whittle it down to a point.

I'll start with that fucker Petri. He throws rocks at me

outside whenever I step away from the Butcher and the twins.

Fuck, it broke.

I guess I'll have to get creative.

The heavy door slides open signaling lunchtime. Damn.

When I step in line, the familiar back of the Butcher is missing.

This isn't what I was expecting.

I sneak a movement forward, and see the huddled form under the blanket on his cot.

Without thinking, I rush in to him.

"Are you okay?" My palm flattens over his shoulder.

This man has protected me from day one. He's never asked for anything in return.

Now, he's lying here shivering under the thin cover.

"Cold." His teeth chatter.

Instinctively, I reach down and touch his hand.

"You're burning up with a fever." Shit.

I jump up and nearly collide with the first of two guards striding in.

"What the fuck are you doing?" He asks.

"He's sick. I was coming to find you." I hold my wrists out and stand still, like I've been taught.

The second moves closer and drops the end of his Billy club to nail me in the gut. "No one touches him," he growls through his face shield.

What? Are the guards protecting him too? Or is that why no one will mess with him?

"He's fine." The Butcher waves the uniformed man away from me.

Holy shit, that worked.

In moments, two more guys with a stretcher appear and whisk the old man away.

Sven and Ben wait for me in the main corridor.

"He wanted us to keep you safe." Sven cracks his knuckles as his brother nods.

"Does that mean I'm the king now?" I grin at them.

We've become pretty good friends.

Sven is the Butcher's enforcer, and I've seen him fight.

I'm glad he's on my side. I bet he'd give Jax a run for his money.

Damn. Jax feels like a distant memory, it's been so long stuck in here.

Lara is the only solid thing I can hope to live for.

Ben grabs my shoulder and squeezes. "There will be trouble. We may need to fight."

I tighten my fist and my smile gets wider. "That's what I'm hoping for."

CHAPTER 72
LARA

A MONTH?

I swear the only reason I'm alive is to keep these birds healthy. Mikhail told me to take as much time as I need, and I am.

When was the last time I went to work? Two weeks ago?

I can't remember.

It's harder to pay attention without Alexei here.

He would keep me on task. Always with which show he wanted us to watch, or which concert to go to.

Now, there's nothing.

A blank schedule, and an empty bed.

With a hollow heart.

He was the only one for me. He accepted me for all my faults.

There won't be another.

It takes most of my energy, but I pull one of Alexei's downy white comforters from his bed out onto the day sofa near the glass door overlooking the veranda.

I can watch the flamingos from here.

Do they have enough food?

They should. I think I checked this morning.

Or, last night?

My head is fuzzy. I'm just so tired. I think I'll take a little nap and then make sure they're okay.

Curling the pillow closer, I struggle to smell Alexei on it anymore.

Is that how long a memory lingers? Only a month?

I let my tears stain the satin. Might as well let the pain replace him.

It's the only thing that can.

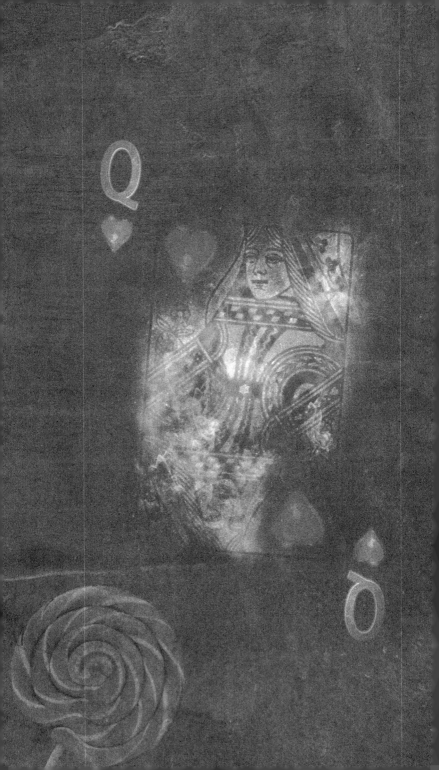

CHAPTER 73

ALEXEI

My foot lands on Misha's face again. "I told you, *I'm in charge now*," I yell into his ear.

Ben pins his feet to keep him from kicking out.

"You smuggle shit in, and don't give me a cut, very bad things happen." I grind my heel into his cheek before I pull away.

"I'm sorry, Alexei. It won't happen again," Misha whines from beneath me.

Sven had suggested taking over with a heavy hand.

I had no idea how far I'd have to push to maintain control.

A murmur ripples through the onlookers as I let Misha stand.

Wait, they aren't looking my way.

"What's going on?" I ask Sven.

He shrugs his broad shoulders then stands on his toes to see over the heads of the rest of the prisoners.

"He's back," Sven grunts, waving at us to follow him.

As I follow him, I try to jump to see over his massive back.

On one jump, I get a glimpse of gray hair and a hunched figure.

There was a part of me worried it was the big bastard whose eyes I gouged out.

I heard he got sent away.

"Boss, it's good to see you again." Ben moves to the side, opening a path for the Butcher to wobble to the row of benches.

"Alexei," the old man steps closer. "I'm glad to see you're still alive." A small smile plays over his silver whiskered lips. "I've heard you're keeping everyone in line?"

"Yep. Was a little touch and go at first, but I managed." I shrug. The blackened eye I got on the second day is nearly healed.

He pats my arm. "Good. You can take over for me when I'm gone." Turning, his fist covers his mouth as he coughs.

"What are you talking about?" I try to look into his eyes, but he turns his head.

"Prisoner five-three-eight-two!" One of the guards calls over the crowd.

Shit, that's my number.

"Here!" I yell as I push my way through the parting bodies.

The others are careful not to touch me while I work my way to the guards.

"Your lawyer is here," he says gruffly and motions for me to hold out my hands for the cuffs.

"I don't have one." I keep my arms still, but I'm thoroughly confused.

Maybe it's Mikhail? Did Enzo find me?

"This way." The head guard turns on his heel and leads me inside.

Following the uniformed back and surrounded by other armed men, we go through a long cold hall to a glassed room with a steel table in the center.

The chain between my restraints gets fed into a lock on the edge by my chair.

As soon as I'm fastened, the opposing door opens and a hulking figure steps through, temporarily blocking the light behind him with his size.

Oh.

That fucker.

"Hello, Alexei." Drago drops a leather briefcase on the metal surface as he sits in front of me.

"You aren't my lawyer," I say flatly.

He's the last person I wanted to see.

"I am today. I'm your only hope of escape." He points one of his darkly tattooed fingers at me. "I learned recently who your friends are."

Why does he look almost remorseful?

"What about them?" I growl. I want to get out of here, so I might listen.

"I didn't know you were friends with the Volkov's. Mikhail saved my life. I owe him everything." His icy blue eyes narrow as he gazes at some spot over my head.

He shakes off whatever memory he was reliving and stares at me. "So I'm going to help you."

"I don't believe you."

His palms turn up. "I get it, I apologize. Tatiana has had to work with, well, bottom feeders sometimes. I thought you were one of them."

"What are you going to do?" I'm starting to believe him.

Do I dare?

"I have the name she wants you to eliminate." He smiles smugly.

Like that's my only problem living in a prison full of people who hate me.

"So, afterwards, you get me out?" I hope it's Misha. I hate that guy.

"I'll do my best." His brows knit in a solemn expression.

Can I trust him? If I'm seen killing someone, I'll be tossed into isolation for the rest of my life.

I guess that means I shouldn't get caught.

"Okay. Who am I supposed to take out?" I don't think I have any choice but to try.

Any chance more than zero is worth doing if I can ever hope to see Lara again.

"His name is Vanos Pushkrov," Drago whispers before looking through the glass at the guards.

I try to go through all of the names of the assholes I've had run-ins with here. I don't think I've crossed that name yet.

Drago must see my confusion, because he leans across the heavy table and gestures at me to move closer. "He's also known as the Butcher of Buresk."

Cold sweat runs down my spine making me shiver.

"No." My answer comes instinctively.

That man has kept me alive, protected me, and taught me the ways in here.

He's more of a father than my own ever was.

"There has to be a mistake." I can't do it.

Drago shakes his head. "That man ruined Tatiana's life. Believe me, he deserves it."

What the fuck? Was her family slaughtered by him?

I've only heard snippets of the rage he brought down on that town.

Damn.

What the hell do I do?

CHAPTER 74
LARA

"Lara? Are you in here?" I can hear Sofia, but I'm too tired to want to talk.

Her footsteps ring through the front room getting closer.

I should tell her I'm okay, I just don't have the energy to.

"Hey, there you are! Mikhail asked Jax if I could check in on you. How are you doing?" She flicks her maroon hair over her shoulder before sitting on the end of the couch near me.

It's only after a moment I catch the smell of something garlicky and savory coming from the bag in her hand.

"I'm fine." My belly growls in argument.

"I brought you some stew. I figured you wouldn't feel much like cooking." Her brown eyes watch me closely.

It's hard to push myself up.

Maybe I should say something mean so she'll leave?

That would also take effort.

"Thank you." I give up. Anger is exhausting.

"Lara? Are you okay? You look, well, pale." Sofia's hand rests over my covered foot. "I know you miss Alexei, but don't you want to be healthy for him when he gets back?" Her thumb moves and she squeezes me.

"He's never coming back," I say hopelessly. "It's been over a month."

The hollow ache comes back like it does every time I think about him.

It hurts so damn bad.

"And if he doesn't? Are you going to just wither and blow away?" She raises one eyebrow then opens the bag. "You need to eat something."

I don't want to be heavy when Alexei comes back.

He won't love me anymore.

I shake my head. "I'm fine, I told you that."

Her lips thin and she pops the top off of the bowl. "Eat." There isn't a waver or question in her command as she thrusts it into my lap. "I brought a spoon, too."

It does smell good.

"Just a little. I'm not very hungry." I'm starving. But I'm terrified to act like it or I'll overdo it.

Sofia frowns. "I'm not leaving until you finish it."

Whatever. Once she's gone, I can get it out of my stomach.

"And, I'm staying for at least an hour afterwards." She adds as she hands me the soup.

That irritates me. "I don't need a babysitter."

"Apparently, you do. I know what it's like to be your own worst enemy. You're not the only person who struggles with it." Sofia looks down at her knuckle before spinning her wedding ring on her finger. "Everyone has their own demons they fight. Sometimes they need help," she says quietly.

I forgot about Jax.

But this is different.

It has to be.

I can't spiral like he did. This isn't the same.

I don't want to die. I just want to be pretty enough to be worthy of love.

It just means I need to be thinner, perfect for Alexei when…if he gets back.

"Lara." Sofia gets my attention. "Please. You need to be healthy. For you, and the life you want to have."

"Maybe the best part is over." I raise my spoon to my lips and sip some of the broth.

My stomach spasms with the rich liquid. I guess it's been longer than I realized since I ate.

"I think you're wrong." Sofia tries to give me a smile, but it looks forced.

Squeezing my fist, my nails dig into my palm until the stabbing pain goes away.

Just one swallow at a time.

Before the bowl is empty, I feel a little perkier. Sofia chats nearly the entire time about her kids and her schooling.

I'm not sure why I forgot she was going into psychiatry.

"This year I have to pick my dissertation project," she sighs, leaning back into the pillows of the couch.

"What does that mean?" How did I eat the entire container? Was I really that hungry?

"I have to choose what my topic is going to be. I think I want to go with something about men's mental health and how depression affects them because of societal pressures." She turns her ring and her eyes drift to the window. "I don't think there's enough talk about it."

"That sounds very noble." I think I might be sick. My belly hurts from being so full.

"It's hard to see the people you care about suffer." She turns and pins me with a hard stare.

Is she talking about me?

CHAPTER 75
ALEXEI

THE WALK back to my cell after Drago left feels like it's miles.

But isn't long enough.

What the fuck am I supposed to do? Kill the only man who's shown me any compassion?

He may be my only protection in here.

There's a very real chance I off him, and I'm still left here to rot.

But if I don't, I'm sure to never get out.

Shit.

Frustration has me punching the concrete wall next to my bed. The pain doesn't bring any clarity, just new scars.

I squeeze my fingers and watch the blood dribble through the scuffs on my knuckles.

Am I ever going to touch Lara again? Will I get to feel the heat of her skin, the warmth of her touch?

She's worth all the risk.

How do I do this?

Tossing and turning on my thin cot all night doesn't help me come up with any kind of plan.

I guess I'll do what I do best, take advantage of the spur of the moment.

I'm dreading it.

When the cell door slides open, I take my usual place in line behind him, and follow his shuffling steps to the mess hall.

Maybe I should just choke him out right here?

In front of everyone and get tossed in a hole? No way.

Sliding my tray on the rails next to his, I wonder if a fast punch to his throat would be enough to drop him.

I fucking hate that I'm even thinking of this shit.

I can't do it today. Just the thought of it makes me nauseous.

He sits in his regular place, and I slide my tray onto the table in front of him.

I can't look at him. Guilt knocks my eyes to my gruel.

"They asked you, didn't they?" he states flatly.

"Asked what?" Shoving another spoonful of the tasteless food into my mouth, I still can't meet his gaze.

"To kill me."

The nasty breakfast threatens to come back up as my stomach churns.

"How did you know?" I'm not going to hide it from him.

He laughs softly, then takes another bite. "You aren't very good at hiding things. And you're far from the first." The white whiskers around his lips twitch as he chews. "But maybe you'll be the last."

His pale gray spoon circles in a broad gesture. "So out of all the people in here, they sent you here for me." He chuckles before scooping another bite. "I suppose I should feel honored."

"They promised me freedom if I did this." Avoiding looking at him is easy when I make little trails through the slimy oatmeal.

"Your girl misses you?" He pushes his tray away and stares at me.

"I worry about her. She needs me." My chest aches just

thinking about her. "I love her," I admit to him. I haven't talked about her much, it hurts too much.

He nods. "My reasons for living are gone. My oldest daughter was killed, then my youngest was kidnapped by that Volkov asshole." His fist clenches. "I was almost relieved to hear she died later in a fire. Better than living under his thumb." He leans back and sighs. "I'm too old for this fight. I think it's time."

"Why not Ben or Sven? They're closer to you than I am." I'm not hungry anymore.

"They are good men. Keep them close. They're too loyal to me to ask that of them." He sniffs and turns away, but not before I catch the sheen of tears in his dark eyes.

I don't know what to say. "Okay. Are you going to tell them?"

He sighs and drops his chin. "Yes, I'll make sure they know. When we're done in the yard and heading back, pick up a pebble about this big." He holds up his arthritic hand with his fingers just a fraction of an inch apart. "You'll lodge that in the locking mechanism of your door before it closes. The dead time just after lights out is the best time."

I let out a long exhale. "You've thought this through."

"When you're as old as I am, every possibility goes through your mind. I've never been the type to hang myself in my cell as so many others have. But I'm, well, tired." He pushes his tray away and leans his jaw into his hand. "Exhausted is a better word."

We both stand and start walking towards the area to stack the empty trays. "At least I know that I'll be setting someone free when I go. Love is a good reason to die." With a last touch of my shoulder, he shuffles to the exit to the outside.

How do I make it as painless as possible?

I've never had to do that before.

Wandering around the inside perimeter of the high fence, I kick rocks and mull over every option I can think of.

By the time I make it back to where the Butcher is waiting, Ben and Sven have solemn expressions.

He must have told them.

Ben nods, although his lips are thin.

At least they won't try to kill me in revenge.

The walk back to my cell is the longest it's ever been. Slipping the stone in place feels final.

I have to do this.

But I don't want to.

This is the only chance I'll have to see Lara again.

Even if it's one percent, it isn't zero.

I lay in my cot and stare at the ceiling, counting every single blemish and pock in the concrete until the heavy click of the switch signals the darkness.

Fuck. Now or never.

My door slides open soundlessly and so does his.

He's lying on his bed, watching me in the dim light.

Without a word, he holds out a whittled down toothbrush, and tilts his head back.

Why is my throat so tight and my arms so heavy?

Is this what dread feels like?

Flattening my palm over his forehead, I pull the makeshift shiv from his fingers.

I mouth the words "I'm sorry" before sinking the point into the bottom of his chin, up into his skull.

He twitches, his hand jerks against my chest, then falls limp.

Maybe I should pull it out, but I don't want to be covered in his blood.

Sneaking back to my own cell, I pull the pebble out of the lock and latch it while I cough to cover the noise.

Now, all I can do is wait for the guards to find him.

"I didn't do it! I swear!" Cries echo through the building as the guards drag Misha down the corridor.

"He didn't have his toothbrush." Sven winks at me as we watch the man getting dragged away.

We're all quiet as the yells fade.

Vanos planned well. I think I'll always call him the Butcher, though.

Sounds better.

"How soon do you find out?" Ben turns and runs his thickly tattooed fingers through his hair.

I shrug, trying to ignore the ache in my chest over what I did last night. "No idea. It might not happen at all. I might be completely fucked."

"What will you do if you can't get out?" Sven crosses his arms over the highest seat on the bench and rests his chin on them.

"Whatever we want. Vanos left us in charge. Can't let everyone fall into chaos." I grin at him and crack my knuckles.

He smiles back. "I like how you think."

"Prisoner number five-three-eight-two!" One of the biggest guards calls for me.

My stomach sinks. Do they know it was me?

"Here!" I call out and jog to him.

I guess my stay is done here either way.

"Your lawyer is here." He twirls his finger at my hands, the signal to hold out my wrists for restraints.

I bet it's Drago.

My heart beats faster. Is there a chance I'm getting out?

Following the guard, it's hard to not want to bolt past him to get there faster.

When the door opens, and Drago's huge frame is standing just outside of the secured area, I let myself get hopeful.

When he folds himself in the seat across from me, the tiniest twitch of his lip betrays him.

"I've heard that everything has been taken care of." His palms flatten on the metal table.

I want to jump up and down and scream at him to let me go.

Instead, I nod.

"I've heard that next Tuesday is going to be exciting." He pins me with his icy blue eyes in a hard stare.

Is he trying to tell me something?

"Yes?" I encourage him to continue with a dip of my chin.

"The northern lights. Explosive, even. From what I've heard, you can see the show best from the west wing at midnight." He doesn't blink.

That's the opposite end from where my cell is.

But with the little trick that the Butcher taught me about the locks, I have a chance of being there.

"I love them. Makes me feel like I'm back home." My head tilts as I watch his reaction.

His smile grows, showing the whites of his teeth.

"Until we meet again." Standing, he tosses me a subtle wink, then raps on the window with his knuckle to the guard.

I guess he isn't so bad.

It's a long ass night waiting until I'm back in the yard with the twins.

"Good news, boys. We're gonna see some fireworks. Now here's the details."

CHAPTER 76
LARA

MIKHAIL

We got word of where Alexei is.

ME

What? Where? Why hasn't he called?

MIKHAIL

He's been in Kamen Prison.

ME

WTF? For what?

MIKHAIL

I don't know the details. I have to go get him. There's a contact there who gave me the info and date.

ME

He's being released?

MIKHAIL

Not exactly...

MY HEART RACES in my ears reading his texts. I have so much to do to get ready for him to come home!

There's tons of housework, and I should buy a new dress to show him.

Running to the bathroom, I make myself lose my breakfast that Sofia made me eat into the toilet.

Catching a look at my reflection, I look the tiniest I have been in a long time, it's a shame I am so pale.

I need to clean in here too.

Weak and shaking, I look around at the mess I made.

Sheila and Bruce are taken care of, I've made a deal with the neighbor to help watch them when I'm too tired to check.

My phone vibrates with another message, but this time it's Sofia asking if I'm home and hungry.

Not anymore.

Alexei is coming back. I'll get back on his meal plan once he's here.

But for now, I have too many things to do than to have her babysit me to eat.

I know she means well, yet it's hard not to feel embarrassed sometimes that she's treating me like a child.

Well, not really.

That's probably just my perception.

I just hate being told I'm doing something wrong. What I eat is the only thing I know how to control.

Alexei is alive. I have to tamp down on my calories and get busy.

CHAPTER 77
ALEXEI

Song, Gasoline, I Prevail

Using the trick that the Butcher taught me, I wedge the lock with a pebble, then crawl into my cot to wait.

I hate it. I'd rather be doing something, anything, than nothing.

But after counting my breaths, and losing track, I know that the time has come.

Silently, I push my barred cell open and pull it shut behind me. Keeping mostly against the rail, I'm out of direct line of sight for most of the prisoners in their beds.

When I step around the corner, I hear a sound behind me.

And run right into a wide chest.

Holy shit.

"Careful," whispers Ben, grabbing me by the shoulders to keep me from falling backwards.

I catch a glance at Sven standing behind him.

Good.

"Let's go." I cut in front of them and lead them further into the west end.

Hopefully, the fun starts very soon.

We find a dark corner to huddle in and wait again.

Every second that goes by is another chance to be caught. I think I'd rather die fighting at this point than be trapped for another minute.

A low rumble is the first clue that something is happening.

Another, this one is louder.

Sirens begin to scream through the stone halls and I can hear the guards scrambling and calling to each other.

Whatever is going to happen, better happen fast. Too many uniforms running around for comfort.

A man in full riot gear steps past, then stops and backs up.

Fuck.

He raises his visor, revealing a black balaclava.

"Alexei? Thought you'd be alone." Mikhail's voice comes through the heavy helmet.

"You made it! Yes! Let's go! They're coming with me." I grab Sven's elbow and tug him to follow.

Mikhail looks at one towering brother, then the other.

With a deep breath, he nods, and motions us to follow him.

Creeping along the concrete walls, the alarms reverberate from every direction and make my ears hurt.

Mikhail gestures towards a single steel door and leads us through. Keeping our heads down, I can still see the orange plumes of fire from the far end of the prison building.

"They blew it up!" Ben exclaims as we run.

Dodging spotlights, Mikhail veers around a section of wall to reveal a cut fence folded open, barely big enough for him to fit through.

I slide to the other side easily enough, but I can hear low curses from the brothers as they force their way between the jagged edges of wire.

"Hurry!" Mikhail yells as he jumps into the open door of a waiting plane. The propeller starts to move and we all climb in through the side.

"We're running heavy, hold on tight!" he yells at us from the front.

"Here." I start handing out parachutes. I feel safer with one on, better than a seatbelt.

The heavy engine of the Kodiak rumbles into high gear when he begins the fast taxi down the short clearing. It whines as he pushes the throttle to the limit.

I think I can almost touch the trees as the aircraft lugs into the dark sky.

A plink is the first sound.

Then another.

"They're shooting at us!" Mikhail twists the yoke making us all roll to the side with the steep turn.

More bullets pierce through the thin metal.

Sven lets out a grunt and grabs his calf. "I'm fine," he says, sticking his finger through the new hole in his prison pants.

Another shot, and there's a popping sound coming from the engine.

"Alexei!" Mikhail shouts. "We're going down! Jump!"

I turn to the brothers. "Have you parachuted?"

They both nod, cinching their straps.

"Go!" Mikhail cries out, almost as if he's in pain.

"Now or never!" Diving out through the side door, I can see the twinkling lights below us.

We have enough distance to pick a decent landing spot.

Past the rushing wind, I point to a clearing below.

Ben and Sven fall just a few yards away. They must have bailed at the same time as me.

But where's Mikhail?

I can't see his chute. Was he wearing one? I don't remember seeing him with it.

The white underbelly of the plane is highlighted against the stars as fire streaks from the engine.

Fuck.

Where is he?

I'm frantic after I pull my cord, twisting in the ropes to try and look around me.

Is he still in the plane?

"Mikhail!" I scream as loud as I can, but my words are ripped away by the speed of my fall.

I'm just about to cry out again, when I see the flaming aircraft plummet from the sky and crash into a fiery ball in the distance.

No!

He had to have made it, didn't he?

My heart lodges in my throat. I can't see another parachute.

Surely he had one?

Oh my god.

Mikhail?

"Did he go down with the plane?" Ben asks before he even stands.

I don't want to, but I nod.

"Shit." Sven whistles low. "Did he get hit by one of those bullets?

I remember the painful sound in his last word.

Damn.

"Maybe. We have to get out of here. I know who to call." I just need to find a phone. Enzo will get us.

CHAPTER 78

LARA

Song, Sleep, Citizen

BLOWING OUT A BREATH, I have to hold onto the side of the couch to stay upright. With every step the world spins a little more.

Placing my hand over my heart, my breathing becomes more ragged. Like my chest is closing in on me.

And my pulse is racing a million miles an hour against my hand.

I shake my head, trying to regain some sense of composure.

It isn't working. It's getting worse.

Slowly, I turn my head to locate my phone. I need Nikolai. This isn't right.

Panic starts to grip me and I feel cold and clammy.

On shaking legs, I take a step towards the coffee table and it's like the life drains out of me. Black dots appear in my vision, like blobs that are getting bigger.

Until I can't see.

I can't feel.

CHAPTER 79
ALEXEI

The Other Side, Ruelle

"I'll take them back with me," Enzo points to Ben and Sven in the back.

"Yeah, I'll call you later." I swing open the passenger door before he can even come to a stop outside my house.

I need a fucking shower. Lara won't mind, I bet she's going to be crazy excited to see me.

She's all I can think about.

I've missed her so much it hurts. I'll never leave her again.

In fact, I am going to ask her to be my wife. She always wanted to be a beautiful bride, I want to give her that.

I'd give her anything she desires.

I just need to get the perfect ring, one that will make her smile every time she looks at it. Maybe a pink one. She loves anything that color.

I sprint to the front door and barge my way through.

"Baby, I'm home!" I call out, heading straight for the living room.

It's eerily quiet.

Sheila and Bruce will be out in the yard. Lara's car is in the driveway.

I round the corner towards the dining room and I freeze when I see a pair of feet.

"Lara?"

My heart almost stops. I rush over to her and drop to the floor beside her.

"Lara, baby, wake up."

She's so still. Peaceful even.

I want to be sick.

With trembling hands, I roll her to face me as gently as I can. Looking down at her pale face, my blood runs cold.

"No, no, no."

Tears roll down my cheeks, I lean in against her, pressing my lips against hers, there's a faint, really faint bit of breath there.

How long has she been here?

Digging out the new cell Enzo gave me, I call him, wiping away my tears and cradling her lifeless body in my lap.

"Come on, baby. You can't leave me. Please."

Enzo's deep voice cuts through.

"Hello?"

"It's Lara. You need to help me. I need a fucking ambulance. Hospital. I don't know. I think she's dying. Help me." The words tumble out of my mouth in pure panic.

"What? You gotta keep it together, Alexei."

I hear the tires screech in the background.

"She got a pulse?" Enzo asks calmly.

I press two fingers on her throat. Why is she cold?

"I think so. It's not strong. Is she going to die?"

I smash my palm against my forehead. I can't lose her. She's my entire life.

I'd sell my soul to the devil to make sure she's okay.

I'd die for her.

I love her so much it hurts.

Enzo's steady voice cuts through this agony. "Alexei, I need you to carry her carefully to the car. Your friends are coming in to help now. Okay?"

"Y-yes."

Now isn't a time to break down.

She needs me to fight for her.

CHAPTER 80
ALEXEI

Song- Sleep Token, Alkaline

I'D DO anything to swap places with her.

Squeezing her frail hand tighter, I try to let her know that I'm with her. That I'm never leaving her side again.

More fucking tears roll down my cheeks, I don't bother wiping them. I don't care.

This is the worst pain I've ever felt in my life. Worse than the beatings my father gave me as a kid.

Watching helplessly as the woman I love lies there in a hospital bed.

I don't know whether the anger is worse than the heartache. How did we all miss this?

I should have done more. I shouldn't have left her.

The doctors told me her body was shutting down from exhaustion. She hasn't been eating, or keeping food down for weeks. Weeks?

I wish I could understand why she does this. She's perfect as she is. She says it's about control, a way to cope with life.

I left and she nearly kills herself. The doctors warned me if she doesn't get help, her body will eventually give up on her.

I'll lose her. Then we will all be without her light in our lives.

My tears turn into full sobs and I don't know how to make it stop.

I don't even hear Nikolai come through the door, but I sit back when I feel his heavy palm on my shoulder.

"Alexei."

I look up at him, not removing my fingers laced through Lara's.

"I-is she okay?"

I sniffle and shake my head.

"Her body started to shut down, Nikolai. Overworking to compensate for her lack of food. She was starving herself to death. So no. She's not okay."

Pain flashes across his face as he looks at his sister.

"Fuck. We've been so busy trying to find you, we thought she was coping. Considering."

That's it.

I fly up out of my chair and get in his face.

"Fuck looking for me. I'm not more important than her." I point to Lara.

"She is everything to me. It would have been pointless even getting me out of that jail if she didn't survive. I'd die without her. Don't you get it? There is no me without her. I'm so in love with that woman."

I'm almost out of breath by the time I finish letting it all out.

He tilts his head and looks back and forth between us.

"What kind of love?" he asks quietly.

"Like you and Mila. Sofia and Jax. The love of a lifetime."

He shakes his head almost in disbelief.

"What?" I press.

"She never said. You never said? How long? I-I, she's my sister? You protect her, you love her, no doubt. But a relationship? Really?"

I step forward getting in his face. He thinks I'm not good enough? That makes two of us. But I am never letting her go.

"What? The man who has dedicated his life to her safety. That would die for her? That will love her with everything he has for eternity?"

Nikolai steps back.

I turn and look at Lara and a fresh wave of sadness washes over me.

"Fuck." I pull at my hair, already feeling guilty for my outburst at my best friend.

Mikhail.

Oh my god. In all of this, visions of the plane going down plague me. When she wakes up, this could break her.

"None of this matters. I just need her back, Niki."

He offers me a sad smile, and wraps a strong arm around my shoulders.

"She's going to pull through and she's going to be so happy when she sees you here. You just gotta be strong for her, okay?"

"You aren't mad?"

He chuckles and stands back.

"We all knew how much you both loved each other this entire time. I just never thought you'd get your head out your ass and realize it."

I blow out a shaky breath.

"You'll look after each other. I know that. I trust you with her."

I take my seat next to Lara, placing my hand over hers again.

Niki lets out a sigh. "And are you okay? After your adventure?"

I shrug. I'm alive. This heartbreak is worse.

"I always wondered what jail was like. Don't recommend it. We gotta stay out of those places."

He chuckles and for the first time in a while, I smile too.

No matter what, this grump has always been family to me.

"What did she make you do?"

I clench my jaw. I'll always hate myself for this one kill. Butcher was a good guy, well, to me anyway.

"Kill an old guy. I swear when I see her again, I'll end her myself. Leaving me in there to rot. I'm lucky Drago saw sense, thanks to Mikhail."

We both stiffen at his name.

My head hangs over her limp fingers. "Fuck. Niki. How do we tell her?"

He steps closer, resting his hand on the edge of the bed.

"First we let her come back to us. We help her heal. And we do everything we can to track him down. Dead or alive, we bring our brother home. I'll let you decide when the time is right, she hates being left out of the loop. So the sooner the better."

I nod in agreement. I can never lie to Lara.

"We just have to wait for her to be ready to come back to us."

And then I'll do everything I can to help her. I don't care what. Or how long it takes.

I just need my pchelka happy and healthy. That's all I ask for in life.

CHAPTER 81
LARA

Song, Euclid, Sleep Token

AM I HALLUCINATING?

Where the hell am I?

The bright lights. The beeping. A damn hospital.

Blinking through the clinical glare, my mouth is drier than a desert.

I can hear Alexei.

My god, am I still unconscious?

It's like he's really here. I can smell him, I can feel warmth on my right hand. His voice.

With all of the energy I can muster I turn my head.

His puffy red eyes are the first thing I see.

But he's alive? He came back for me.

"Pchelka," he whispers.

"Sladkiy." A tear slips down my cheek. There's so much I want to say. To explain.

I'm just so tired.

He rests his forehead against mine and I close my eyes, the calm to my storm.

Alexei gets the doctors in, who proceed to check me over. I

hear them saying things to me, but it's difficult to concentrate. I just want to talk to Alexei.

They're discussing a program for my eating disorder. The word starvation came up a couple of times. Body shutting down. I've kind of tuned my brain out.

I know what I've done to myself. I know it has to stop.

I look over to Alexei, who is taking every word in from the doctor and squeezing my hand for reassurance.

He is now, and will always be, my protector.

Piecing me back together again bit by bit. I've hurt him. Seeing me like this will be killing him.

I let myself down. I let him down. And my family. I spiraled too far this time.

I just wish I knew how to fix my broken.

A doctor in bright blue scrubs stands over me. "You get some rest, Lara. We will be back in to keep checking on you and once you're feeling up to it, we can discuss your plans, okay?"

She pushes her glasses back up the bridge of her nose and smiles at me.

"Thank you."

I let out a sigh of relief when the door closes and I turn my head to face Alexei.

"I missed you, pchelka." The raw emotion in his voice makes me want to burst into tears.

"I missed you most," I say back.

Silence washes over us, we lost each other and we fell apart.

"I love you, Lara. I'm so sorry I left you. I thought I was doing the right thing. That this would keep everyone safe. I nearly lost you. How was I ever supposed to live a life without you in it?"

He's speaking so fast it's hard to understand.

"I'm okay, Alexei. I'm going to be fine. I missed you. I

thought I'd never see you again." My eyes burn. I've never been so lost in this world without him.

"I was always making my way back to you. I promised, remember." He lifts up my hand and places a kiss. "Getting back to my girl was the only thing keeping me going in there. When I found you—"

My stomach sinks. "Shit. You found me?"

No wonder he looks so distraught. I can't believe I let this happen.

"You need to get help for this, baby. I am not smart enough to do that on my own. We need clever people, like Sofia. I won't let you leave me, not like this."

He shakes his head. I keep quiet to let him continue. "The way I love you means I have to die before you. You can't go first, Lara. And the way this is going, you will, baby. I vowed to protect you, and if it's from yourself then I will. This is not how we end."

It's like a stab through the heart. The thought of losing him kills me. I can't imagine the pain he's going through.

I'm petrified of dying. I can't leave Alexei nor my family. I just can't make this stop. I punish myself to feel in control.

"I don't want to, it was never about that. The thought of leaving behind you, Elena, my brothers, that rips me apart. I never wanted to die. I just didn't know how to keep living."

Seeing the tears roll down his cheeks guts me even more. Guilt washes over me. I'm hurting everyone I love.

"I'll do whatever it takes. I promise. I'm not giving up. Not on us. Not on life."

"I won't let you. I swore to protect you, and if that means from yourself, that's what I'll do."

He raises my arm and places my palm on his warm cheek.

He's so handsome. I don't deserve his kindness.

"W-what if I'm too broken to fix? Do you really want to spend the rest of your life worrying about me? I'm holding you back."

"Don't," he says sternly. "You think I'm not how you say, broken, too? Sometimes I'm not sure what goes on in my brain."

I hiccup a laugh. That's true.

"But you know what?" he continues.

I lean into his touch as he strokes my cheek and let his words sink in.

Two halves that fit together perfectly.

Both imperfect, yet together, we make a whole.

Maybe it isn't all about being perfect.

"We can be a little bit broken together?" I finish the sentence for him.

He nods and smiles at me.

As he leans over me, I suck in a breath. I've been waiting for this moment for what feels like a lifetime.

"One kiss won't ruin everything, right?" He smirks, rubbing his nose softly against mine.

"No, handsome. It's going to fix us, the only way we know how."

Waking up from a nap, I dreamt of the cabin. Of cuddling up to Alexei by the lake. Just silencing the world for a while.

I always ran there to avoid everyone. Except I've realized that home isn't a place, not for me.

It's a person. It's Alexei.

"I'd like to go to the cabin, if that's okay?"

He bows his head with a frown.

And then it hits me. He thinks I don't need him right now.

"I'd like you to come with me."

He strokes the front of my hand with his thumb.

"You think I'm ever leaving your side again, do you? Huh?"

That wide grin emerges on his lips and I can't help but smile too.

This is what I need. Space from the world but not from my person.

I need him with me.

I know that with Alexei, I can conquer anything in my path and this battle with bulimia is one I have to fight now.

No more hiding. I can't keep hurting the people I love. I can't keep hurting myself anymore.

I will do anything to take back control of my life, even if it is small steps every day.

I never want to see tears fall from his eyes because of me.

"I won't let you leave me. You're mine, Alexei."

He brings my hand up to his mouth and presses a kiss to my knuckles.

"You've been the sole keeper of my heart since the moment I laid eyes on you. That will never change. We will get you through this, pchelka. I promise."

He leans over and brushes my cheek.

"Because I simply cannot lose you. My world stops spinning when you aren't there. My fire goes out. I will love you through the hard times, I'll fight for you when you're too exhausted to fight for yourself. I'll take care of you when you need it. I'll do anything in my power to keep you smiling, because that is what I live for Lara. You. Us. No matter what, it will always be us against whatever battle we come across."

I choke on a sob. Those are the kindest, most beautiful words anyone has ever said to me.

"I will fight for us, Alexei. I'll fall with you, I'll love you every single day. I'll do whatever it takes to make sure we do life together. Because I live for you, too. And I'm sorry. I'm sorry I lost control, that I hid my battles from you."

He shakes his head.

"Don't apologize, baby. We've got this. Now get some rest, I'll get the cabin ready and we can escape for a little while."

451

As he stands I grab his wrist.

"No kiss?" I give him an exaggerated pout.

He laughs and runs a hand over his face. My poor man looks broken.

Bending over, he kisses me so softly, like I'm a piece of glass that will crumble.

"You won't break me, sladkiy."

He smiles against my lips and kisses me properly.

"I love you," he whispers.

"I love you, sweets."

CHAPTER 82

ALEXEI

Closing the door behind me, as soon as it clicks I rest my back against it and rub my hands over my face.

"Fuck."

I want to punch something, anything. I just want to make this all better for her, snap my fingers and it's okay again.

Why can't I save her from the demons in her head?

I know I can't. But I'll do everything in my power to help her.

It's up to me to remind her every day how perfect she is. On the inside and out.

I'll worship her until the day I die.

Starting with fixing up the cabin. I have no idea how I'm going to break the news about Mikhail. Especially when we have no idea what happened.

I can't believe he's dead. But until I see that giant body, I won't believe it.

Nikolai clears his throat and I look up.

"Go spend some time with her, I have some things to take care of," I tell him, sliding out my phone.

He nods.

"Don't mention Mikhail until I get back, okay?"

Niki raises a brow and looks through the glass.

"You saw the plane go down?" Niki asks sternly.

"Yea."

I clench my fist, a fresh wave of nausea washing over me.

"He can't be dead, Niki. We all need him. Her most of all." I point towards Lara's door.

It's like the world is crumbling around me. I take a deep breath.

"Enzo is on it. We can't plan his funeral yet. Mikhail is a clever fucker. We can't rule him out so easy. We've seen him survive the unsurvivable once before." Nikolai clenches his jaw as he stares at his sister.

I remember vividly.

I saw what happened to him. I knew the man before and the man he turned into after the fire.

"But how many times can you cheat death, Niki?"

He shakes his head and shrugs.

"I could ask you that every day, Alexei."

He has a point.

We just have to hope Mikhail is like me and he hasn't already used up his last one.

CHAPTER 83

LARA

Song- Ocean, Martin Garrix, Khalid

I'M EATING. I'm not throwing it back up.

I'm in my safe space, away from the world.

I just found out my brother is missing. Or worse, dead.

I'm not sure I've fully processed that. I can't until I know the truth.

But, I'm glad Alexei told me. That he didn't treat me like I couldn't cope.

Because I can. I am strong. Well, I'm trying to be.

Maybe this was the wake up call I needed to become better, to finally regain control of my life.

We've been at the cabin for three weeks now. Mainly just snuggling up and watching crap TV. And resting.

We both needed that, even Alexei, after his ordeal.

And it's the first time I've seen him remorseful over taking a life. I knew all along deep down Alexei is a kind soul to those who deserve it. But I think even this new emotion is taking him by surprise.

"Your brain sounds busy, pchelka. Anything I can help with?" he asks, running his fingers through my hair idly.

459

I nestle closer to him, feeling the warmth of his body as I squeeze my arms around him.

"Just thinking about Mikhail, about you being stuck in a jail, and how peaceful it is here."

"We can live here. I have all I'll ever need."

His response brings a warm smile to my face.

"You'd go stir crazy here, not being able to run free."

"I'm never running far again. But yes, people need us back home."

Especially with Mila about to give birth, I'd like to be around for my nephew and Elena.

"Don't forget Sheila and Bruce."

Much to Nikolai's delight, he's on flamingo duty. But Elena loves seeing them, so it was easy to get him to agree. He does anything for that little girl.

The room is filled with the loud grumbling of my hungry stomach.

"Time for dinner?" Alexei chuckles.

"Sounds that way."

I'm opting for small, frequent meals to start with. Alexei had the place stocked with just about every food you could imagine, so there is always something I fancy.

"I'll cook." He taps my ass, meaning it's time for me to untangle myself from him.

When he stands, I can't help but ogle the outline of his cock in those gray sweatpants.

With a knowing look, he twists his head to glance at me and playfully winks, before continuing on his way to the kitchen.

I quietly get up and tiptoe behind him, trying not to make a sound. As he reaches up into the cupboard, I quickly lunge forward and yank down his sweatpants, causing them to drop to his ankles.

I gasp as his bare ass is exposed.

So I slap it. Hard.

I watch as he unabashedly turns to face me, his erection already becoming noticeable.

"My turn." He smirks, and as he leans forward, I jump out of the way and dart towards the bedroom.

Fuck, I'm laughing so much when I slam the door behind me. I lean over the bed to catch my breath.

The sound of his heavy footsteps approaching behind me fills the room.

"You've been a naughty girl, Lara."

My eyes go wide and I hiccup before turning to face him.

"Ah, you lost the pants rather than pull them up."

I can't stop staring at his enormous dick, the piercing catching my attention. God, it looks so good.

He stalks towards me, and excitement courses through me.

Grabbing the front of my delicate lace nightgown, he tears it apart in one swift motion.

Licking his lips, his eyes travel up my body until our gazes meet.

Instinctively, I wrap my arms around my exposed middle, and he places his hand over mine.

"You were made to be worshiped by me, baby. Let me show you?"

Maybe I need this? I take a deep breath, trying to calm my racing heart.

"O-okay."

Gripping both shoulders, he guides me in front of a full-length mirror opposite the bed. I focus on him as he stands behind me and rests his chin on my shoulder.

"Don't look at me. Look at yourself."

I shiver as he lightly traces his fingertips down both of my arms and then slides the ripped dress from my body.

I squeeze my eyes shut for a moment. It's almost painful being so exposed.

"Open them, pchelka." His tone is firm yet soft.

I do as he says and make eye contact with him in the reflection. His face lights up with a smile, while his eyes gleam with desire. All for me. My belly erupts with butter-flies, distracting me from zoning in on my imperfections.

I ignore the instinct to wrap my arms around my stomach to hide it. I can do this.

"Such a good girl." He brushes away my long hair over my shoulder.

"I want you to watch. See how much I admire every single inch of you. Even the parts you hate, I'll show you exactly why I love them, one kiss at a time."

I can feel the tears prickling at the corners of my eyes as his words sink in. When I lower my chin to my chest, he deli-cately lifts it back up, guiding my gaze upward.

"You are enough. You are more than that. Way more. You're everything."

His touch is gentle as he traces his index finger along my lips, leaving a tingling sensation.

"I love how your lips feel against mine. So soft and plump."

His fingers glide through my hair, sending sparks down my spine as he pulls my head back to rest against his shoulder.

"Your smile and your cute little nose. The way you bite your lip when you're concentrating, the way your blue eyes pierce into mine. You see right through me, you always have."

"I love kissing you here." He licks all the way down my neck. "And I really like how my hand feels wrapped around your throat."

As I clench my thighs together, I can hear a subtle chuckle escape from him.

I gaze into the mirror, and notice the red flush slowly spreading across my neck. My nipples stand at attention. There's a hunger in my eyes for him.

Every kiss he peppers down my right arm ignites a spark that courses through my entire body.

"I love the way it feels when you wrap your arms around me. It's like home."

With a tender gesture, he presses his lips to each finger, saving the thumb for last.

"Some days it's okay to feel like you're not enough. Everyone has bad days. But I need you to tell me. Promise you'll tell me, so I can take the time to prove to you, on my God damn knees if I have to, why you're wrong. Why you are worthy. I'll remind you every day how perfect you are if that's what you need."

I give him a little nod. If I speak, I might cry. Just out of pure admiration for this man.

Next, he cups my breasts and squeezes.

"And these. Fuck. These are perfect. Look at them in my hands. Enough to squeeze, to tease."

He rolls my erect nipples between his finger and thumb.

"Look how responsive you are to my touch."

He pushes his hips, his hard dick digging into my ass, and a little moan slips out of me.

"Feel how hard I am. That's just by looking at you. I have to fight it every second I'm with you, or thinking about you. So every minute of the day, I'm redirecting blood from my cock."

As I sway my hips, a mischievous smirk appears on his face.

"Do I get you wet just by thinking about me?" He nibbles on my neck.

"Y-yes. All the time. It's distracting."

When his hands glide down my sides, I exhale a deep breath.

"Look." He nods to the mirror.

"All of you. I love it all. I don't see your imperfections

because to me, you have none. You never have. You've always been my perfect girl."

That's it. I can't hold it in. I've tried to hold back the tears. And fail. I see them rolling down my cheeks.

"And do you know what? I should remind you of this. I love you. I want you to feel special, like you are the most beautiful woman on the planet."

"I love you, Alexei," I whisper, looking into his eyes through the mirror.

He grabs my jaw, tilting my head to the side, and presses his lips against mine.

His tongue glides across my cheek, gently collecting the salty trails of my tears.

"I'll kiss away all your fears." His hand gently cups my pussy. "And fuck away all your bad thoughts." He smirks.

"And this is mine. All fucking mine. You know how good it feels when I sink inside you? I told you before, I never want to leave. You know what else? I could sit and eat you for days. Days, pchelka. I could just sit you on my face and make you come over and over."

A gasp escapes my lips as he plunges his fingers inside of me.

"Oh, you like the sound of that? Hear how wet you are for me?"

He thrusts in deeper and it's all I can hear.

Removing his hand with a naughty glint in his eye, he wraps his forearm around my neck and sucks them clean.

"Mmm. So fucking good. Put your hands on the mirror and bend over," he whispers against my lips.

I feel a sense of emptiness and longing as he retreats, leaving me without the reassuring presence of his touch.

But I do as he says, adrenaline running through me as my palms meet the cool mirror. There's a thud behind me as he drops to his knees.

"Remember the rules. Eyes on you. See how pretty you are when you come for me."

His strong grip tightens around my thighs, sending a shiver down my spine. With one slow, deliberate lick, a rush of pleasure courses through my body, causing me to gasp and stumble forward.

With his firm grasp, he effortlessly pulls me back into position and holds me there.

"You taste so fucking good. Ride my face."

Holy shit.

With each lick, my body trembles and I roll my hips. I swear every time his tongue connects with my clit, I almost come on the spot.

"A-Alexei. I'm close."

"You better be watching yourself." Is all he replies before his tongue dives inside of me and I scream out.

I study my reflection and the world around me blurs.

This flushed, starry-eyed girl stares back at me. The man of my dreams has his face buried in my pussy making noises come out of me I didn't know possible.

A man who just declared his love for every inch of me.

He makes me feel worthy. Loved. And safe.

Confident even. For the first time in what feels like my entire life, I want to let go, and be free.

For him.

CHAPTER 84

ALEXEI

Song- DIAMONDS, MIKOLAS

HER CRIES FILL THE ROOM.

The only ones I plan on her doing again, the ones out of pleasure.

I lick up all of her release as she comes so hard on my face, her body shuddering against the mirror.

She better have watched every moment of that. I wish I had her view.

Although, being face first in her pussy is a good second option.

With one last lick, she rests her head against the mirror to regain her breath.

Now is my chance.

Before I sit back, I bite down hard on her ass cheek and grin at the tooth marks I've left behind.

"Alexei," she whines breathlessly.

While she's distracted in her post-orgasm state, I crawl to the left as silently as possible and pull open the top drawer, snagging out the little pink box.

I always knew I'd do this at the cabin.

467

The place she feels safe and secure.

I don't want this retreat to be about running anymore. I want it to be our sanctuary.

A place of love.

Where the world is quiet and we can just enjoy each other.

Our place.

I promised her forever, and this is my way of showing I can give her the whole world.

I remember when she was a teenager, how her eyes would light up when her and her friends would talk about their dream guys and weddings.

The thought of her marrying another man, even back then, made my skin crawl.

I am the only man that will give her the happily ever after she deserves.

I'll marry her tomorrow.

There isn't a single thing I wouldn't do for this woman.

Shuffling back behind her, with that gorgeous view of her ass, my dick is so painfully hard. But I'm doing my best to ignore that.

Positioning myself on one knee, I hold the box out in my palm.

"Pchelka. Turn around."

My stomach tightens with nerves out of nowhere. I shake my head and swallow any doubts.

She turns to me, looking down at me on the floor. I watch her face switch from confusion to excitement. Her hands fly over her mouth and she gasps.

"Alexei," she gushes.

"Lara." I respond with a grin.

Holding out my hand, she places her dainty one in it, and I tug her closer.

I'd wear her as a second skin if I could. I'm that obsessed. I never want her out of my sight.

"I have a very important question that there is only one correct answer for."

I flip open the box to reveal the masterpiece I designed. A square-cut diamond, the biggest one they had, surrounded by little pink gems. Set on a silver band, because all of her jewelry is that color. Apparently it matches her skin tone best. I remember everything she tells me.

I wanted to make it really pretty, just like her.

So she looks at it every day and smiles.

"Yes, Alexei."

I smile so hard my cheeks hurt.

"Hang on. Let me ask it properly. Will you, Lara Volkov. Pleasure me in being my wife?"

She bursts out laughing.

"What?"

"I think it's 'do me the pleasure of'?"

I shrug.

"You can pleasure me whenever you want to."

She bites her lip, and it's taking all I have not to pounce on her.

"Will you marry me, pchelka? Please?"

I bat my lashes at her for the full dramatic effect.

"Yes, sladkiy. One hundred million times, yes. Infinite yes."

My heart almost explodes. Springing up, I wrap my arms tightly around her, my hand cradling her neck as I press my lips against hers, savoring the moment with my fiancé.

I kiss her until we're out of breath then slide the ring onto her shaking finger.

"That's so beautiful, Alexei. You have a good eye. It's perfect for me."

I tug her closer by the waist.

"I'm an expert in Lara. I've been studying for twenty years, remember? Maybe I could get a certificate."

As her hand touches my chest, I can feel her warmth seeping through my skin.

"A marriage certificate? That's probably the best one."

When she pushes on my ribs, my eyes widen in surprise, causing me to stumble backwards and land on the mattress

"My girl wants to take some control back? Hmm?"

I stroke my cock as she saunters towards me, so I spread open my thighs.

"Be my guest. Do your best." I wink at her.

This should be fun.

A sassy Lara is one of my favorites.

I want her to feel powerful.

I am weak for her, I always have been.

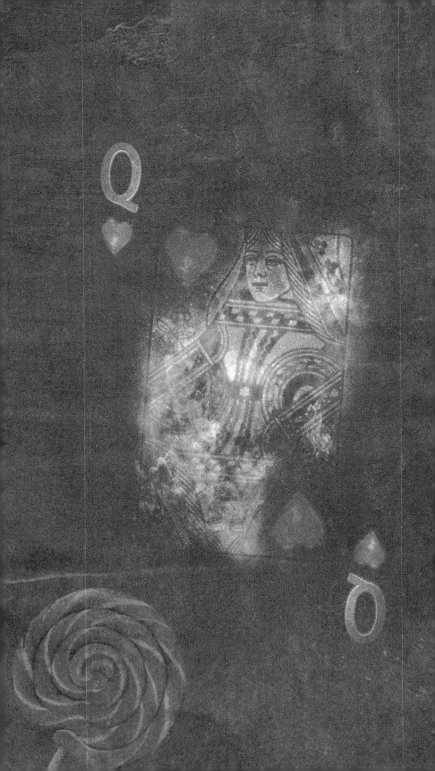

CHAPTER 85
LARA

Song- Body Loud, SWIM, Limi.

I'M giddy with excitement and so turned on I could explode.

He wants me in control?

Where do I even start with this?

Stepping between his thighs, his eyes darken as I move his hand away and replace it with my own. Purposely using my new sparkling left hand for him to see.

"Damn, that looks good."

He's made me feel like the sexiest woman to exist, so I'm embracing that.

He's created a safe space to allow me to be whoever I want to be with him.

And right now. I want him needy, desperate, and begging for me.

Hmm.

Heading over to my drawer, I dig out a belt.

"Hands above your head, sladkiy."

The moment he bites down on his lip, a sly smirk forms on his face. God, he's hot.

I'm lucky.

He does as I say and I admire the veins in his arms as he tenses. Climbing up his body, I purposely let my pussy rub against his dick and he groans.

"You want more of that?" I whisper in his ear while securing his wrists together with my gold belt.

"You know I do."

"Hmm." I tap my finger against my lips.

Sitting back on his stomach, I have an idea.

"Put your knees up for me."

He tilts his head, eyeing me suspiciously, but does as I say.

I lean my back against his thighs.

"You got a good enough view now?" He tips his head forward as I spread my legs over each side of his chest.

"Hell yeah. Come closer, let me eat."

I shake my head and tut.

"No. I'm in control, remember? I wanna tease you. I want you to beg me to ride you. I'm going to get you so desperate for me you come inside me the second you thrust in. I won't stop until you're feral for me."

I cup my breasts in both hands and run my tongue along my lower lip while he tugs at his restraint.

"Understood?"

He purses his lips and nods, fidgeting with the belt around his wrists.

Working my hands lower down my front, he lets out a groan the same time my two fingers circle my clit.

"Please sit on my face, baby," he pleads, but not desperate enough yet.

I shake my head. "Beg better."

"Fuck," he hisses as I spread my legs even wider and slide two fingers inside.

Leaning forward, I trace over his lips. He opens his mouth, but I don't slide them in. Instead, I lean back and let him enjoy the view.

"Such a tease, pchelka." He drops his head back to the pillow with a grin.

Not good enough. He needs to be more needy.

So I flip myself over, carefully positioning my legs on either side of his head, my pussy just far enough away that he can look but not taste.

I lick all the way down his shaft. As I flick my gaze up, I catch myself in the mirror.

Damn, this is hot.

I watch as I take him as far down my throat as I can. I can hear him grunting and groaning behind me.

"I need to be inside you, Lara."

"Hmm, mmm," I moan around his cock.

"Please baby, I'm begging. I'll do anything. Let me come inside you. I don't want to come down your throat. I want to fill you up and watch it spill out of you. Then I want to fuck it back inside of you with my fingers. Please. Lara."

There it is. His words are laced with desperation.

Inching my hips back, I let him have a taste. And he does.

"Fuck. You're so wet. So delicious. Do I get to sink inside you yet?"

I nod, still with him in my mouth. Pushing myself up, I turn around.

He's flushed and looking feral. I crash my lips over his and line his dick up before pushing myself back.

"Shit," I cry out.

He brings his arms up, still restrained, over our heads and grabs my ass.

"I can't keep my hands off you," he mutters against my lips.

"I'm good with that. Now fuck me."

In one swift movement, he thrusts his hips up, hitting so deep. The belt clatters to the floor and he grabs my throat, flipping me onto my back.

"You want me crazy for you?"

My arms splay above my head with his grip tightening.

"So. Fucking. Perfect," he grits out between each thrust.

With his spare hand, he grabs hold of the headboard behind me and uses it to dive deeper inside me.

"Oh my god," I cry out.

The sensation of my toes curling and the ringing in my ears overwhelms me.

"Come for me." His words send my world crashing, my name a chant on his lips as he spills inside me. He steals all my breath with a kiss.

He's all I can feel. Every sense of mine belongs to him.

And it's perfect.

We are each other's missing pieces.

"I'm so proud of you." He nuzzles into my neck.

CHAPTER 86
ALEXEI

THE SUN BEAMS through the window to our cabin bedroom. Lara is tangled up between the sheets, resting her head on my chest.

"Good morning, pchelka."

I had a text from Nikolai, they need me back. It sounds like Ivan's guys are sniffing around the casinos.

And Mikhail isn't there to scare them away.

We can't let them know he's gone.

"Morning, Alexei. You're awake early."

"Hmm, I like watching you sleep."

Maybe one day I'll tell her how many times I have watched her.

"Lies. Something is on your mind, spill."

Her nails start scratching at my throat and I groan.

"Leave marks and I'll get them tattooed there too," I tease, but I am being serious.

She stifles a yawn.

"Please do, those back ones you had done are so hot. Marked and mine. But stop deflecting, talk to me."

I can't help but grin at how well she reads me.

"Fine. You got me. Nikolai needs me. Well, us."

She pushes herself up, blowing her blond hair out of her face.

"Then we go. Family is important. Especially now. Plus, we have news." She holds up her hand and wiggles her fingers in front of my face.

"That we do. I was also thinking…" I trail off.

"Oh, God. What?"

I slap her ass and yank back the cover, revealing her naked body.

So gorgeous. And distracting.

Pinning her hands above her head, I roll over and settle between her legs.

"I was thinking, we move into the place I bought you and we do it up, together?"

She wraps her legs around my ass and pushes me into her.

"Deal. Let's do that. Shall we make a movie theater room?"

"Whatever your heart desires, baby. The world is yours."

CHAPTER 87

LARA

Song- I Wouldn't Mind, He Is We

SMOOTHING DOWN the front of my wedding dress. I opted for one that sits above the knees and puffs out a little, but it hugs me in all the right places. I even had a diamond waist band added. And for the first time that I can remember, I look at my reflection in the mirror and I smile. I like what I see.

And Alexei is going to go nuts over this. I can't wait for him to rip it off later.

We only wanted a small wedding, especially with Mikhail gone.

Fuck.

I didn't want to cry today. I miss my big brother. We have no idea where he is. He could actually be dead for all I know. I'm holding on to the hope that he's just used another one of his lives.

Except I know, someone can only live so recklessly for so long before it catches up with them.

My gut is telling me he's still alive.

And I know Nikolai, Alexei and Enzo won't rest until he's back with us.

There's a knock at the door that distracts me from my little spiral.

I open it up and I'm met with a huge bouquet of lilac and white flowers and a platter of strawberries and a little white envelope with scribble on.

Alexei.

Holding back the tears, I put the tray and flowers on the table and rip open the letter.

I have loved you since the moment I laid eyes on you.

No matter what, you are the other half of me.

The strongest, the wisest and the most beautiful woman in the universe.

There is no Alexei without his pchelka.

I can't wait to do the rest of my life with you as my wife.

I am proud of you and I love you more than I can ever explain.

But I love you for everything that you are today, everything you ever have been or will be.

Whatever version of you,

For eternity, Lara.

I bet you look so fucking pretty right now.

Now be a good girl and come and marry your man.

I've waited long enough for this.

Let's do this crazy life thing together, just like I promised you twenty years ago.

Love your sladkiy.

Dammit Alexei. I hiccup and wipe away my tears. They say everyone is put on this planet to search the other half of them. The one love of their life. I'm lucky to have had mine in my life for as long as I can remember.

Every milestone, I've had him by my side.

Through the good, the bad and the horrifying, he's held my hand.

He's cried with me, he's held me and made me laugh until I forget the pain.

He's made it his life purpose to see me smile.

Even when I hated myself, that man dragged me out of my head.

On days I didn't want anyone to speak to me, he made sure I still knew he loved me.

That I was worthy of it.

He spoke louder than the voices telling me I was useless and ugly.

I may never truly be able to see my own beauty, but I'll always be able to see it in his eyes when he's looking at me.

We truly have always done life together.

There's another knock at the door as I place the letter on my pillow.

"Come in!"

Nikolai fills the space. God he looks so uncomfortable in his suit.

"You look smart, bro." I tease.

"And you look stunning, little sis."

He scratches his stubble, looking over at the flowers and strawberries.

"Have you... eaten?"

I nod.

"I had breakfast with Sofia and Mila. Oatmeal to be exact."

Sometimes I feel like a kid with them checking in on my food intake, but I understand after starting my therapy that it's because they care.

I scared them. And myself.

I never wanted to die. I don't want to leave them, I couldn't.

My family and Alexei are everything. I just lost control.

My eating habits were the only thing that made me feel like I wasn't spiraling, even if it was slowly killing me.

But it's something I'm going to have to manage for the rest of my life. There is no magic fix here.

We're just taking it one step at a time.

"Are you okay?"

I look up at Nikolai and rush into his arms. We aren't a cuddly family, but he sure does make me feel safe.

"Today, you marry that crazy man downstairs that makes you so happy. You're getting better, we're searching for Mikhail. We've all got your back. We always have and we always will. You hear me?"

I squeeze him tighter. "I miss Mikhail."

"That makes two of us. You know him, whatever the hell he's up to, he'll be safe. Have faith in his brutal ass."

I can't help but laugh.

I've seen him at his worst. He's scary as hell. But a heart of gold.

"We better get going before those damn flamingos run rampant and get us all kicked out."

I roll my eyes.

"They aren't house trained. But they do listen to Alexei."

He chuckles. "They understand broken English I guess."

"They must."

CHAPTER 88
ALEXEI

"I CANNOT BELIEVE you dressed up your flamingos and brought them to your wedding. You're lucky we own this place."

I stroke the top of Sheila's head and she rests against my bicep.

"They love me and Lara. They are our babies, I couldn't leave them at home."

Jax takes a wary step past Bruce.

"I swear that thing hissed at me." He scratches the back of his head, eyeing the bird.

I shrug.

"Maybe I'm training him up to be security at one of Enzo's clubs."

Enzo rolls his eyes.

"Why not. If he can scare Jax, he's doing something right."

"Hey! I'm not scared. I'm just not sure about his intentions."

Nikolai bursts out laughing and winks at Mila, who's waddling like a penguin as she strokes her baby bump.

"Can I have your gun, I need the bathroom." She smiles sweetly at her husband, who leans in and kisses her cheek.

We have extra security in place today, even though it's a small wedding, we don't trust Ivan. Especially if word starts to go out about Mikhail's disappearance.

We refuse to say his death.

We won't accept it.

Once he hands her the weapon, he turns his attention to me.

"I never thought I'd see the day. Alexei, married. To my sister."

"Like we didn't all see it coming," Jax jokes and Nikolai raises an eyebrow.

Enzo shrugs.

"It's true. It was obvious from the outside. We were all just waiting to see how long it would take for the donkey to realize."

"Really? Even on my special day, I'm the donkey."

Bruce steps forward and Enzo points at the bird.

"That thing tries to bite me, I'll shoot it. Don't test me."

I stand between them and tap Bruce on the beak.

"You shoot my Bruce, I'll return the favor." I give Enzo my best unhinged smile.

"Now, now, play nice. You need me," Enzo replies smugly.

He's right.

Ushering Bruce back to Sheila, I readjust his bowtie and she lays her head on his.

"Awww, look." Elena points to the birds from her seat.

Yea, they are kind of cute.

The priest clears his throat from behind us and my heart almost skips a beat.

"If we could all take our seats, the ceremony is about to begin."

I shuffle over to stand underneath the pink flower arch and tug on my collar.

Fuck. It's hot in here.

I turn to Jax in the front row.

"Can we open a window or something, I'm on fire."

He laughs and shakes his head.

"Have you never been nervous before?"

I frown.

"No. I don't think so."

The main doors open up and I swear time stands still. Her eyes instantly lock onto me and she smiles.

It lights up the whole room. Just like it always has.

She brightens my life, she breathes life into my soul. When she blows me a kiss, clutching onto her pink bouquet of roses in her right hand, I pretend to catch it.

It's like time moves in slow motion with each step she takes.

I want her to be my wife, right this second.

I launch myself down the aisle and pick her up into my arms, holding her close and darting back to the spot.

"Honestly, Alexei. Sixty seconds and you couldn't wait?" she says with an amused grin.

I lean in and kiss her cheek.

"No. I want forever now."

CHAPTER 89
LARA

Song- Lollipop, Framing Henley

As soon as the elevator doors close, he's already pressed against me. I just about manage to hit the button to take us to the penthouse that I've borrowed from Mikhail.

It has the best views of Vegas, complete floor to ceiling windows. I have plans to be slammed up against that glass and railed until I pass out.

It is our wedding night, after all.

Between fervent kisses, at some point the elevator dings.

The rush of air escapes from my lungs as Alexei leans down and gently scoops me up, cradling me in his strong embrace.

"I've seen them do this in the movies." He winks, stepping into our suite.

With me still nestled in his arms, he confidently strides towards the dining table, and my excitement grows as I catch sight of the surprise I had prepared for him.

"Wow." His mouth drops open, looking at the dining table.

I sneak a glance.

The entire eight foot glass dining table in the center of the room is smothered in candy. There's so damn much of it you can't even see the table.

Every type, every flavor. It's there.

"You happy?"

He looks at me and back at the array of sweets.

"Happiest damn day of my life." He presses a kiss to the side of my head and somehow hugs me tighter.

"You can put me down, you know?" I tease.

He shakes his head in disbelief, then leans forward to snatch one of the sugar-coated gummies.

He puts it between his lips and sucks, then holds it out in front of me.

"Wanna taste?" He licks his lips.

Opening my mouth, he inserts it, resulting in a strawberry explosion on my taste buds.

"Mmm. Nice."

"You know what else tastes good?" he asks, brushing the candy back to create a pile and making space for me to be placed down.

"Oh, I have no clue." I pretend to not know what he's talking about.

Taking a step forward, he spreads open my legs and positions himself snugly in the center.

"You tease," he murmurs against my lips, taking my chin between his index finger and thumb.

"My wife's pussy is so sweet." He nibbles on my bottom lip making me moan.

When I lean back, I take a handful of treats and hold it up between us.

"Better than these?"

"I'm addicted to you more than anything in the world. Candy included." He takes them from my palms and tosses them on the table.

His hands glide up my thighs, and he begins to delicately lick from my jawline to the curve of my ear.

"Be a good girl for me and lay back."

I cast a glance over my shoulder at all the candies scattered around.

"Do it." He commands, raising a brow. I love his deep voice when he gets into his more dominant side.

Holding back my words, I obey his demands, and he spreads my legs against the table.

My breath catches as he traces his finger along the side of my panties.

"What a perfect wife, crotchless white lace for her husband. Wanted to get eaten out on your wedding day? Hmm?"

"Eaten out? I need more than that. Choke me on your cock. Press me up against that glass and rail me. Pull my hair. Spit in my mouth. I want to forget how to breathe when your hand squeezes my throat. Fuck me like you mean it. Fuck me like I'm your filthy little whore."

Seeing his jaw drop, I quickly sit up and gently tap his chin to close it.

"And maybe spank me nice and hard for good measure. Mark your wife. Be my caveman and claim ownership over me."

He looks at me, blinking a few times, while running his thumb across his lip. A smug smile spreads across his face as he swiftly grabs hold of my throat.

"On your knees, pchelka."

He yanks me away from the table, causing me to collapse in front of him. I gaze up at my incredibly handsome husband.

My gaze fixates on him as he unbuckles his belt and pulls it through the hoops of his pants, the sound of the leather slapping against his palm echoes in the room.

I press my thighs together. Fuck. I want that on me.

"That made your eyes light up. You want to be spanked?" He pulls back my bottom lip and pushes down his pants and boxers.

"Go on then, baby. Blow my brains out with that sassy mouth of yours."

His dick stands at attention in front of my face. As I take him in my mouth, I focus on the tip and his piercing with my tongue.

I run my hand along his shaft, and raise my eyes to find him watching me with a hint of amusement in his expression. He has a red lollipop sticking out from his lips.

"Go deeper. How much of my cock can you take?"

Candy clatters against his teeth, and I relax my throat, wanting to impress him. His eyes darken as I get further down to the base. Tears well in my eyes and he casually wipes them away. When he hits the back of my throat, I tense and gag.

But the moan that comes out of his mouth pushes me to keep going. Bobbing up and down on his cock, I trail my nails into his thick thighs.

As soon as he starts to tense under my touch, his fingers tangle in my hair and he pulls me back. His dick pops out of my mouth and I swipe the side of my lips.

"That good you couldn't stop yourself coming down my throat?" I tease.

Bending down, he gently lifts me up, his strong arms supporting my unsteady legs.

As he gets down on one knee, a soft tap on my ankle catches my attention. Placing it on his thigh, I stabilize myself with a hand on his shoulder while he takes my heel off, repeating the process with the other foot.

He gives a kiss to the inside of my thigh before standing up.

"Drop the dress. Let me see every inch of your beauty, pchelka."

With trembling fingers from excitement, not knowing what his unpredictable ass is going to do next has me all kinds of riled up.

Following his instructions, I unzip the side and let it drop. This is exactly why I opted for a shorter dress. Easier to take off.

It gathers around my feet, leaving me vulnerable and exposed to him.

His eyes trace my body with intense desire.

"Hold this." He shoves his lollipop in the air, so I take it and pop it into my mouth.

That earns me a grin.

"Hmmm." His fingers trace along my ass.

I let out a shriek as he grabs my waist and bends me over his shoulder, then stands.

The next thing I know, I'm on all fours on top of the dining table surrounded by candy, but I'm the main course.

"Back it up, baby. Gimme that ass."

Shuffling back as best I can, I wait patiently for him.

"I want you to just feel. You good with that, baby?" He traces his finger up my spine and I arch my back.

"I trust you."

"Good girl. Close your eyes."

I do as he says and a wave of anticipation rushes through me as he secures what I think is his pink tie over my eyes.

"Head down. Butt up. I'm about to do things to you that will make you scream, just like you wanted."

He slaps my outer thigh, and I jolt forward in surprise.

I bite down on the inside of my mouth as he runs his finger along my pussy and spreads me open. His hot breath beats against my sensitive skin. The second his tongue connects, I cry out. It feels so good. My heightened senses are solely focused on the sounds of his moans and the sensations of his licks against me.

He knows what I need. I never have to tell him. He was right.

He knows me better than I know myself.

CHAPTER 90
ALEXEI

Snaking my hands around her thighs, I pull her back so her cunt is smothering my face.

And I'm loving every fucking second.

She's sweeter than candy.

I'm addicted to her. Plain and simple. And now she's mine forever.

Mine to explore. To push. To protect. To mark. To love. To cherish.

To eat out on our dining room table.

As soon as her legs shake against my palms, I pull away and her chest heaves.

"Patience, baby. I have more plans for you yet."

Before she can respond, I sink two fingers inside her and I'm rewarded with a moan.

They're soaked when I pull them out, so I spread her ass and trail them back towards her back entrance.

She becomes quiet and that makes me smile.

"Saved your ass for me, hmm?"

That makes my dick twitch. Her ass is mine and only mine.

"Y-yes."

Stepping back to regain some composure, I run my hand over my jaw.

I snatch another red lollipop from beside her and peel off the wrapper.

Cherry. My favorite.

Getting it as wet as I can, I take it out of my mouth and run it along her pussy.

Hmm. I wonder.

Dragging the sweet between her cheeks, I push down on her shoulders to bring her ass up higher. Spreading her open, I swirl the ball of the lollipop over her puckered hole and lean in, alternating between my tongue and the candy.

Pulling back, I push the lollipop in enough to tease but not all the way in and spin it.

"Ohhh," she pants out, almost in surprise. She likes it.

"I might not have been the one to pop your cherry, but I just made your ass taste like one. I bet no one has ever done that to you before," I tell her, pulling out the sucker and replacing it with my tongue.

"M-more," she says breathlessly.

Keeping my attention on her ass, I sink three fingers in her dripping pussy.

"Better?"

Once I'm all the way to the knuckle, I curl my fingers to hit the spot I've learned she goes crazy for.

And on cue, my hand is soaked.

This is fun. And so fucking hot.

I wonder what else I can try.

Scanning the colorful array surrounding my girl, I stop on the packet of popping candy and a lightbulb moment happens in my brain.

I want her to watch this one.

Stepping around the table, I carefully remove her blindfold. She blinks a few times and looks up at me with her flushed cheeks and glassy eyes.

I can't help it. I grab the back of her neck and slam my lips over hers. As our tongues explore each other, I skillfully maneuver her onto her back, where she lies flat. As I guide my hand down her stomach, deepening the kiss, her legs open for me and I grin against her lips.

"Desperate for more, huh?"

Her fingers tangle in my hair as she tugs me closer and I circle her clit softly.

"I'm so fucking needy for you."

"Good. Because I'm obsessed with you." With one last hard kiss, I pull away and rip open the popping candy with my teeth.

Her mouth forms a perfect 'o' when I lick a straight line from her clit to her belly button. Pushing her thighs back even further, I tap the packet and watch the little pink crystals fall all over her pussy.

With my head between her legs, we lock gazes. I can hear it popping already.

"Oh my god, that tickles!" She shimmies her hips and I get to work, licking up every bit and letting them dissolve on my tongue.

Before I swallow, I let them crackle in my mouth and lean over her, taking her by the throat and prying her lips open with my thumb.

Gathering all the candy and saliva on my tongue, I tower over her and spit the contents from mine into hers and tug her closer before crashing my lips over hers.

She moans in my mouth, and fuck, I'm so hard it's almost painful.

CHAPTER 91

LARA

My MOUTH TINGLES and so does my pussy. I grab onto his shirt to pull him close so his weight is almost crushing me. Wrapping my legs around him, I roll my hips.

"Fuck. Me. Please." I grit out each word desperately.

He's had me on the edge so many times I can't take it anymore.

A growl erupts from him and it's all a blur, as he whips me up and presses my face against the glass. My hands instinctively splay out on each side of my head and he presses himself against my back.

The coolness of the window provides a sharp relief from the raging fire within me.

"Fuck. I love you," he whispers against my shoulder, kicking open my legs.

"I love you too."

"Good." He taps my ass lightly.

"Now—" He wraps his hand around my neck and pulls my head back. "—you're going to look at that pretty view while your husband rails you and watches your pretty reflection."

He lines up with my entrance and holds me in place by the hip as he thrusts inside me, hard and fast, pressing my breasts against the glass. I suck in a breath as I adjust to his size.

He presses the points in my neck, enough to make me go fuzzy and have blood pounding in my ears.

He consumes me. He ignites me. He completes me.

It doesn't take long for him to get me back to the edge of release.

"Fuck this." He grunts out.

"I need to look you in the eyes as you fall apart for me. And you need to witness just how crazy in love with you I am, as I claim your sweet cunt."

"Yes." I pant out.

He spins me around, pressing my back to the glass and lifting me. I wrap my legs around him. He holds me in place by my thighs and slides back in.

"Much better. Look at you, being such a good girl for me,"

Holy shit.

I bite down hard on my lip.

"I'm so fucking close, Lara." Fisting his hand through my hair, he drags his lips over mine.

It's a frantic and hungry kiss, leaving me breathless.

"Now," he whispers against my lips, signaling me to fall apart for him. His fingers dig into my cheeks as he forces me to look at him.

His dark eyes burn into my soul.

And this is it. My entire life in one man. The one who sees me for who I am.

Who doesn't try to fix me.

He accepts me for all of my broken and cherishes every part of me.

The man who made me believe something seemingly impossible…

I am worthy of the love that I crave.

THE END.

EPILOGUE
ALEXEI

"ALEXEI! Alexei! Oh my god!" Lara screams from downstairs.

I throw my paintbrush on the ground and gray paint splatters up my jeans.

"Fuck."

No time to deal with the mess. Lara needs me.

I sprint down the stairs, my heart pounding, and I stop when I see her standing in the living room, tears running down her cheeks and her hands over her mouth.

She turns to face me and mouths "be quiet".

"What?" I frown.

She nods her head over to the corner of the room.

Sheila and Bruce's little area we penned off.

I tiptoe over to Lara and wrap my hand around her waist, following her line of vision.

"Our babies," I whisper.

Sheila and Bruce are both fussing over a tiny little white ball of fluff.

"It hatched. We have a baby." Lara presses her fingers over her mouth.

Fuck. Why do I want to cry?

"I'm so proud of them. Look at how good they are."

Lara nods to our birds, pure elation on her face.

Lara would make an amazing mom. Maybe one day. Not yet. We don't think it would be good to have that pressure on her body.

She's doing so well with her recovery. She seems happy. She's eating.

Once we find Mikhail, things will be perfect for her.

Her palm rests on my wrist. "Do we need to call a vet or something?"

Shit, why didn't I think of this?

"I don't think so. They seem healthy. I'm not sure a vet would let us keep them."

"I'll find a corrupt one. I'd never let them go."

I squeeze Lara closer to me.

"Baby flamingos are so cute. I'm obsessed."

"You're cuter," I tell her, pressing a kiss to her temple.

We moved into the house I bought Lara for her birthday right after our wedding. It's only been three weeks but we've got a few rooms decorated.

It keeps us occupied while we search for Mikhail. Enzo is doing his best but it's like Mikhail's become a ghost.

There's no remains of the plane.

No sign of him.

I know what I saw.

But I also know Mikhail.

That man's been to hell once already and survived.

I have no doubt he can do it again.

WANT SOME MORE ALEXEI AND LARA??

How about a halloween mask scene…

You can sign up to my newsletter to receive a bonus spicy scene.

Grab it here: https://dl.bookfunnel.com/c2zp9iorlg

MIKHAIL CAN'T REALLY BE DEAD?? CAN HE??

I guess you'll have to wait until Claim releases in January 2025!

The king will be unmasked.

You can pre-order CLAIM here: https://mybook.to/ndUnT

Have you read the first book in the series, CHAOS yet?

A brothers wife, biker, boxer and a vibrating tongue piercing, you're welcome.

It is available on Amazon and Kindle Unlimited.

READ IT HERE- https://mybook.to/qyAgjg

MORE BY LUNA MASON

Beneath The Mask is Luna Mason's first series, in the same universe as Beneath The Secrets. If you haven't had a chance to read the series, they are all now live on Kindle Unlimited.

Distance, book one, Keller and Sienna- https://books2read.com/u/mgPk2X

Detonate, book two, Grayson and Maddie- https://mybook.to/3tlYU

Devoted, book three, Luca and Rosa- https://books2read.com/u/brB0xA

Detained, book four, Frankie and Zara- https://mybook.to/PfoRNy

Roman Petrov, a marriage of convenience novella, part of the Petrov Family Anthology will be releasing July 12th 2024. You can pre-order ROMAN here: https://mybook.to/I5APQd

ABOUT THE AUTHOR

Luna Mason is an Amazon top #12 and international best-selling author. She lives in the UK and if she isn't writing her filthy men, you'll find her with her head in a spicy book.

To be the first to find out her upcoming titles you can subscribe to her newsletter here:

https://dashboard.mailerlite.com/forms/232608/79198959451506438/share

You can join the author's reader group (Luna Mason's Mafia Queens) to get exclusive

teasers, and be the first to know about current projects and release dates.

https://facebook.com/groups/614207510510756/

SOCIAL MEDIA LINKS:

http://www.instagram.com/authorlunamason

https://facebook.com/groups/614207510510756/

https://www.tiktok.com/@authorlunamason?_t=8j38HlkCYmP&_r=1